The Dirt Peddler

THE DIRT PEDDLER

A Dick Hardesty Mystery by

Dorien Grey

 PUBLISHERS®   San Francisco

Published in the United States by
GLB Publishers
P.O. Box 78212, San Francisco, CA 94107 USA

Cover by GLB Publishers
Photography by Karl Overholt

ISBN 1-879194-72-4

Library of Congress Control Number:

2003093612

Published 2003

To those who,

in the darkest night,

still know the dawn will come

Chapter 1

If you're like most people, whenever someone lobs a cliche into the conversation, you tend to mentally roll your eyes toward the ceiling and heave a sigh. I'm usually guilty of the same response unless I stop to remember how it is that cliches become cliches in the first place. In a way, cliches are a lot like fortune cookies—pretty bland on the outside, but more often than not with a bit of universal truth tucked in the middle.

"The pen is mightier than the sword" has always been one of my favorites because the overlooked truth in that one is that our entire culture is in fact set upon a foundation of written words. Words move us, inspire us, sooth us, anger us: they're the building blocks of civilization.

Writers as a group tend to be pretty much aware of the power of words and use them responsibly, but some choose to indeed use words as their personal swords, which they wield either to defend or attack. But swords have double edges, and if the wielder is not careful, one of the people they hurt, even unwittingly, can be themselves.

And that's exactly what happened to the Dirt Peddler.

* * *

"Can we get our money back?" Jonathan asked as we left the theater.

"I don't think so," I said. "You didn't like it? It was your idea, you know."

"Well, it sure wasn't what I was expecting. The guys in the ad were really hot."

"And the title didn't clue you in? 'L'amour Triste'?"

"Oh, sure," he said. "Like I speak fluent Hungarian."

I looked at him to verify that he was pulling my leg, and he grinned. "Okay, okay: 'Sad Love'. But the guys in the ad were really hot. How was I to know they were just going to sit there and moon over one another for two and a half hours?"

"There was that one pretty interesting love scene at the end," I said.

"How could you tell?" he asked. "It looked like it was being photographed through the bottom of a fish tank."

"Live and learn," I said.

"Gee, let me write that down," he said, and I grabbed him by the back of the neck with one hand and squeezed until he yelped.

Actually, 'L'amour Triste' was part of the city's first gay film festival playing at what was normally The Central's gay porn house.

Jonathan and I were still at that stage of our relationship where even monthly anniversaries were special occasions, and for this one, our...uh...our "several-th," we chose a night at the movies before going out for our "traditional" anniversary dinner.

I had also bought him a book he really wanted: *An Illustrated Guide to Decorative Shrubs of North America.* He'd just completed his first semester toward his Associate Degree in Horticulture Technology and really loved anything and everything that had to do with plants, trees, flowers, and shrubs—just about anything with roots.

Not surprisingly, it had to be special-ordered and I'd decided to show my support for Bennington Books' having opened a big new store in The Central, the city's ever-expanding gay district. That a large, established chain had chosen The Central was further evidence of how the times were changing, and how far the gay community had come. And Bennington was not in real competition with the smaller, independent community-oriented bookstores which had provided so much support for gay and lesbian authors over the years. This was just my way of saying "thanks" to a mainstream company for recognizing the buying power of the gay community.

I'd gotten a notice the day before saying the book was in, so after we left the movie and before going on to dinner, we stopped by Bennington's. It was within walking distance of the theater, and as we approached the store I suddenly remembered that as part of its grand opening, there was a big to-do scheduled for that night: a personal appearance and book signing by Tony T. Tunderew, author of *Dirty Little Minds*, which had been at the top of the NY Times Best Seller List for three weeks.

I've always been somewhat leery of people who insist on using their middle initials as part of their name—and especially those who appear to be overly fond of alliteration.

Dirty Little Minds was Tunderew's first book, a steamy, barely-fictionalized guided-sewer expose of Governor Harry Keene, who had recently resigned in the wake of widespread rumors involving his alleged financial ties to the operator of a prostitution ring, whose services were widely available to the state's executive branch.

Neither Tunderew nor the book was gay, so it struck me as a little odd that he'd be doing a signing in the heart of the gay community, but then I realized again that times were changing, and it was to promote the new store, no matter where the store might have been. And that it drew people from outside of the community was yet another sign of the times.

There was a line stretching out onto the sidewalk of people clutching their copies of the book, awaiting Tunderew's signature. Jonathan suggested we should just forget it and come back the next day, but I grabbed him by the hand and "excuse me'd" past those blocking the door. The line inside snaked its way past tables and racks of books to the rear of the store, where a crowd surrounded what I assume had to have been some sort of table. It was impossible to see either the table or whoever…uh, Tunderew, maybe?…might be sitting behind it.

There was no one behind the counter when we walked up to it, but a moment later a clerk, who had passed us headed for the front tables with an armload of *Dirty Little Minds*, hurried over.

"Sorry," he said. "A real madhouse tonight."

"So we noticed," I said, and told him why we'd come. He smiled, glanced under the counter and, like a magician pulling a rabbit from a hat, reached down and pulled out the book. Jonathan's face broke into a huge grin as the clerk set it on the counter.

"Wow! This is great!" he said excitedly, immediately beginning to turn through the pages. "Thank you, Dick!"

The clerk gave us both a knowing grin.

* * *

A week or so later, as I was making out my final report on a just-completed case, the phone rang.

"Hardesty Investigations," I answered, picking up the phone on the second ring as always.

"Dick," the familiar voice said: "It's Glen O'Banyon."

O'Banyon was one of the city's leading attorneys, for and with whom I'd worked on a number of cases. I was a little surprised to hear directly from him, since he usually went through his secretary, Donna.

"Glen, hi," I replied. "What can I do for you?"

There was a slight pause, then: "I was wondering if you'd like to meet me for a drink this afternoon—say around 4:30 at Hughie's?"

Now that came as something of a surprise. I almost always met him at his office when he had an assignment for me. And at Hughie's? Hughie's was a hustler bar about two blocks from work, and I had met him there a couple times on a much earlier case, but...

"Sure," I said, figuring I'd find out exactly what was going on when we met. "I'll see you then."

"Good," he said. Another pause, then: "Well, I've got to get to court. Later."

I called the apartment to leave a message telling Jonathan I'd be a little late getting home.

* * *

Ah, Hughie's. I hadn't been there, I don't think, since I met Jonathan. But it hadn't changed. Hughie's never changed. It was exactly the same when I walked in at 4:15—early as ever—as it had been the first time I wandered in for a beer right after I'd first opened my office.

Bud, the bartender, saw me come in and automatically reached into the cooler for a frosted mug, drew me a dark draft, and had it on the bar by the time I reached it.

"How's it goin', Dick?" he asked, as though I'd been in yesterday afternoon.

"Fine, Bud," I said. "You?"

He just shrugged, took my money, and moved off to the register.

The place was starting to fill up. The hustlers—those who hadn't already been there most of the day—were drifting in from the streets in anticipation of the imminent arrival of the johns as the local offices and businesses closed. I recognized a couple of them, but most were new: the turnover rate in hustling was always high, and I didn't care to speculate as to the reasons.

One of the guys my crotch had been concentrating on—a really good looking, rough-around-the-edges blond started looking, then moving, in my direction.

Shit! Now what'll you do? my mind asked.

Yeah, like this is your first time, another mind-voice responded.

Luckily, at that moment I felt a hand on my shoulder and turned to see Glen O'Banyon standing beside me. As the other times we'd met at Hughie's, this was not the executive tower, dressed-to-impress lawyer; this was a guy in a baseball cap, a Green Bay Packer sweatshirt, and pair of pretty threadbare Levi's. Not one person in twenty he saw every day would readily recognize him.

"Thanks for meeting me, Dick," he said, one hand on my shoulder while he signaled Bud with the other.

The blond number had stopped in mid-step when he saw O'Banyon come up, and looked at me with one raised eyebrow. I gave him a quick half smile and a shrug, and he turned and went back to where I'd first spotted him. My crotch was *not* happy, though the rest of me was guiltily relieved.

"No problem," I said. "It's good to see you in civvies."

Bud had come over and O'Banyon waited until he'd ordered

before turning to me with a grin. "Yeah," he said. "I really need to get out more."

He scooped a bill out of his pocket and exchanged it for the beer Bud had brought him.

"So what can I do for you?" I asked, knowing full well this wasn't strictly a social get-together.

He pushed himself away from the bar, picked up his beer, and gestured for me to follow him to the far corner of the front of the bar, where no one else had gathered yet. We set our drinks on one of the tall, steering-wheel sized tables flanked by two high stools.

"I may have a case for you," he said, immediately piquing my interest.

"Great," I said. I didn't have to ask or say anything else: I knew he'd tell me.

He took a long swig of his beer and pulled one of the stools closer to sit down.

"I've got a client with a whole shitload of problems," he said, "most of which he brought on himself. Strictly between you and me, he's a pain in the ass. Less than a year ago he was a very junior executive at Craylaw & Collier and today people are falling all over themselves to cozy up to him and his ego has completely run off with what little common sense he might have had to begin with."

"And what did he do to deserve all this sudden attention?" I asked.

O'Banyon sighed, took another swig of his beer and set the bottle on the table. "He wrote a book," he said.

He sat there watching me in silence for a moment until I said: "Not one titled *Dirty Little Minds*, by any chance?"

"*Dirty Little Minds*," he said.

Interesting, I thought. "And where might I fit into all this?" I asked.

O'Banyon smiled: "Oh, we're just getting started," he said. "And by the way, I know I don't have to even mention that I'm telling you all this with the full confidence that none of it will go any farther than between the two of us."

"Of course," I said, and he nodded.

He stared out the window for a moment, then said: "Tunderew is currently working on a second book, which promises to be an even bigger blockbuster than his first. He's got every major publisher in the business practically throwing advance offers at him."

"What's the new book about?"

O'Banyon shook his head. "He won't say, but he's got a lot of people very nervous. As you probably know, Craylaw & Collier is a very big outfit with its fingers in a lot of pies. It's primarily a consulting firm but they have branches throughout the county doing public relations, financial planning, you name it. By no small coincidence, it handled the P.R. for Governor Keene's last gubernatorial campaign. Tunderew left the company shortly before his book came out. I wouldn't be surprised if Tunderew wasn't keeping some sort of little black book on some of C&C's other clients." He finished his beer and pointed to my nearly empty mug. "Want another?" he asked.

"Sure, thanks." He got off his stool and moved to the crowd at the bar, which by now was sprinkled with business suits as well as tee shirts and tank tops. The blond I'd seen earlier was talking earnestly with a forty-something guy in a white shirt who had his back to me. Every now and then the blond would glance over the guy's shoulder and lock eyes with me.

Hardesty! Knock it off! my mind commanded, and I pulled my eyes away and concentrated on staring out the window until O'Banyon returned. Even our relatively empty corner of the room was beginning to fill up, so O'Banyon pulled his stool closer to me when he sat down and continued our conversation in a somewhat lowered voice.

"Tunderew had originally submitted *Dirty Little Minds* to every single publishing house that is currently chasing after him. None of them would touch it. Finally Bernadine Press took a chance with him, published it, spent a little money on promotion, sent copies to the right reviewers and…the rest, as they say, is history. But Bernadine is a very small house, and was on the verge of going under before *Dirty Little Minds* came along. They had enough faith in Tunderew to offer him a two-book, no-advance contract, which he signed."

I saw where this was going. "So now he wants out of the contract for the second book," I said.

O'Banyon took a deep swallow of his beer, stifled a belch, and nodded. "Yep. He's hired me to break the contract with Bernadine. So much for loyalty. Without Bernadine he'd be standing in line at the unemployment office, but as I said, the guy's a real piece of work. Oh, and I forgot to mention, on the subject of loyalty, that as soon as the book showed signs of taking off, he filed for divorce from his wife of thirteen years. Conveniently before his first royalty check could be considered community property."

"Why did you agree to take the case?" I asked.

O'Banyon shrugged, staring at the beer bottle in front of him. After a moment, he looked up at me.

"For one thing, weak as it may sound, because it is not up to lawyers to determine right or wrong. Lawyers present the case, the courts judge on the basis of law. And like it or not, Tunderew does have a case under law. I don't have to like my clients: just present their case to the best of my ability."

I took another drink of my beer before saying: "So what, exactly, is it you'd like me to do for you?"

O'Banyon sighed. "Well, it seems he's also being blackmailed."

Probably couldn't happen to a nicer guy, I thought.

"Can I ask what for? Though from what you've said of this guy, I'd imagine it could be about just about everything."

O'Banyon smiled. "Yeah, and that's another interesting thing, and why I approached you. The guy's a rabid homophobe, and the blackmailer apparently has evidence indicating that Tunderew's gay."

That one caught me by surprise. "Is he?" I asked.

He gave a cursory shrug. "Certainly not according to him, but the point is that he can't afford to have his public image 'sullied' as he put it—an oddly Victorian word—which is rather laughable, considering. But since he writes about scandals, it wouldn't do his reputation much good to be caught up in the middle of one of his own. So he wants to quash the whole thing before any damage can be done."

I polished off about half my remaining beer, then said: "So he wants a gay private investigator to prove he's not gay?"

O'Banyon's face broke into a slow grin. "Ironic, isn't it?" he said. "Of course I didn't tell him you were gay…you can do that if you want to, and knowing you I'm sure you will. I just told him I knew of a very good private investigator who was uniquely qualified to do the job. He didn't ask what I meant by 'uniquely qualified,' and I didn't tell."

"Does he know *you're* gay?" I asked.

"I haven't a clue," he said. "Maybe he does, maybe he doesn't. It's not as if I really gave a shit. But I've found out one thing over the years: if you're rich enough, or powerful enough, or if someone needs you badly enough, it doesn't matter who you sleep with."

I shook my head and joined him in the grin. "You're getting a big kick out of this, aren't you?" I asked.

He gave a raised-eyebrow shrug, still grinning. "Hey, I get so little pleasure out of some of these cases, don't begrudge me."

We small-talked while we finished our beers, and I noticed the blond walk out with the guy he'd been talking to. As he reached the door, he turned to me, gave a small shrug and a wink, then left. My crotch was muttering curses, but I ignored it.

As O'Banyon and I were getting ready to leave, he reached into the back pocket of his jeans and pulled out a business card, which he handed me.

"Here's Tunderew's number," he said. "I told him to expect your call."

I took it without looking at it, and stuck it in my shirt pocket. "If he's as big a pain in the ass as you say he is, I just might tell him to go fuck himself," I said.

"Yeah, you might," O'Banyon said with a grin as we walked toward the door. "I made it clear to him that this was just a referral and you were your own man when it came to deciding what cases to take, so I'm off the hook. If you turn him down and he blames me and wants to find himself another lawyer, I wouldn't lose much sleep over it."

We shook hands as we reached the sidewalk, and went our separate ways.

* * *

Walking back to my office, I pulled out the card and looked at it: "Tony T. Tunderew, best-selling author of *Dirty Little Minds*" No ego there. There wasn't any address, but there was a phone number. I stuck the card back in my pocket, found my car in the lot across from my office building, and went home.

Jonathan was in the kitchen, talking to Phil and Tim, his two goldfish, and Matthew, Mark, Luke, and John, recent Tropical Something-or-Other additions to the new, larger aquarium Jonathan had conned me into getting for him as atonement for a minor argument which I obviously lost.

When he saw me, he grinned as though he hadn't seen me in years, then quickly turned to the refrigerator from which he extracted my evening Manhattan. Apparently I was a little later getting home than I'd thought. He started to reach into the freezer for some ice cubes, but instead set the glass down and came over to give me a lung-emptying hug.

"Glad you're home," he said.

"Me too," I replied as we released the hug. He started to turn back toward the refrigerator, but I stopped him. "I can get it," I said. "You want a Coke?"

"Sure," he said. "How did it go with Mr. O'Banyon?"

I handed him his Coke before I reached into the freezer for my ice cubes. "Fine," I said. "I met him at Hughie's for a beer. He referred a case to me."

Plopping a couple ice cubes into my glass, I closed the freezer door and turned to put my free arm around Jonathan's shoulders. "Let's go in and sit down, and you can tell me about your day. Have a good one?"

We sat, as always, side by side on the couch, thighs touching.

"As a matter of fact, yeah," Jonathan said. "We delivered

some trees to New Eden today, and guess who I saw?"

I of course hadn't a clue. "Who?" I asked after an appropriate pause.

"Remember when I first met you I told you one of the other hustlers from Hughie's used to let me crash at his place every now and then?"

"Uh…yeah, I remember, sort of." Jonathan has his own logic and his own way of getting from point A to point B. I'd learned just to go along and it would all become clear in time.

"Randy," he said. "Randy Jacobs. You remember. Anyway, he's at New Eden now! It sure was good to see him. I'm really glad he got off the streets. He's doing really well out there; he's working in the office and everything."

New Eden was one of a number of very large, very profitable, tax exempt farms run just outside major cities across the nation, owned and operated by the Eternal Light Foundation. In turn, the Eternal Light Foundation was, when all the governing committees and advisory boards and assorted boards of directors were stripped away, two people: the Reverends Jeffrey and Barbara Dinsmore, rising stars in the Conservative skies of this great nation. The purpose of these New Edens was to take in homeless, throwaway kids; the ones no one wanted or everyone else had given up on, and put them in an environment of hope. Sort of like the local M.C.C.'s Haven House, but on a much larger scale, and it was of course not limited to gay/lesbian kids as Haven House was.

Each New Eden was as self-sufficient as possible. Eternal Light kids worked the farms, built the barns and sheds, repaired and maintained all the farm equipment in exchange for room, board, rehabilitation, education, and counseling. The profits from the farms were plowed back into the expansion of the Foundation's good works.

Surprisingly, from all accounts the approach appeared to be actually working, and the Dinsmore's had recently been featured on the cover of Time. While there was absolutely no doubt that Eternal Light was set in rock-solid Christian fundamentalism, the Dinsmores were smart enough to keep it very low-key. No fire-

and-brimstone bible thumping; no mandatory seven-days-a-week religious services; no passing out religious tracts at the airport or selling flowers on the streets. You had to give them credit for that. And since they were able to walk such a fine line between the religious and secular aspects of their foundation, they had access to corporate funding not available to more overtly religious organizations.

"I'd like to ask him over sometime," Jonathan said, bringing me back to the moment. "I think you'd like him."

"Sure," I said. "That'd be nice. Can they come and go as they please?"

He took a sip of his Coke before answering. "I think they can have one night a week, as long as they say where they're going, and they have a ride back and forth to town...and they have to be back by midnight."

"Whenever you want," I said. "But I'm curious why you'd be delivering trees to New Eden. It's a farm; you'd think they'd have enough trees of their own."

Jonathan grinned and nudged my leg with his. "Well of course they do," he said. "But these are for around the Dinsmores' new house: some flowering dogwood and Japanese Cherry."

"A new house, huh?" I asked. "A little 97-room cottage with an indoor polo field and trout pond?"

He gave me a look of mock disgust. "Jeez! What a cynic! No, no trout pond or polo field. It's a nice house, but it's just a house. Maybe four bedrooms?"

Now that came as quite a surprise, given the tendency to excess of some other doers-of-good-works who had been making the headlines in the past few years.

"Well, you ask Randy over whenever you want," I said.

Jonathan beamed, as only he can. "Great!" he said. "We'll be going out there again tomorrow. I'll ask him then."

* * *

At the office the next morning, I waited until about ten o'clock to call the number on Tunderew's business card. I figured rich and famous authors probably liked to sleep-in in the morning. They could afford to.

There were two rings at the other end of the line, then a "click" and a woman's voice: "Mr. Tunderew's office."

An office! I'm impressed! I made a note to remind myself to write a book someday.

"Is Mr. Tunderew in?" I asked.

"No sir, he's not. May I take a message?" There were sounds in the background which I couldn't quite make out, but seemed familiar.

"Could you tell me where your office is located? Perhaps I can drop Mr. Tunderew a note."

"Ah, well, I'm afraid I couldn't tell you that, sir. I really don't have an address. This is Mr. Tunderew's answering service."

Aha! The sounds in the background were other operators taking other calls for other clients. 'Mr. Tunderew's office!' Right! So much for my writing a book.

I gave her my name and number and told her that I was calling in response to his conversation with his attorney, Glen O'Banyon. She thanked me, and we hung up. Well, at least he had a pretty high class service—I didn't hear her popping gum.

While I waited, having no idea how long the wait would be, I looked in the phone book for the address and phone number of Bernadine Press. I figured I'd be needing to contact them at some point.

Somewhat to my surprise, the phone rang just as I was turning the yellow pages to "Publishers."

"Hardesty Investigations," I said, picking up on the second ring.

"Mr. Hardesty, this is Tony T. Tunderew…"

Gee, thanks for putting the middle initial in there, Tony, I thought. *I wouldn't have had a clue which Tony Tunderew this was without it.*

"…my secretary just told me you'd called."

Sure, Tony.

"Yes," I said, "Glen O'Banyon tells me you're having some sort of problem."

He gave a dramatic sigh. "I'll tell you, Mr. Hardesty, since *Dirty Little Minds* first hit the NY Times best seller list..."

Just in case I didn't know, I thought.

"...I've had nothing but problems. Fame is a hard taskmaster."

Okay, so now that we've firmly established the fact that you're famous _and_ a pompous ass, can we get on with it? my mind asked.

"So which particular problem can I help you with?" I asked, although of course I already knew. I just wanted to see how he'd handle it.

There was a slight pause and the sound of throat clearing, then: "Well, I really can't go into it on the phone," he said. "We should really get together to discuss it. And I like to get the measure of the people I deal with before committing myself to anything."

Hooo, boy! Like _he's_ doing _me_ a favor! "Of course," I said. "Why don't I come by your office and...."

"Uh, no," he said hastily. "Why don't we meet for lunch today? At the Brambles, say?"

The Brambles was a caviar and truffles restaurant located in the main building of the Birchwood Country Club—the city's most exclusive. The Brambles deigned to accept reservations from non-country-club members, as long as they were rich and famous. However, it did have its own entrance to keep any non-Birchwood members from getting too close to the real members. I sincerely doubted that Tunderew was a member of the country club, but I knew damned well he'd like me to *think* he was.

"Well, that's very nice of you, Mr. Tunderew," I said, "but I've got a pretty full schedule today, and the Brambles is quite a distance. Could we make it at Michael's?"

I could have, of course, just suggested he come by my office, but I suspected that he preferred to be out among his adoring public. Michael's was one of the oldest restaurants in the city; good food, not cheap but not in the Brambles' price range by any means. It was quite popular with the business set, so I figured Tunderew wouldn't consider it too far beneath him.

There was another slight pause and then: "Yes, Michael's will be fine. I'll call for a table. Twelve or twelve thirty?"

"Twelve thirty will be fine," I said. "I'll look forward to it."

"Fine," he said. "I'm sure you won't have any trouble spotting me. I look exactly like the photo on the dust jacket of my book."

I did not want to burst his little bubble by admitting I'd never so much as picked up a copy of *Dirty Little Minds* and so hadn't a clue what he might look like. Well, there was a bookstore two doors down from Michael's, which I'm sure he knew. I'd take a quick run in there and check. And I was mildly bemused by the fact that he didn't ask how he might be able to spot me. I'm sure he didn't care.

* * *

Michael's was within walking distance of my office, so thanks largely to a blustery wind at my back all the way, I made it in plenty of time to go into the bookstore to see if I could find a copy of *Dirty Little Minds*. Since fully one half of an entire display window was stacked with them, that didn't prove to be much of a problem. I went in, idly picked a copy off the nearest table, and turned it over. Tony T. Tunderew turned out to be a rather handsome man who for some inexplicable reason reminded me of a used-Mercedes dealer or an unctuous maitre d'. He was wearing a bulky-knit turtleneck sweater of the type favored by Cape Cod fishermen and famous authors, leaning against some sort of rough-wood wall, staring intently into the camera, his arms folded across his chest.

I laid the book carefully back on the pile and left.

I paused briefly, upon catching a glimpse of myself in a window, to quickly run a comb through my hair so I didn't look quite so much like I'd just stuck my finger in a light socket. When I entered the restaurant, I made a quick look around the crowd—Michael's always did a good business and it was, after all, the lunch hour—but no sign of Tunderew. I noted there were two tables—one toward the far wall and one in the center of the large front window, with small "Reserved" cards, and I was pretty sure I knew, if Tunderew had called for reservations, which one was for him.

A moment later the door opened and a dapper-looking Tony T. Tunderew entered, wearing a neat blue blazer over a smoke-grey turtleneck sweater. He looked as though he had just gotten out of the barber's chair, and despite the gale-force winds didn't have a hair out of place. I hate people like that.

He didn't even look at me as he headed toward the door to the dining room, until I said: "Mr. Tunderew?"

His eyes immediately went from my face to my hands, apparently to see if I was an adoring fan carrying a copy of his book. Seeing that I wasn't, he must have made the connection, because he said: "Mr. Hardesty?"

We shook hands and exchanged the usual requisite greetings as a waiter came up with two menus.

"Mr. Tunderew's table, please," Tunderew said, and the waiter smiled, nodded, and gestured us into the room. We followed him to—where else?—the table in front of the window.

"I'll have a Vodka Gimlet," Tunderew said as soon as we were seated and as the waiter was handing us the menus. "Three onions," he added, and the waiter nodded again, then looked at me.

"Whiskey sour," I said. I figured if we were into slightly obscure drinks, I'd go along.

After ascertaining that we would wait a few minutes before ordering, the waiter went off to get our drinks.

"So exactly how might I be able to help you?" I asked, not seeing much point in wasting time.

Tunderew tugged at the collar of his turtleneck with an index finger, then reached for his glass of water.

"I'm being blackmailed," he said after taking a sip of water and replacing his glass on the table.

I tried to look as if I hadn't known all along. "Any idea who?" I asked.

He looked at me with mild disdain. "I know exactly who," he said, which rather caught me by surprise, since O'Banyon hadn't mentioned that part—if Tunderew had even told him.

The waiter arrived with our drinks and asked if we were

ready to order. We asked for more time, and he left.

"And exactly what does the blackmailer think he has against you?" I asked.

He leaned forward and lowered his voice. "Totally circumstantial bullshit," he said.

Somehow I doubted that. "If you know who it is, have you confronted him...or her?" I asked.

Tunderew shook his head strongly from side to side. "Oooh, no! I'm not going near that little piece of shit! I don't want to give him an ounce of encouragement!"

Well, that was all pretty cryptic, I thought. "May I ask why?" I asked.

"Because I can't afford a scandal, no matter how ridiculous, of course."

"And this particular scandal might involve...?" I urged.

His look changed to one of total disgust: "My being a faggot," he said.

Chapter 2

I couldn't resist the temptation.

"And are you?" I asked, taking an oddly perverse delight in watching him turn beet red.

"Of course not!" he spat, a fate-worse-than-death look of revulsion on his face.

"Then on exactly what is he basing the blackmail?" I asked. "And how did you find out about it?"

We both took a healthy swallow of our drinks while he regained his composure. Then he reached into his jacket pocket and pulled out an envelope, which he slid across the table to me. I took it and opened it. There was a single sheet of paper inside with the typed words: "Check #2501 is worth a hell of a lot more than $375. Say, $10,000? Cash. POB 324, 1815 Mercer Blvd. By the 15th."

I returned it to the envelope and slid it back across the table to him.

"And exactly why might Check #2501 be worth more than $375? What was the $375 for?"

He stared at me for a long moment, slowly rotating his glass with his thumb and middle finger. Finally, he took in a deep breath and said: "There was this faggot who worked at Craylaw & Collier in the research department...Larry Fletcher...a real pansy...."

Well, now, there's a word that went out of fashion somewhere around 1927, I thought, in a not very successful attempt to remain calmly objective.

The waiter returned to the table and we broke off the conversation long enough to look quickly at the menu and order. Actually, I didn't really have to look: Michael's was one of the few places in town that served a Monte Cristo sandwich, complete with a powdered sugar top and mint jelly on the side, and I ordered it every time I had occasion to come in. And while our conversation thus far had pretty much taken my appetite away, I wasn't about to deny myself a Monte Cristo.

Tunderew watched the waiter depart, then resumed his story. "Anyway, this little Nurse Nancy took a real shine to me, always hanging around, always asking if there was something he could do for me—well, I sure as hell could figure out what that little fudge-packer had in mind."

Where in hell does he come up with this stuff? my mind asked casually, as an alternative to my reaching across the table and ripping his lungs out.

Apparently mistaking my silence for intense interest, he kept right on.

"I had a pretty high-pressure position at C&C, so I let him do some little look-up things for me. He was in faggot heaven! All I had to do was ask, and he was right there. I used to get a kick out of giving him a best-buddy smile or maybe a little wink—especially when I knew that he might have to bend company policy to get what I wanted. He'd practically cream his jeans. I even had him running errands for me during his lunch hour. Made my life a lot easier, that's for sure." He gave a little self-satisfied chuckle. "We had enough faggots at C&C to open an interior decorating studio—I've heard that old man Collier was a little light in the loafers himself, and liked to hire his own kind."

Oh, please let's punch him! Can we? several of my little mind voices said eagerly.

"You still haven't told me just how the check enters into it," I said.

He shook his head slowly from side to side. "You know that old saying that no good deed goes unpunished?"

"I've heard it," I said.

"Well, I go out of my way to help somebody—some little fruit, no less—and it comes back to bite me on the ass!"

He had my full attention. "You wrote a check to Mr. Fletcher?"

He pulled his head back quickly as if ducking something I'd just thrown at him.

"Are you out of your fucking mind?" he asked, rhetorically. "I wouldn't be caught dead writing a check to some little faggot!"

Well, you're going to be writing one soon to a not-so-little faggot if I'm crazy enough to take this case, I thought.

He gave a dramatic sigh and continued. "Okay, it's like this. I told you that I had him do some little research projects for me on the side—nothing important, just stuff I didn't have time to do myself. Granted, as I said, some of them involved looking into places he shouldn't have been looking, but...anyway, he comes to me one day and tells me he has to quit work and move back home to Bumfuck, Arizona or someplace. Seems some other faggot he was living with threw a hissy-fit and told him he had to move, and he'd found a place, but he didn't have the money for the deposit. So I gave it to him—strictly a loan! I realize now, though, that it was just the first step in his little extortion scheme. But I guess I was just too naive to recognize it at the time."

Naive. Uh huh.

"As I say, I wasn't stupid enough to make it out to him. I made it to the apartment building's management company. Still, it wouldn't take much to link the two things together if anybody wanted to—and I know damned well there are people out there who'd love nothing better. Well, that's what I get for being a nice guy."

I was glad I wasn't in the process of taking a sip of coffee or I'd probably have choked on it.

"Anyway," he continued, oblivious to the small wisps of steam curling up from my ears, "he apparently took my generosity as a sign of true love, and I could tell from the looks I started getting from some of the other office fruits that little Larry was telling his girlfriends stories about me. That did it. The week before I quit myself, I saw to it that little Larry got his faggot ass fired."

"Which brings us to what you expect me to do about all this. If you're so sure it's Mr. Fletcher, you could just go down to the post office and wait to catch him opening the box."

"For one thing, it's not a post office box," he said. "It's one of those commercial places where they just forward mail on to somewhere else. They told me I'd need a court order before they could reveal who took out the box, but they didn't have to. As I told you I know who it is."

The waiter arrived with our food, and it's a tribute to Michael's chefs that I was able to override my loss of appetite. We waited until the waiter had left and we'd picked up our forks to begin eating.

"So what exactly would you like me to do?" I asked finally.

Tunderew snorted in disgust. "I just want to you to let him know he's not going to get away with it. All I know is that I sure as hell am not going to start showing up in the tabloids as a queer! I've got a reputation to protect!"

Oh, I'm sure you've got a reputation, my mind agreed. *But why in the world would you want to protect it?*

I'd concentrated on trying to eat while he talked, partly as another form of distracting my urge to get up and walk out, after first shoving his three-onion Vodka Gimlet up his ass. "Well," I said after taking time to carefully put a dab of mint jelly on a piece of my Monte Cristo, "if you'll excuse me, I can't see that as really a very solid basis for blackmail. People spread rumors all the time; that doesn't mean they're true."

"Well *this* one sure as hell isn't," he said defensively.

Uh huh, I thought. "I'm curious, though," I said, "who else might have had access to your checkbook, or who else might have made an association between a check made out to a management company and any relationship, real or imagined, between you and Mr. Fletcher? Seems like quite a leap."

He looked uncomfortable and shrugged. "Well, I did have to write 'L. Fletcher Deposit' on the 'Memo' line of the check."

Aha!

"It seems to me your wife might have found that a little odd."

Tunderew laughed briefly. "My wife?" he said, contemptuously. "She's so self-centered I don't even think she knows I'm gone. She wouldn't have the guts even if she had the intelligence, and she's dumber than a lamp post. And my checkbook is *my* checkbook," he said firmly. "Besides, she has no reason to resort to blackmail. She's getting more than enough alimony to keep her happy. It's that fruit Fletcher."

That's it, Charlie, I thought. *One more 'pansy' or 'fruit' reference and I'm gone.*

"You always keep your checkbook on you?" I asked

Tunderew carefully speared an onion that had fallen from its blue plastic pick to the bottom of the glass before looking up at me.

"No," he said. "I keep it in my briefcase, which is usually locked."

"But not always," I said, making an obvious assumption. "And you don't have your briefcase with you every minute. Ever leave it lying around open?"

He thought for a moment. "Uh…I had it with me at that little dipshit publisher's one time, and I had it open to put in a galley proof of the book, and…" he pursed his lips "…and I left the office to take a piss, but I remember when I got back it was just where I'd left it. And what in hell reason would Bernadine have to rummage through my checkbook?"

"Did they know at that point that you were planning on dumping them with your second book?"

"No," he said casually. "I hadn't officially accepted the advance offer yet. I didn't tell them until my agent had everything all sealed up with the new publisher."

It wasn't beyond the realm of possibility that an open briefcase might be somewhat tempting if Bernadine Press knew or suspected he was planning to jump ship…and check #2501 would have been the top check in a new set of 25. Just lifting the cover of the checkbook would have shown it in carbon copy.

I took a long sip of coffee, carefully replacing the cup on the saucer, before speaking.

"Well, to be honest with you, Mr. Tunderew, knowing your aversion to faggots and considering that I am one, I might suggest you could be better served by going to the yellow pages and picking a private investigator with whom you might feel more comfortable."

I was watching his face for any reaction to my letting him

know I was gay myself, but there was none. He didn't bat an eye. "I of course could have contacted a heterosexual private investigator, but the nature of this…issue…would be better addressed by someone more familiar with it on a personal level. I deliberately asked Glen O'Banyon for a reference because I was pretty sure he'd recommend…a fellow traveler," he said with a small, condescending smile. "I'm a very open-minded and practical man when it comes to my own best interest."

I said nothing, having earlier decided against mopping the floor with him, but was still debating just getting out of my chair and leaving.

"I appreciate your candor," I said, again vaguely pleased by how calm I sounded. "Not very many bigots have the courage to be so open in a one-to-one, face-to-face situation."

His smile returned. "Since I doubt we will ever be spending much quality time together, we don't have to like one another, Mr. Hardesty," he said. "But I understand that you are both discreet and good at what you do. And for you to turn me down, as I'm sure you've been considering doing, would only prove that you were as bigoted in your own way as you claim I am in mine. As a final incentive, I'm willing to pay half-again your normal rates in an effort to appeal to *your* own practical best interest."

Well, I hate to admit it, but he had a point or two in there. And it occurred to me that probably the main reason he chose me was because he was so firmly convinced the blackmailer was Fletcher. His paranoia didn't want anyone straight—even a p.i.—to know someone might think he was gay. Tunderew may have been positive about Fletcher, but I'd bet the line of people with a good reason to blackmail him would stretch around the block.

"And if, on some very outside chance, it *isn't* Mr. Fletcher?" I asked again.

He just shrugged, removing the little pick with the two remaining onions from his glass. He closed his teeth just past the second onion and pulled the now-empty pick slowly from him mouth, then drained his drink, and dropped the pick back into the empty glass.

"It is," he said. "No question. He follows me around to book signings, keeps sending me love letters—I just tear them up without opening them."

"How do you know they're 'love letters' if you never open them?" I asked.

"I suggest you use your rubber hose on someone else, Mr. Hardesty. Larry Fletcher would be a good choice. Do you want the job or not?"

I knew that if I didn't take it, he would manage to find someone to go after Larry Fletcher and, guilty or not, he didn't deserve to be hounded by some ham-fisted straight p.i. with a Mickey Spillane complex. So while it was still against my better judgment, I found myself saying: "Okay, I'll take the case. I'll bring the contract, including a revision of my rate schedule, to your office—or..." I thought the mention of his office would spark a response and it did, because he broke in immediately.

"We don't need a contract. I just want you to put the fear of God into that little turd."

"Well, I'm sorry," I said, "but I don't take any case without having a signed contract to protect both parties' interest."

He gave an exasperated sigh. "Very well, then. But just mail it to my post office box. I don't want anyone to know of our arrangement, and the post office box is more private. I'll sign it and get it back to you."

"Fine," I said, wondering idly why, if he didn't want to be seen hobnobbing with faggots, we were sitting in the front window of a popular restaurant within two doors of a bookstore promoting his book.

Oblivious to my thoughts, he nodded. "You'll go see him immediately, then?" he asked. "We only have until the 15th—that's just two days after I get my next royalty check, and I have far better things to do with the money."

"The minute I get the signed contract and retainer," I said as pleasantly as I could. I could see he wasn't too happy about that, but I couldn't care less. A big part of me was just looking for the slightest excuse to tell him to forget it.

* * *

On the walk back to my office after lunch—I'd insisted on paying for my own, and he didn't object—I tried to figure out just why in the hell I had agreed to take this case. I've turned down cases before. Okay, not many, but... Actually, I think it had something to do with his remark about his trusting that I wasn't as much a bigot as he was.

And I was just nosy enough to want to know exactly what Fletcher—if it was Fletcher—*really* had on the guy. A check made out to a rental agency might look a little incriminating, but I couldn't really see it's being much of a basis for blackmail. There was more going on here than Tunderew was letting on, and that he apparently thought I was too stupid to figure it out really pissed me off. But Fletcher or not, I suspected Tony T. Tunderew had quite a few skeletons rattling around in his...uh...closet. If it turned out Tunderew was gay, I might seriously consider turning in my membership card and joining a monastery. But I knew full well that being gay is not an automatic nomination for sainthood—straights don't hold a patent on obnoxious jerks.

As soon as I got in the door of the office, I filled out a contract, drew a line through my normal rates and wrote in the new figure above, and increased the amount of my retainer by the same percentage. I really sort of suspected...with no small element of hope in there...that I'd never hear from the guy again.

I checked the business card Tunderew had given me (I now had two, so I pitched the one Glen O'Banyon had given me at Hughie's) for his P.O. Box number he'd written on the back, addressed an envelope, and went out into the hall to drop it in the mail chute beside the elevators.

When I returned to the office, I called O'Banyon's office and left word with his secretary, Donna, that I had met with Mr. Tunderew and would be taking the case.

I determined to put Tunderew out of my head until and unless I got the contract back with a check. But me being me, my mind kept going back to my meeting with the guy, and especially to Larry Fletcher. I was very curious about him for some reason.

It was obvious that Tunderew had taken full advantage of the poor guy, though how Fletcher could possibly, as he apparently had done, fall for such an arrogant sonofabitch I couldn't imagine. Well, some guys like to be treated like doormats. And I was very curious as to exactly what sort of "research" Fletcher was doing for him. That part was fairly easy to figure out: *Dirty Little Minds* just happened to be about a character everyone immediately recognized was based on Governor Keene—and Governor Keene had been a client of Craylaw & Collier. I'd be willing to bet that Tunderew had quit his job the minute he knew his book was sold, to avoid being canned. And he had to get rid of poor Larry Fletcher so there wouldn't be anyone around to verify that Tunderew had been snooping around the company's files. Whether Fletcher was the blackmailer or not, Tunderew was sending me after him as a warning to keep his mouth shut.

* * *

Jonathan was waiting at the door with my Manhattan—I'd glanced up at our apartment as I walked through the courtyard toward the door and saw him in the window with a spray bottle he used to mist some of the 14,000 plants we'd accumulated from his job at the nursery. Apparently he'd spotted me coming in.

We exchanged grins and a hug, and as always went directly to the couch to sit down. Jonathan already had his Coke on the coffee table.

"I saw Randy today at New Eden," he said, "and asked him over for dinner. I told him Friday, if that's okay. I would have made it Thursday, but I've got class."

"Friday's fine," I said. "How's the Dinsmore's new house coming along?"

He took a sip of his coke. "The Dinsmores have already been living there for a couple of months now. We're just finishing up the yard. We just planted the last of the new trees today." The look on his face told me he had something else to say, but was hesitant to do so for some reason.

"Something else?" I asked, and he gave me a quick, small grin.

"Can I take the car to work Friday?" he asked. "That way I can go directly from work out to New Eden to pick Randy up and bring him home. But that means you'd have to take the bus, and..."

As usual, we'd had our free hands resting on each other's thighs, and I gave him a quick squeeze. "You take the bus every day," I said. "I think I can manage to do it for one."

His smile became a broad grin. "Thanks!" he said; then his face changed slightly into his 'naughty little boy' look and he said: "Ya wanna play a game before dinner?"

"Sure!" I said. Jonathan was very much into the "Let's Pretend" brand of eroticism, and he'd gotten me pretty much hooked, too. It added a lot of spice—not that we really needed more—to our sex life. Usually they'd be set off by something specific: picking him up from class might spark an infinite number of variations on "The Hitchhiker," or just coming home from grocery shopping would lead to a rousing "The Manager and the Stock Boy", or...well, you get the idea. He always kept me on my toes, that's for sure.

"What do you want to play?" I asked, noticing that my crotch was already responding enthusiastically to the prospect.

Jonathan set his Coke aside, got up, took my Manhattan from my hand and set it on the coffee table, then pulled me up from the couch.

"How about 'The Hardworking p.i. and the Appreciative Lover'?" he asked as he led me to the bedroom.

Sounded good to me.

* * *

I could tell Jonathan was really looking forward to having Randy over for dinner, and I realized with some sense of empathy and maybe a touch of irrational guilt that Jonathan really didn't have any gay friends of his own—all our friends had been my friends first. He hadn't been in town all that long when

I met him, and he'd been hustling all that time, so he really hadn't had a chance to make friends. I got the impression that he and Randy hadn't actually been that close, but it was as close as he got. And I suspected that while Jonathan might not realize it himself, he wanted to let someone know how far he had come since that time. He had every reason to be proud of himself.

As for Randy, from what Jonathan had told me of him, his life had been a classic horror story of abuse, abandonment, and neglect. His father had died in prison, his drug-addict mother walked out on him when he was six. He was placed in the revolving door of the foster care system, where he became a chronic runaway. At 13, he ran and never came back. He'd been living on the streets, and hustling, ever since. I could not comprehend a life like that. With New Eden, he had the chance for some real stability for the first time in his life.

Jonathan had insisted on buying all the ingredients for dinner himself, including a very large roast. He got up early Friday morning to peel potatoes and carrots, arranging them carefully around the roast in a dutch oven, then rearranging the refrigerator to make room for it. He'd done all this by the time I got up, and before he left for work instructed me to put it in the oven at 350 degrees the minute I got home. I assured him I'd try to set the table before he arrived.

* * *

Taking the bus to work really wasn't all that bad, and I probably would do it more often were it not for the fact of never knowing when I might need the car during the day for work. And since I paid monthly for a parking space in the lot across the street from my office building, it was foolish not to get my money's worth from it.

I did my usual morning things, sent out a couple of bills on completed cases, wrote a reminder letter to a client whose bill was long overdue, and generally puttered, awaiting the arrival of the mail.

Sure enough, there was an envelope (no return address)

containing Tunderew's contract and a cashier's check for the retainer. I suppose he was being paranoid and didn't want to repeat his mistake with Larry Fletcher by writing out a check traceable to a known faggot. Instead, he had his name clearly written on a contract hiring one. What an idiot. But that was fine with me—at least I didn't have to worry about a money order clearing the bank.

So, like it or not, I was on the case. I put the contract in my file cabinet, returned to my desk, and got out the phone book, turning to the "F"s. There was an "L. Fletcher," a "Laurence Fletcher," and a "Lawrence C. Fletcher." Since "Lawrence C. Fletcher"'s address was on Ash within two blocks of Beech (and therefore almost directly in the middle of The Central), I opted for him. I tried calling, but there was no answer and no machine. Well, I'd try to call when I got home, before Jonathan and Randy arrived.

* * *

Though I left work about half an hour early, anticipating a long wait at the bus stop, one pulled up just as I approached the corner, and it didn't take all that much longer to get home on the bus than it did with the car. I went immediately to the kitchen to turn the oven on to exactly 350 degrees and to say hello to Phil and Tim and the other fish (Jonathan had me brainwashed). I set the table in the dining area, which we very seldom used, figuring Jonathan would prefer that to the kitchen table. I then went to the phone to call Larry Fletcher and had just started to dial when it occurred to me that perhaps the roast might cook faster if I took it out of the refrigerator and put it in the oven. (Hey, I can't be both devilishly handsome *and* smart at the same time!)

Returning to the phone, I dialed Fletcher's number.

"Hello?" a pleasant-sounding voice said after the second ring. Subtly but definitely gay, though.

"Larry Fletcher?" I asked, not knowing whether Fletcher might have a roommate and not wanting to plunge ahead without being sure I had the right person.

"Yes?"

"Mr. Fletcher, my name is Dick Hardesty, and I'm a private investigator. I'd like to talk with you about Tony Tunderew."

I could almost see his eyes narrowing in suspicion, which was more than evident in his voice when he said: "What about? I won't say anything bad about Tony, if that's what you're after. He's been very good to me, and…"

Well, that was certainly an interesting couple of sentences, I thought, making a mental note to follow up on them the first chance I had.

"No," I hastened to say, "this is on a totally different matter. Would it be possible for us to meet in person to discuss it as soon as it might be convenient for you?"

There was a long pause, and then: "Well, I don't know. I suppose so. But I don't know when. I work Monday thru Friday, and…"

"How about tomorrow?" I asked. "Perhaps we could meet at my office sometime during the day—you name the time. It shouldn't take too long, really, and it is rather important." I could have suggested that I go to his apartment, but thought he might feel a little less intimidated if he came to my office. It's easier to just get up and leave someone else's place than it is to try to get someone to leave yours.

I heard a long sigh. "All right. One o'clock? Where is your office?"

I told him, thanked him for his cooperation, said I was looking forward to seeing him, and we hung up.

* * *

I'd held off having my evening Manhattan, deciding to wait until Jonathan got home and to see if Randy might want something. I was pretty sure he drank, since Jonathan had picked up a bottle of wine for dinner. I was also quite curious about meeting Randy. I was sure he would provide me with a little insight into Jonathan's hustler past, although he'd really only hustled for a couple of months before we met.

I was in the kitchen checking on the roast when I heard the front door open, and Jonathan's voice calling: "We're here!" I hastily closed the oven door and went into the living room. Jonathan came quickly across the room to give me a hug, and then turned to the young man standing just inside the door.

"Dick," Jonathan said, taking me by the hand and leading me over to Randy, "this is my friend, Randy."

Randy extended his hand, looked me over from top to bottom, glanced at Jonathan with a slightly raised eyebrow, and said: "Hi."

"Hi, Randy," I said. "I'm glad to meet you." As we shook hands, I looked him over, too—or as much as I could see from the short distance between us.

A very nice looking guy, probably very close to Jonathan's age, though he looked older; about 5'10", dirty-blond hair cut short, hazel eyes, with a small scar at the side of his nose just below his right cheekbone. And if I hadn't known that he was—or had been—a hustler, I could easily have guessed. He had that indefinable...what?...hard-edged?...look and body language I immediately see in most hustlers. Hustling is a hard life, and it takes its toll. In Randy, it showed in his eyes. His body language gave off almost an aura of cockiness, bravura, and guardedness. I inwardly shuddered to think that if Jonathan had stayed in that life, he would be very much the same as Randy was now.

As soon as we had disengaged our handshake, Jonathan said: "Come on, Randy, let me show you the apartment, and then I'll show you my fish!"

There really wasn't all that much to see in the apartment, of course, but Jonathan was very eager that his friend see everything, and made a point of showing Randy the small picture of a cat Jonathan had bought at an art fair, and which now hung in the hallway right outside our bedroom door. I left the tour before they got that far, and went back to the kitchen.

"I'm going to have a Manhattan," I called out over my shoulder, loudly enough to be sure they could hear. "Would you like something, Randy?"

"Yeah," he called back. "A Manhattan'd be good. Thanks."

I had both Manhattans made and opened a Coke for Jonathan when they entered the kitchen, Jonathan leading Randy directly to the fish tank.

"That's Tim there," Jonathan said, pointing, "and that one down there's Phil. They were my first two, so they're special." Apparently concerned that he may have hurt the feelings of the others, he quickly bent forward and said, obviously addressing them: "Not that you're not all special." As I've said before, Jonathan marched to his own drummer.

When the fish introductions were over, we all moved into the living room and sat down, Jonathan getting immediately back up again to go check the roast.

"Nice place," Randy said, looking around. "Jonathan's lucky he found you."

I grinned. "I'd say I was the lucky one," I replied, and he gave me a smile from somewhere beneath his hustler shell. It made me oddly sad, somehow.

"So how do you like New Eden?" I asked to divert my thoughts.

Randy took a sip of his Manhattan and shrugged. "It's okay," he said. "I won't be there too much longer, though."

"Oh?" I said, curious to learn just how the New Eden system worked. But I'd have to wait to find out.

"Yeah, I'll be getting my own place pretty soon," he said. "Maybe go back to school."

"That's great," I said. "What do you want to study?"

Jonathan had come back into the room and sat beside me on the sofa, retrieving his Coke from the coffee table and taking a long swallow.

"I think I'd like to be a dental technician," Randy said. "Jonathan says they offer that at Grant, where he goes."

"Randy got his G.E.D. through New Eden," Jonathan said, obviously proud of his friend, and I was impressed not only by Randy's willingness to get it, but by the fact that New Eden helped to make it possible.

I really was increasingly curious about just how New Eden

operated. I'd heard the kids who went there—and had a sudden realization that Randy was hardly a kid anymore; another source of curiosity—worked the farm in exchange for room and board, but obviously there must have been some way they could make money in order to be able to move on with their lives at some point, as Randy was apparently planning to do.

* * *

During dinner, I could sense subtle cracks developing in Randy's hustler shell as he allowed himself to relax ever so slightly. I knew, though, that the cracks were only temporary. He and Jonathan talked a lot about shared experiences and times and former fellow-hustlers of which and of whom I knew nothing, but I didn't feel left out. I was fascinated to watch Jonathan relate to his friend...*his* friend...and I was truly happy for him.

Several times Randy hinted at his prospects for a very bright and prosperous future, and there seemed to be something other than idle bravado in it, though I couldn't pin it down and certainly couldn't ask directly. Well, normally I might have, but I realized I was being on my best behavior for Jonathan's sake.

We drove Randy back to New Eden around eleven-thirty. I'd suggested that Jonathan could take Randy back by himself, to give them a little more time alone together, but Jonathan insisted I go along.

As we got back on the highway leading into town, Jonathan said: "That was nice, wasn't it?" and I agreed. "Did you like him?" Jonathan asked.

"Yes, I did. And mostly because he's your friend."

Jonathan sighed and looked out the window for a long time without speaking. Finally he said, almost to himself and without looking at me: "It's so different."

"What is?" I asked, though I think I knew.

"Me then and me now," he said. He turned to me and put his hand on my leg. "Can you imagine where I'd be if I hadn't met you?" he asked.

34

The Dirt Peddler   *Dorien Grey*

I didn't even want to think about that, so I turned to him and smiled. "Well, the important thing is that we did meet. And I'm very glad that we did."

"Yeah," he said softly, then turned to look out the window again.

* * *

I usually try very hard not to work at all on weekends, but since I was anxious to get this case going, I figured I'd better catch Larry Fletcher as soon as I could, even if it was on a Saturday. Jonathan had been carefully nurturing a bunch of plants he wanted to take over to give to the residents at Haven House.

"A lot of these kids have never had anything of their own that depended on them," he'd said. "Plants need attention, and they're almost as good as pets." Then, with typical Jonathan logic, he added: "Except you don't have to walk them."

We agreed that he could drive me to the office, since it was almost on the way to Haven House, go deliver the plants, then come back and pick me up. I didn't think it would take too long with Fletcher.

I got to the office at about quarter to one. Though the building was open until five, it was nearly deserted. The diner and newsstand were closed, no one was in sight, and the sound of my footsteps echoed through the lobby. I made a pot of coffee more out of habit than need, figuring maybe Fletcher would like a cup.

Well, that was fun, my mind voice said as I flipped the "on" switch on the coffee maker. *Now what will we do?* I didn't have a Saturday paper for the crossword puzzle, and there was little point in trying to start any sort of project. And it was all so damned quiet.

I finally settled for opening the middle drawer of my desk, which hadn't been cleaned out in decades and started rummaging idly through it, finding enough pencils—a couple with points—to build a small log cabin, and more pens than I could ever use, most of them without ink.

I heard the elevator doors open and footsteps approaching. Not a moment too soon. I slid the drawer closed and got up to go to the door.

Larry Fletcher turned out to be...well...average, and "average" is a pretty hard thing to describe. Hot guys are usually easy to describe—just let your fantasies run wild. Singularly unattractive people usually have some distinctive features that make them so. But "average"...well (again), average looking people look pretty much like everyone else. Fletcher was one of them: early twenties, average height, average build, long-ish brown hair, glasses. Walk down a busy street and eight guys out of ten you pass could be Larry Fletcher. But he certainly was not, at first glance, the flaming faggot that Tunderew had led me to expect.

If I could think of one word to describe my first impression of him, it would be "meek."

We shook hands, and I noticed that while his grip wasn't limp by any means, it wasn't exactly the confidence-filled handshake of a motivational speaker. After an exchange of greetings, I gestured him to a chair near the desk as I closed the door behind him.

"Coffee?" I asked before I sat down.

"No, thanks," he said, looking and sounding a bit nervous.

I sat down behind my desk and waited while Fletcher's eyes reflected his discomfort by slowly circling around the room in smaller and smaller sweeps—like water draining from a sink—to finally meet my own, briefly.

"Why, exactly, did you want to see me?" he asked. "I told you on the phone I won't say anything against Tony."

Tony, eh? Interesting.

"What makes you think I'd want you to say anything against Mr. Tunderew?" I asked.

"That's what the lawyers from Craylaw & Collier wanted," he said. "They threatened to sue me, but I just told them to go ahead and try. I thought you were working for them until I saw you just now."

???? "I'm sorry?" I said, my face probably reflecting my confusion.

Fletcher gave me a shy smile. "I've seen you in the bars," he said, "several times. You never noticed me, of course."

What do you mean "of course?" I wondered. And why did that make me feel like a ten pound bag of bat guano?

"…and I could tell those lawyers are so uptight I'll bet their sphincters would slam shut at the very idea of hiring a gay p.i. "

I broke out laughing, and after a quick trepidatious look to see if I were laughing at him or with him, he joined me, covering his mouth with his hand like a kid. The ice pretty much melted away after that.

"What were Craylaw & Collier's lawyers wanting you to say?" I asked.

"They thought Tony had been breeching company security and stealing files."

"On Governor Keene," I said, not having to make it a question.

He nodded. "And they thought I was helping him."

"And were you?" I asked, watching closely for his reaction. "Closely" was hardly necessary. I could have been a block away and still caught it; he lowered his head and dropped his eyes to the floor. I don't imagine the guy was very good at playing poker.

"It wasn't that way at all," he said, looking up at me with his head still lowered.

"What way was it?" I asked.

He waited until his head had caught up with his eyes. "How do I know I can trust you?"

"Well," I said, "for one thing because it was Mr. Tunderew who asked me to talk with you."

"He did?" Fletcher said, his entire face lighting up.

I nodded.

"Well, then you know why I wouldn't tell those lawyers anything—not with Tony doing undercover work for the FBI."

!!!! I thought.

He nodded his head somberly and continued. "He needed to get all the information on the Keene case he could from C&C's

files. The FBI thinks some higher ups at C&C were in on the scandal. But Tony couldn't draw suspicion to himself by getting the files himself, so he asked me to help him."

My first reaction was: *You're pulling my leg, right? Nobody can be that gullible!*

But then I thought of what little I knew about the charming Mr. Tunderew, and the vibes I was getting from a young man who practically exuded low self esteem, and I realized exactly what Tunderew had done. The kid obviously had a crush on him. Tunderew had zeroed in on it like a rattlesnake on a mouse hole, and the poor kid didn't stand a chance.

And any idea at all I might have had of Larry Fletcher being the one blackmailing Tony T. Tunderew went right out the window. I'd been wrong before—a lot—but I didn't think I was this time.

"I'm curious," I said. "Did Mr. Tunderew ever give you any indication that he might be gay?"

The downcast eyes again, and a furious blush. Finally he looked back up at me. "Not in so many words," he said. "I mean, I know he's married and all that, and he likes to pretend he hates gays, but..."

My opinion of Tunderew was rapidly sliding from dislike to loathing. I had not the slightest doubt that he had deliberately led Larry on with those "best buddy" smiles he himself had alluded to. I despise people who take advantage of the naivety of others to get something for themselves.

I decided to just forge ahead. "Did you ever...uh...socialize with Mr. Tunderew outside of the office?"

Fletcher looked truly surprised, and shook his head vigorously. "Oh, no. Never. I'm sure we would have, but his wife is a real witch. He had to go right home every night after work or she'd make his life miserable. I really felt sorry for him. He talked several times about wishing he could take me out for dinner to show his appreciation for everything I did for him, but his wife would never allow it."

Sigh.

"I understand Mr. Tunderew loaned you some money toward

your apartment?" I asked.

"Yes," Fletcher replied with a happy smile. "That's just like Tony. When I told him I was going to have to quit work and move back home, he offered to lend me the money to get my own apartment."

Somehow I didn't think I had to ask him if Tunderew's generosity might have coincided with the time Fletcher was copying files for him. If Fletcher had indeed quit, Tunderew would probably would have had a tough time finding someone else to do his dirty work.

Of course that thought had probably never occurred to Fletcher, who was still talking. "He's a wonderful man," Fletcher was saying. "I've tried to repay him, but he's never cashed a single one of the checks I send him."

Checks? He was sending Tunderew checks and that arrogant asshole just tore them up without opening them because he assumed they were love letters!

"Where do you send them?" I asked.

"He has a post office box. When I'd copy a file for him, I'd stay after work to do it, and then mail it to him at his box. He didn't want me to just give it to him there at work, and I couldn't send it to his home because of his wife. I don't have his home address anyway."

"And did you ever find anything incriminating any Craylaw & Collier personnel?" I asked.

He shook his head. "Oh, I never read anything I copied. That wouldn't be right. Tony would just tell me which file he wanted and I'd find it and copy the whole thing."

I wondered if he knew it was Tunderew who had gotten him fired. "You're no longer working at Craylaw & Collier, I understand," I said.

He looked embarrassed, and again lowered his eyes. "No. I…I was fired. I think someone found out I was copying files, though they never asked me anything until later when the lawyers talked to me. When he found out I was fired, Tony went right to Mr. Craylaw to ask him to give me my job back."

"He did?" I asked, surprised. "How do you know that?"

"Tony told me," he said.

Dear God! I thought.

"When did he tell you that?" I asked, curious.

"I ran into him in the hall when I came back to the office the next day to pick up some of the things I'd left."

"Were you aware that Mr. Tunderew is being blackmailed?" I asked, again watching closely for any reaction that might indicate I was wrong in thinking it wasn't him.

He looked truly shocked. "No! What for? Who'd do something like that?" He paused and then nodded his head up and down slowly, eyes narrowing. "I'll bet it's his wife!" he said. "I heard that he finally filed for divorce. I'll bet she's trying to get even!"

The guy had a good point. Now that I'd ruled him out, she'd be the next logical place to look. I was still amazed at how incredibly naive Fletcher was about Tunderew and what he was really up to.

I couldn't resist asking the obvious: "Didn't you think it a little odd that after Mr. Tunderew had you do all that file copying on Governor Keene, he comes out with a book on the scandal?"

He shook his head. "No...well, maybe a little bit at first, but I went to his very first book signing and waited for him afterwards until he came out, and I talked to him and asked him about it. He said the FBI had given him permission to use anything he'd found out about the scandal for helping them, except he couldn't mention Craylaw & Collier because the investigation is still going on."

And the kid actually believes it! my mind said, incredulous. *How can any one human being be so stupid?*

And the minute I thought that, I was ashamed of myself. It wasn't a matter of being stupid, just a matter of seeing what one wants to see. Fletcher sincerely thought Tunderew was his friend, and that alone made me truly sad.

There was one other thing I thought I should clear up, just for my own satisfaction.

"Mr. Tunderew says he's seen you at a couple of his book signings," I said.

Fletcher nodded. "Yes, I wanted to be one of the first ones to buy his book, and I did have those questions for him, so I went to that signing I told you about. And then I went to Bennington's opening of their new store in The Central to have him sign a copy to send to my folks. He was so busy, he hardly even had a chance to look at me."

Uh huh.

"Well," I said, getting up from my chair, "thanks very much for coming in, Mr. Fletcher. I'll let Mr. Tunderew know I've talked with you. And he told me to tell you to just forget about repaying the loan. He owes you a lot more than that."

Fletcher got up and followed me to the door. He was obviously delighted that Tunderew had been thinking of him. I was very glad he did not know in what way.

"Please tell Tony hello for me, will you?" he asked as we shook hands.

"I'll do that," I said.

Smiling, he left.

Chapter 3

Jonathan showed up about five minutes after Larry Fletcher left, and we got on with our weekend. I was pleasantly surprised to find that from the moment I closed the office door behind me until I opened it again on Monday, I hadn't given more than a total of five minutes of thought to my current case—largely, I'm sure, because other than my empathy for Larry Fletcher, I knew I really didn't *care* who was blackmailing Tony T. Tunderew.

Well, with Fletcher eliminated, in my mind anyway, as the blackmailer, it was time to move on to the wife...or ex wife by now. After I'd gone through my coffee/paper/crossword puzzle ritual Monday morning, I dialed Tunderew's "office" number. I needed him to call me so I could tell him about Fletcher, and get the number and address for his ex.

"Mr. Tunderew's office," the switchboard operator said. I wondered idly if she even had any idea who he was.

"Is Mr. Tunderew in?" I asked, just to see what this one would say.

"I'm sorry, sir," she said, and there was a slight pause. When she continued, it was obvious she was reading from a prepared text. "Mr. Tunderew will be out of town until Thursday of this week on a book signing tour. He will be a guest on 'A.M. New York' on Channel 14 on Tuesday at 9:45 local time and invites you to watch."

God, what a sweetheart that Tunderew is! one of my little mind voices whispered reverently. *He wants you to watch him plug his book. Almost brings a tear to the eye, doesn't it?*

"Uh, thank you," I said, "but I'll be having an elective root canal at that time. Could I just leave him a message, please?"

I left him my number and told him to call me.

After I hung up, it occurred to me that with Tunderew having been so dead certain that Larry Fletcher was the blackmailer, and having hired me primarily because both Fletcher and I are gay, he never made it clear what he wanted me to do if it *wasn't* Fletcher. I could either sit back and wait for him to call or proceed on the assumption that he'd still want me to find out who the blackmailer was. In the back of my mind, I suspected that when I told him I didn't think it was Fletcher, he'd think I was lying to protect a fellow faggot and fire me. Well, I wasn't just going to sit around and twiddle my thumbs for that to happen. I'd been hired to find his blackmailer, and I'd do my best to do just that. And you can be damned sure I would bill him for every minute spent on the case up to the point of getting the ax.

While I was almost certain that he wouldn't be listed in the phone book, I picked it up and turned to the "T"s. I was right. 'Tundeman, James' was followed by 'Tundfell, Stanley'. Nary a 'Tunderew' to be found.

I decided to call Glen O'Banyon's office on the assumption that he might know how to get in touch with Tunderew's ex. O'Banyon, of course, was in court, but I left a message with his secretary, Donna, asking her to see if I could get Mrs. Tunderew's first name and current address and phone number. She said she would get back to me.

* * *

Around two o'clock, Jonathan called. Unusual for him to call at that hour, but I was glad to hear from him anyway.

"What's up?" I asked.

"Can you do me a favor?" he asked, then paused. "I mean can *I* do *Randy* a favor?"

He had me confused, but it wasn't a first-time for that. "Sure, I suppose," I said. "What does he need?"

"He wants to come into town tonight. He, uh, he's got some stuff he wants to do, and he needs a ride in and back. Would that be okay if I went and got him and took him back later?"

"Uh, I guess," I said, not wanting to press him for details.

"Great! Thanks! I'm at the office at work now. We were out at New Eden this morning and I had to run back to pick up some fertilizer, so I thought I'd better call now so I can tell Randy when I go back out there. Thanks a lot! I'll see you at home."

"Okay," I said, and we hung up.

I really hoped Randy wasn't going to look on Jonathan as a regular taxi service. It didn't occur to me to wonder what "stuff" Randy had to do in town.

* * *

"What time are you supposed to pick Randy up?" I asked as we sat on the sofa in our just-home-from-work mode.

"Six thirty or seven," Jonathan replied, taking a long swig from his Coke. "I really hope you don't mind. I know it's kind of an imposition, but he said he had something he wanted to talk to me about, and we can't talk there."

"That's okay," I said. I didn't ask why Randy didn't just come over here, because I realized he probably wouldn't feel comfortable talking about whatever it was in front of me.

"So you're just supposed to take him into town and pick him up later, or...?"

Jonathan blushed and looked uncomfortable. "Yeah," he said.

I cocked my head and looked at him with a slightly raised eyebrow until he gave a huge sigh and said: "He wants to come in to town so he can...uh, make a little money. He says he needs some cash to tide him over until some big deal he's got going comes through."

I could sense that wasn't the whole story.

"So you're just supposed to take him into town and pick him up later?" I repeated.

He took his feet off the table, chug-a-lugged his Coke and didn't meet my eyes. "Yes, that's what I'm going to do," he said a little defensively. "What's the matter, don't you trust me?"

That took me aback. "Of course I trust you," I said.

We sat quietly for a moment, I looking at him, he looking at the floor. Finally, without looking up at me, he said: "He, uh...he wanted me to go with him. He says he knows this guy who likes three-ways with hustlers. I told him 'no way.' Even if I was single I wouldn't get back into hustling for anything! He wants to hustle, that's his business, but he can do it on his own."

I had to admit I had a queasy feeling in my stomach when he first mentioned the subject, but I realized it was just a flush of the old Scorpio curse: jealousy and possessiveness. Still, I was a little pissed at Randy for even suggesting it...he knew Jonathan was in a relationship.

Same song, Hardesty, my mind-voice said, and I knew it was right.

"Any idea what he wants to talk to you about?" I asked.

He sat back on the sofa as the tension dissolved. "Not really. I think it's got something to do with this big deal he's working on. He mentioned it at dinner the night he was over, if you remember."

I remembered.

He shrugged. "Hustlers talk big," he said, "but he really sounds like he's got something. I'll find out."

I reached out and gave his leg a squeeze. "Nice to know I'm not the only detective in the family," I said.

* * *

Rather than bothering to fix dinner, we decided to run out to a local fried chicken place, after which Jonathan dropped me off at the apartment and headed off for New Eden. I sat around the apartment watching TV...all right, all right, and looking at the clock...until Jonathan came in at around 7:30.

"Everything go all right?" I asked.

Jonathan came over and plopped down beside me on the sofa. "Yeah. I think this'll be the last time I'll be playing taxi, though."

"Oh?" I said, noncommittally.

He sighed. "Yeah, if he wants to come over and hang around sometime, that's fine, but I don't want to be in a position of having to lie for him."

"Why would you have to lie for him?" I asked.

"Everybody who stays at New Eden can leave one night a week, supposedly, as long as they say where they're going. Randy told them he was coming over here with me. And he told me he gets to leave any time he wants to."

"Yeah?" I said. "How does he manage that?"

Jonathan pursed his lips and looked at me closely. "Well, I'm not supposed to tell anybody, but…" he paused, and I managed to keep quiet and let him finish his sentence when he was ready. "…Randy's having sex with Jeffrey Dinsmore."

Well, surprise, surprise!

I looked at him. "He *is*? Or he *says* he is?"

Jonathan shrugged. "I think he *really* is," he says. "Apparently Mr. Dinsmore has a fondness for hustlers—that's why so many of them end up at New Eden."

"Does his wife know?" I wondered aloud.

"Oh, I really doubt it," he said. "Dinsmore's very discreet, Randy says. He only does it with guys when his wife is out of town. And she's out of town a lot."

"Well, that is a fascinating little bit of news," I said. "And exactly how does Randy benefit from all this? Other than the privilege of changing Mr. Dinsmore's oil—or having Mr. Dinsmore change his?"

Jonathan grinned. "New Eden has a work referral program. They train the street kids who go there in lots of different fields, and then when they're ready to move on, New Eden helps find them a job. The Dinsmores are pretty well connected, so they can come up with some pretty good jobs. Randy's been working in the office…filing and making travel arrangements for the Dinsmores and stuff like that, and he's managed to get in pretty tight with both of them, but especially *Mr.* Dinsmore, of course. He's pretty sure they can find him a really good job when he's ready."

He was silent a moment. "Somehow I get the idea there's more to it than that. But Randy wouldn't say anything. Just hints that sounded to me like he was expecting a lot more than a good job."

"What time are you supposed to pick him up—and where?"

"Eleven o'clock…at Hughie's. Will you come with me? I know it's late and we both have to get up early, but I really don't want to go into Hughie's by myself."

I wasn't wild about the idea either. "Sure, if you want."

We watched some TV and left the apartment a little before 10:30. Traffic was fairly light at that hour on a Monday night, and we even managed to find a parking place just down the block from the bar—probably partly because not many hustlers had their own cars.

As we walked toward the bar, we saw one hustler leaning against one side of the entrance, apparently hoping to snare a John before he had a chance to check out the competition inside. But as we got closer, I saw the guy couldn't have been more than 16. Even at Hughie's they check IDs.

Jeesus! I thought.

Jonathan leaned toward me as we approached him and said: "I'll meet you inside, okay?"

I knew he wanted to talk to the kid, so I said "Sure." I nodded to the kid as I passed him and opened the door, while Jonathan stopped in front of him and said: "Hi."

The bar itself was pretty quiet. Again, it was a weeknight and some of the hustlers who'd normally come in earlier had probably left to work the streets, where the odds of being picked up might be slightly higher. And they didn't have to waste money on even one beer.

It was close to eleven, and no sign of Randy, which irked me somehow. I went to the bar and ordered a beer and a Coke from a bartender I didn't recognize. I was so used to seeing Bud behind the bar that this other guy's being there caught me rather by surprise. But then I realized Bud had to have time off sometime.

I'd always found it fairly easy to tell the hustlers from the johns, and of the ten guys in the place other than the bartender and me, I'd say it was seven to three in favor of the hustlers. So when the bartender brought the drinks and took my money, I set the Coke on the bar in front of the empty stool next to me to dissuade anyone from thinking I was looking for a pickup.

Jonathan came in about five minutes later and sat down beside me. He looked pensive and distracted as he picked up his

Coke.

"I told him about Haven House," he said.

I'd figured. "Good," I said.

He was quiet, staring at the back bar. "I really hate this place," he said.

The door opened and I turned to see if it was Randy. It wasn't. A well-dressed, good looking guy in a business suit came in and walked to the stool on the other side of Jonathan. He ordered a beer, then glanced at Jonathan and broke into a grin that had more of Little Red Riding Hood's wolf than casual pleasure in it.

"Hey, how's it goin'?" he asked. "Haven't seen you in a while."

Jonathan looked embarrassed and glanced quickly from the guy to me. "I'm okay," he said.

"Lookin' good," the guy said, staring at Jonathan with a look that left little doubt where he was headed, and giving me the feeling that I must be invisible to him.

Poor Jonathan was obviously excruciatingly uncomfortable. Finally he looked at the guy and said: "I'm with someone now."

For the first time the guy seemed to realize I was there. "Oh," he said, "Okay." Then he turned his grin to me. Obviously he assumed I was a just another john. "I can vouch for this one," he said, with a head jerk to Jonathan that reminded me of a cattle auctioneer. "You'll sure get your money's worth."

On rare occasions, I can be very proud of myself. This was one of them. While a very large part of me—okay, the Scorpio part, which *is* a very large part of me—wanted to get up and throw the guy through the wall, which I think Jonathan was afraid I might try to do, I managed to control myself, nodded, and said nothing.

"Well, I'll see ya around," the guy said, picking up his beer and moving off toward the other end of the bar, where a tall, thin kid in a worn leather jacket watched him coming over with a sly smile.

Jonathan just stared at his Coke and shook his head slowly back and forth. "I'm sorry, Dick," he said. "He picked me up here once, just before I met you, and..."

I reached out to put my arm around his shoulder. "No problem," I said. "Don't worry about it."

He gave me a weak smile and said: "Have I mentioned that I really hate this place?"

I glanced at my watch and noticed it was ten after eleven, and no Randy. Jonathan then looked at his own watch and said: "Let's give him ten more minutes, okay? Then we'll go, and he can find his own way back."

We finished our drinks in relative silence, noting the guy in the business suit—who one of my mind voices insisted on referring to as "Jonathan's ex"—left with the kid in the leather jacket.

At eleven twenty, we got up to leave. Just as we reached the sidewalk—the teenager was gone—a battered pickup truck pulled up to the curb and Randy got out. He shut the door without looking back and came quickly over to us.

"Man, did you see who that guy *was*?" he asked in lieu of any other greeting as the pickup made an illegal U-turn and headed back in the direction from which it had come. He directed the question to Jonathan. "Chad Brownell!" he continued without waiting for an answer. "Doctor Carstairs on 'Life Goes On!' He denied it, but I knew it was him the minute I saw him."

"Life Goes On" was one of the most popular of the prime time New York based soaps, and Chad Brownell was one of its hottest stars. I knew Brownell was originally from here, and that he was both widely known to be gay and had a penchant for hustlers. But what he was doing in a beat-up pickup truck I didn't know. Good for his butch image, maybe.

"I sure am meeting a lot of famous people lately," Randy said as we headed for the car.

* * *

We dropped Randy off at New Eden at three minutes to twelve, and headed home, again in relative silence.

"Not the best of all possible nights," Jonathan said, looking out the window.

I turned and grinned at him. "But hardly the end of the world, either," I said.

He shrugged and turned to me. "True," he said, his spirits obviously lifting. "Think we'll have time to play a game when we get home?" he asked.

"Sure," I said. "Which one?"

"How about 'The Asshole John and the Vengeful Hustler'? It could get a little rough."

"Sounds like fun," I said.

And it was.

* * *

Tuesday morning, at about the same time that Tony T. Tunderew was scheduled to oil his way into the hearts of A.M. New York's national viewing audience, I got a call from Donna at Glen O'Banyon's office. She apologized for not having gotten back to me sooner, and gave me the telephone number and address of Catherine Tunderew, Tony T.'s recently exed.

"If you talk with her," Donna said before she hung up, "would you please tell her that her number one fan sends her best regards?"

"I'm sorry?" I asked, confused.

"You don't know who Catherine Tunderew is?" she asked.

Should I? I wondered. "No," I said, "I'm afraid I don't know of her."

Donna sounded mildly embarrassed when she said: "Catherine Tunderew is one of the top children's book illustrators in the country," she said. "My daughter Amy loves her work, as do I. I thought everyone knew who she was."

"Well, I've not been too much into children's books for the past couple of years," I said. "But I appreciate your telling me. And I'll be sure to pass on Amy's—and your—regards."

"Thank you, Mr. Hardesty. Good bye."

It occurred to me that if Catherine Tunderew was a well known illustrator, it was probable that the picture her ex-husband painted of her might be as inaccurate and unfair as his description of Larry Fletcher.

Donna had not indicated whether Mrs. Tunderew worked out of her home or for a company, but I tried calling the number I'd been given anyway. I could always just leave a message, if she had a machine.

I heard a click, and then: "Catherine Tunderew."

"Mrs. Tunderew," I said, feeling a little awkward addressing her by a title she no longer officially held, "my name is Dick Hardesty, and I'm a private investigator. I wonder if I might talk with you about your ex-husband."

"And which sweet, innocent young virgin cruelly seduced and despoiled by the heartless but famous and newly rich writer do you represent, Mr. Hardesty?"

"I beg your pardon?" I said. "I'm not sure I follow you."

There was a pause, then: "Ah. Then perhaps I've mistaken you for one of the two other private investigators to whom I've spoken recently."

Despite the definite undertone of bitterness in what she said, her tone was light. "I'm sorry," I said, following her lead. "I haven't represented a despoiled virgin in quite some time. I'm working for Mr. Tunderew, as a matter of fact."

She laughed. "Well, then," she said, "in that case it's been a *very* long time indeed. What other mischief has my darling Tony been up to?"

"Would it be possible for us to talk in person?" I asked. "I'll be happy to explain everything then."

"Of course," she said pleasantly. "If there is anything I can do to add to dear Tony's problems, I'll be glad to contribute what I can. I assume you are licensed and listed in the phone book?"

Now that was a first, I thought.

"Yes, of course. It's under Hardesty Investigations…" and I gave her the address and phone number.

"Thank you," she said. "I'll call you right back." And she hung up.

A very interesting if somewhat odd lady, I decided.

Less than a minute later, the phone rang. This time I did not wait for the customary two rings, but picked up the receiver immediately.

"Hardesty Investigations," I said.

"One can never be too careful," Catherine Tunderew's voice said. "I was quite serious when I said if there was anything I could do to add to my ex-husband's problems I would, but that does not include catering to the tabloids or the money-grubbers. You'd be surprised the innovative lengths to which some people will go to get information they can turn into cash."

"I can appreciate your caution," I said, and on thinking it over, I certainly could.

"Would you like to come by at two?" she asked. "I assume you have my address."

"Yes, I do," I said. "I'll see you at two, then. And thank you."

"You're quite welcome," she said pleasantly, and hung up.

* * *

Catherine Tunderew's address proved to be a small, well maintained but unassuming apartment building probably built in the 1930s. A small, neat entry with a panel of eight brass-plated mailboxes was just to the left of the door. No locked security door, no buzzers.

I took the stairs—there was no elevator—to the second floor and walked down the hall to the back of the building, where I found Apartment #8. A small bracketed sign to the left of the door said: "C. Tunderew." I knocked.

"Who is it?" a voice said from just the other side of the door.

"Dick Hardesty, Mrs. Tunderew," I replied, and I heard the security chain being slid aside and the door opened.

Catherine Tunderew was a pleasant-looking woman about 40, no make up, greying hair pulled back into a ponytail, dressed in jeans and a man's sweatshirt, over which she wore a paint-smudged, dark blue smock.

"Come in," she said with a smile.

I followed her into the living room, half of which was set up with a large drafting table, a couple smaller easels, and a small work table upon which was a jumble of art supplies. Leaning against the legs of the drafting table were several varying-sized tablets of drawing paper.

She led me to one of two comfortable-looking chairs facing each other beside the large window and separated by a large coffee table. There was no couch. On one wall were about six framed brightly-colored illustrations, obviously from children's books.

"Would you like some tea?" she asked as I sat down. She had a rather pleasant, almost musical quality to her voice—the kind of voice I somehow associated with a storyteller reading to small children.

"No, thank you," I said, and she smiled as she took the seat opposite me.

"So what has Tony gotten himself into this time?" she asked.

"He's being blackmailed," I said, deciding to get right to the point.

She did not look surprised. "*Poor* Tony," she said with a Mona Lisa smile.

I waited for her to ask what he was being blackmailed for, but she didn't. I couldn't tell whether it was because she already knew, or she just didn't care.

"Would you have any idea who might want to blackmail him?"

The small smile became a broad one. "My darling Tony has the ability to attract enemies the way a dog attracts fleas," she said. "I can imagine very few people who have ever met him who *wouldn't* want to blackmail him if they had the chance. He's just 'that kind of guy.'"

"I don't mean to be rude," I said, "but would that include you, by any chance?"

She looked pensive for a moment, then said: "Why, I suppose it might, if I wanted anything from him, which I don't. I make enough on my own to get by. I would far rather be rid of him and poor than still married to him and rich."

"And you get alimony?" I asked.

"Oh, yes," she said. "Very generous. It almost covers my grocery bill each month. But I didn't and don't want anything from him. You'd have to have been married to him for thirteen years to fully understand."

She certainly sounded convincing, but I really found it hard to believe she wouldn't be harboring at least some resentment.

"Could you tell me a little about your relationship with Mr. Tunderew?" I asked.

"Current or past?"

"Both, actually." I said.

A whistling sound from the kitchen caught her just as she'd opened her mouth to speak, and she got up quickly from her chair. "Are you sure you wouldn't like some tea?" she asked.

"I'm sure," I said, "but please don't let me stop you from having some."

She smiled and moved toward the kitchen. "I'll only be a moment," she said.

While she was out of the room, I turned my attention to the framed illustrations. Mostly watercolors with a few pastels, they were really wonderful: A fine balance of not-quite-realism and pure whimsy, I could see why kids would love them.

She returned a minute or so later with a heavy white coffee mug of the type I automatically associated with just about every all-night diner I'd ever been in. The tab of a tea-bag draped over the edge. She also had a piece of paper towel and a large spoon, which she placed in front of her on the coffee table as she sat back down.

"So," she said, leaning back in her chair, ignoring the cup for the moment, "my life with the famous Tony T. Tunderew...an overview or a thirteen-year day-by-day account?"

I grinned. "The overview will be fine," I said.

She leaned forward, picked up the tab of the tea bag with one hand and the spoon with the other, and bobbed the bag up and down several times, finally removing it from the cup and placing it on the spoon. She twisted the string several times around the bag to force the excess water out, then set the spoon and bag on the paper towel.

"We met," she said, picking up the cup and again leaning back in her chair, "in Chicago. I was at the Art Institute, and Tony was working at an insurance company in the Loop, taking night classes at Roosevelt. He wanted to go to Northwestern, to the Journalism school, but he couldn't afford it."

She sipped her tea and smiled. "Tony can be incredibly charming when he wants to be," she said, then added "...as you may have noticed."

I certainly had not, but was curious as to the implication. I chose not to ask.

"My parents had recently died," she continued, gazing out the window in reflection, "and left me their small house on the South Side. Tony and I started dating, and then he moved in with me to save money. I got a job at an ad agency doing commercial art, and after a while, Tony quit his job at the insurance agency to go to school full time."

"And you supported him?" I asked.

She returned her eyes to me and shrugged. "Basically, yes," she said, "but I didn't think of it that way. We were in love, he was going to be a great writer...you know the story."

I nodded.

"We moved here so Tony could get a journalism degree from Goodlee," she said. "It's not really that good a school, as you know, but then Tony wasn't that good a writer, I'm afraid. I sold my house at a nice profit, and we lived on the proceeds. I got another ad agency job and began to do freelance illustrations for children's books. Tony did some freelance work, too, doing sleazy features for the tabloids. When it reached the point where the money ran out and I simply couldn't support us both, he got a job at Craylaw & Collier, and the rest is history. The week he signed the contract for *Dirty Little Minds* he filed for divorce."

"I'm curious. How long did it take him to write *Dirty Little Minds?*"

She thought a moment. "Not all that long, really, once he got going on it. I must say in his defense, however, that he had already started the book even before the Governor Keene scandal started hitting the papers. It certainly was marvelous timing, though."

I wondered if she knew—and was pretty sure she didn't—that

Governor Keene had been a client of Craylaw & Collier. Tunderew had somehow gotten wind of the looming scandal and recognized its potential.

We were quiet for a moment while I tried to phrase my next question diplomatically. When I realized there wasn't a diplomatic way to do it, I just plunged in.

"Might I ask how you feel about the divorce?" I did not add "in light of his now having more money than he knows what to do with?"

She gave me that Mona Lisa smile again. "It was exactly what I could have expected from dear Tony," she said. "He has never been burdened by a sense of morality. He was always a firm believer in the philosophy that what was mine was his, and what was his was his. He didn't even bother to tell me he had *signed* a contract. I only found out about that part after the divorce papers were signed."

I couldn't resist: "And you're not bitter for what he did?"

She shrugged, still smiling. "I've always defined 'bitterness' as 'surprised disappointment,'" she said. "Absolutely nothing Tony did or does could surprise me, therefore I couldn't be disappointed."

Again, I couldn't help but wonder how honest she was being—either with me or with herself, but I decided to move on.

"You'd mentioned on the phone that you'd been contacted by a couple of other private investigators?" I asked.

She finished her tea and set the cup on the coffee table.

"So they claimed to be, but I wouldn't know. They mainly wanted me to provide details on Tony's notoriously roving eye. Nothing like a juicy scandal to sell tabloids...or books."

"Might his roving eye have included men?" I asked.

For the first time, she looked surprised. It was a quick reaction, quickly contained. Then she laughed.

"Oh, my!" she said. "What an interesting thought, though I can't see where he would have found the time from his bimbo collection. But then again, this is Tony T. Tunderew we're talking about. I wouldn't put anything past him. I'd heard that shortly before he left Craylaw & Collier, he'd been having yet another little affair with one of his co-workers. And you think it might have been a man?" She smiled. "I sincerely, sincerely doubt it. But why in the world would you ask that?"

"Just curious," I said. "Did you by any chance have access to his checkbook?"

"No," she said. "Has he been writing checks to young men?"

Now there's an interesting question, I thought. I didn't answer. "Tony always had his own bank account," she continued. "In the thirteen years we were married I never once knew how much money he made, or how much he spent, or on what, other than the rent on our apartment and the mortgage on the cabin. I paid all the other household expenses…food, utilities, insurance…from my own account."

"The cabin?" I asked.

"Yes, our…excuse me, *his* since he paid the mortgage and therefore claimed it in the divorce…cabin on the Oak River, near Neelyville. He used it as his 'writer's getaway.' He spent every weekend there—supposedly writing, but usually with his conquest of the moment. Dear Tony is not nearly as clever as he thinks he is. He thought I didn't know, but it wasn't that I didn't know so much as that I didn't care. Toward the end of the marriage, he was up there most of the time. He may well be living there now, but I'm not positive. We don't exactly keep in close touch."

I sensed that it was about time to call our little meeting to an end.

"Well, I really do appreciate your talking with me, Mrs. Tunderew…" I began.

"Catherine, please," she corrected. "The only reason I'm keeping the last name is because that's the name I started out with in my illustrating, and it would be just too complicated to try to switch at this stage of the game."

I smiled. "I understand," I said. "I wouldn't have bothered you except that Mr. …your ex…is really concerned about this blackmail thing, and I thought you might be able to give me some ideas. I'm sure you know that he now has the wherewithal to make life miserable for whomever is responsible, if he ever finds out for sure."

We both got up from our chairs at the same time.

"Well," she said as she walked me to the door, "I'm sure he'll be spending a great deal of money one way or the other, then, won't he?"

* * *

By the time I'd reached my car, I'd pretty much placed my bets on Catherine Tunderew as being the blackmailer, though short of beating a confession out of her with a rubber hose, I didn't know how I could actually prove it. But if she was the one, I hope she might have gotten the message. I'd also gotten the impression that if she was, she might be doing it more to bedevil her ex than to seriously expect him to pay up.

Fletcher ruled out, Catherine Tunderew ruled in. That was about it, right? Not quite. The publisher was still in the picture, though on the periphery. That he had every right to be pissed at Tunderew (as did, I'm sure, just about everyone who knew him other than Fletcher) was a given. Tunderew had said he'd left his briefcase, with checkbook, on the publisher's desk while he went to the bathroom. But again, people don't normally go rummaging through other people's briefcases just on a whim—and even if the publisher might have been looking for evidence that Tunderew was playing footsie with other publishers, how would he know that a check stub made out to a realty company might be potential blackmail material?

Unless...

I made a mental note to call Larry Fletcher when I got home.

Chapter 4

Though it was almost time to go home, I went back to the office and called Bernadine Press.

"Bernadine Press," a pleasant female voice answered after the first ring.

"Is Mr…Bernadine in, please?" I asked. I would normally have assumed 'Bernadine Press' was just a generic name, but Tunderew had referred to the publisher as "Bernadine," so…

"Senior or Junior?" she asked.

There are two of them? "Senior, please," I said, wanting to sound as though I had known all along.

"May I tell him who's calling?"

"My name is Hardesty. Dick Hardesty," I said.

"And may I ask what company you are with?"

"Hardesty Investigations," I said.

"One moment, Mr. Hardesty." There was a click and then the sounds of Vivaldi's "Four Seasons." *Well, the place has class,* I decided.

A moment later, another click and a male voice. "Donald Bernadine."

I introduced myself as a private investigator and explained that I would like to speak with him about one of his authors, Tony T. Tunderew. I didn't mention I was working for Tunderew. I could do that later.

"I do not discuss our professional associations," he said, politely but firmly.

"I understand," I said. "But this is a matter of some importance which might affect Bernadine Press, and I would really appreciate it if we could talk in person for a few minutes."

After a moment of silence, he said: "Tomorrow at10:30? I have a meeting at 11:00, so it will have to be brief."

"10:30 will be fine, Mr. Bernadine. Thank you. I'll see you then."

* * *

At home, right after dinner, while Jonathan sat cross-legged on the floor studying, I called Larry Fletcher. I hoped he was in, since I really wanted to talk to him before I went to see Donald Bernadine.

Luck was with me.

"Hello?" Fletcher's voice said.

"Mr. Fletcher, it's Dick Hardesty. I had another question I wonder if you could answer for me?"

"Will it help Tony find out who is blackmailing him?" he asked.

"I hope so," I said. "I understand you were nice enough to run some errands for Mr. Tunderew during your lunch hours."

"Oh, yes," he said. "I was glad to do it. I don't eat lunch very often anyway. And Tony was always so busy..."

Uh huh, I thought. "Did he by any chance ever have you go by Bernadine Press for him?" I asked.

There was no hesitation. "Yes, a couple of times Tony asked me to take things over to them. Mr. Bernadine is a very nice man; very friendly."

I found it a little odd that Tunderew would be so brazen as to keep anything having to do with *Dirty Little Minds* at work.

"So he would just hand you a package and ask you to deliver it to Bernadine Press?" I asked.

"Oh, no, not during working hours. Tony is very conscientious about not taking up company time for his personal affairs."

Right, I thought. *Why should he when he can sucker some naive kid into doing it for him?*

Unaware of my thoughts, Fletcher kept on talking. "Whenever he'd have something he'd like me to take over to them, he'd ask me to meet him in the parking lot before work. I'd put it in the trunk of my car, and then deliver it during my lunch hour."

Sigh.

"Did you by any chance mention to Mr. Bernadine that Tony had helped you get your new apartment?"

"I don't think I…wait, yes I did. I stopped by to drop off an envelope on my way to the apartment management company with the check. I was so touched by Tony's kindness I'm sure I told Mr. Bernadine about it. Tony'd made me promise not to tell anyone at work, but I had to tell someone! Why do you ask?"

"I was just curious," I said, only half truthfully. "And I was wondering, were there any rumors around work about Tony and any of the women he worked with?"

I sensed the question bothered him a bit. "There are *always* rumors," he said. "Tony's a very, very handsome man. Every girl in the office had a crush on him, I think."

And at least one of the guys, I thought.

"Any one in particular?" I asked.

"Well, maybe Judith. She was a temp and worked for Tony on a project he was doing. She was only there a month or so, but she really liked Tony. He was just being nice, as he is with everyone, but I think she thought he liked her…well, you know."

I knew.

"Do you know Judith's last name, or the temp agency she worked for?"

He paused. "Her last name was Francini. I remember that because our next door neighbors when I was growing up were Francini's. I asked her if she might be related, but she didn't think so. And Craylaw & Collier uses Manpower for all their temps. But she left about halfway through the project and they got someone else."

"Any idea why?"

"Not really. You know temps…they come and they go."

I wondered if the reason this particular temp went might have anything to do with the charming Mr. Tunderew.

"Well, thanks again for your help, Mr. Fletcher."

"I'm always glad to help Tony," he said.

There are none so blind… my mind-voice sighed, as I reached for the pencil and notepad beside the phone to write down "Judith Francini/Manpower."

* * *

The offices of Bernadine Press were in an older, seen-better-days office building much like my own. The last door to the left of a long hall was a windowless solid brown slab with cracked laquer and a wooden engraved sign which announced: *Bernadine Press*. I turned the brass knob and entered a 12'X12' room, at one end of which, directly in front of me, was a short hallway to a single venetian blind window, beside which stood a water cooler. I could see three doors on either side of the hall. The room I had entered had a secretary/reception area to the left, and one door on the right, on which was a brass plate with the words: "D. Bernadine, Publisher."

The receptionist/secretary was a comfortable-looking heavyset woman in her early 50s who reminded me of my aunt Ethel, and I immediately sensed she'd probably been with the company since she got out of secretarial school. As I walked over to her desk, she smiled and said "May I help you?" in a voice I recognized from my phone call the day before.

"I'm Dick Hardesty," I said. "I have a 10:30 appointment with Mr. Bernadine...Senior."

"Please have a seat," she said. "He'll be with you in a moment."

I took one of the three chairs against the wall and sat down as she returned to whatever it was she'd been doing. The walls in the reception area, including the one behind my chair, were hung with framed dust jackets of Bernadine Press books and photos I assumed to be of authors. I didn't recognize any of the titles, or any of the people in the pictures. Surprisingly, Tony T. Tunderew and *Dirty Little Minds* were not among them.

My curiosity about the rest of the place got the best of me, so I got up from the chair and said: "Could I get a glass of water, please?"

"Of course," she said, and started to get up.

"Don't bother," I said. "I noticed the cooler at the end of the hall. I can just get it myself if that's all right."

She smiled and nodded, and I headed down the hall. The first door to my right, next to Bernadine's office, was closed with no indication of what may be behind it. Directly opposite it was a closed door with a sign saying "Bookkeeping." The next door on the right was an open door with a small sign on the wall beside it saying "Art Department." As I passed I glanced in to see a crowded room cluttered with drafting tables, file cabinets, two windows, and two desks. A young man with a white dress shirt rolled up to his elbows sat with his back to me at one of the drafting tables. There was the faint smell of rubber cement.

In the hall across from the Art Department was another open door showing a small lunch room with a table, several chairs, a coffee maker, and an older refrigerator. The last door to the left had a sign saying: "S. Evans, Editor", and across from it an identical door and a sign saying "P. Bernadine, Editor."

Interesting.

My curiosity satisfied, I poured myself a cup of water from the cooler, observing the somehow satisfying " *Blurrrrurp*" and the accompanying large bubble of water rise from bottom to top.

I returned to the reception area just as the door to Bernadine's office opened and an elderly gentleman with white hair in a crumpled-looking brown suit emerged. I was still in the hallway and, apparently expecting me to be in the reception area, he looked at the secretary with a puzzled expression. She gave a subtle jerk of her head in my direction, and he turned to me. He did not smile.

"Mr. Hardesty," he said as we shook hands. "Please, come into my office."

He stood aside while I entered, then closed the door beside me and motioned me to a seat.

The office was...well*old*...but a comfortable "old." There was a sense of having stepped back in time. The furniture was solid, practical, rather worn, and comfortable. That everything in the room was in shades of brown, including the brown drapes flanking the window—when is the last time you've seen drapes in an office?—undoubtedly contributed to the effect. Bookcases lined one wall, filled with books which all showed the letters "BP" at the bottom of the spine. On one side of his desk was a stack of what I assumed to be manuscripts.

"Now," he said, as he moved behind the desk and sat down,

"just what is this 'important matter' you wanted to discuss?"

His tone and his posture did not suggest hostility, but there was no casualness in it either; strictly business.

I decided to get right to the point. "Were you aware that Tony Tunderew is being blackmailed?" I asked.

The mention of Tunderew's name cause his eyes to narrow slightly, but other than that there was no reaction.

"No, I was not, though I'm neither surprised nor, I must admit, particularly sorry to hear it. Though I take offense at the implication that Bernadine Press might somehow be involved."

"I apologize; there was no implication intended," I lied. "I was mainly concerned with what you might know of an associate of Mr. Tunderew—a young man named Larry Fletcher. I understand you met him on a couple occasions."

He shook his head. "Not that I can recall."

"Mr. Tunderew sent him over a couple of times, and…"

He nodded. "Ah, then he probably spoke with my son, Peter. Peter is Tunderew's editor. I personally have had almost no contact with Tunderew at all. To be frank, I had serious hesitation about becoming involved with someone of Mr. Tunderew's ilk. It turns out I was right."

"I'm sorry," I said, "I don't think I understand. Why did you agree to publish *Dirty Little Minds*, then? I'm sure it has been very profitable for Bernadine Press."

He shook his head slowly and his face, for the first time, broke into a small, wry smile. "Bernadine Press," he said, "was started by my father nearly fifty years ago. We are, and always have been, associated with offering quality books of high literary merit…until now." He picked up a pencil, sharpened to a needle point, and began to tap it on the desk top.

"In recent years, things have gotten tight for the entire publishing industry and for Bernadine Press in particular. Reading habits have changed, and reading itself is becoming something of a lost art. We were, to be brutally honest, in a very precarious financial position. It was my son, Peter, who brought Tunderew to my attention. He knew Tunderew casually, and when sked for a synopsis and outline." He sighed and then went on.

"Under normal circumstances, I would have rejected it out of hand, but Peter convinced me that if Bernadine Press was to survive, it must make accommodations with literary trends—though by no stretch of the imagination would I consider *Dirty Little Minds* 'literature.' He felt very strongly that Tunderew's book would be a great financial success.

"Peter's instincts proved to be correct, and ironically it is *Dirty Little Minds* which has given Bernadine Press a chance for survival. We are, as a result, in negotiations with our bank to completely modernize and expand our operations. If his second book turns out to be as profitable as his first, we will be in a solid financial position to explore new avenues which will allow us to continue publishing what we set out to publish—quality books of high literary merit."

We were both quiet for a moment, until I said: "I understand you are suing Mr. Tunderew for breach of contract."

He nodded. "The contract for *Dirty Little Minds* stipulated that we were to have first rights on his second book, which he had begun working on even before *Dirty Little Minds* was completed, and first refusal rights on his third—if there was to be a third."

"Is it customary to, in effect, tie a writer down like that?"

Bernadine shrugged. "No one held a gun to his head," he said. "He was perfectly free to say 'no'. We were, after all, taking a huge risk with this project. We knew full well he had few options if he wanted to see the book published at all. And if it did turn out to be the success Peter predicted, well… neither Peter nor I had the slightest doubt that 'loyalty' is not a concept familiar to Mr. Tunderew, and that he would try to dump us the instant he became successful and thought he could make more money with another publisher. We felt it only natural to protect our interests:"

"Do you know what the subject of this second book is to be?" I asked, genuinely curious.

Bernadine shook his head. "Peter knows more than I. Another potentially explosive scandal involving another well known national figure, but that's all I can say. Peter thinks it will be even a bigger seller than *Dirty Little Minds*. I'm letting Peter handle it. Frankly, I would be just as happy to let Tunderew break the contract, but I must think of the survival of Bernadine Press. I'll be retiring in a year or so, but I want Peter—and the company—to have a future, even though it may be a very different future from one I would have chosen. So yes, we are suing Mr. Tunderew. A contract is a contract, and since Mr. Tunderew so obviously lacks any sense of moral obligation, he might be made to understand that legal obligations are not so easily dismissed."

He glanced at his watch and said: "Now, if you'll excuse me, I have a few things to do before my 11 o'clock meeting."

"Of course," I said. "I very much appreciate your having taken the time to talk with me. But do you suppose I could talk with your son for a few minutes? I would like to find out more about this Larry Fletcher situation."

Bernadine nodded and reached for the phone hidden behind the stack of manuscripts. "I'll see if he's available," he said.

* * *

I waited in the reception area for another few minutes until the intercom on the secretary's desk buzzed.

"Mr. Bernadine will see you now," she said. "The end of the hall, on your right."

I remembered.

When I reached the door, I knocked—again reflecting on our odd social customs, since I knew he was expecting me and I doubted he'd be doing anything that would require advance notice.

"Come in," a surprisingly deep voice responded, and I turned the knob and entered. Peter Bernadine's office was smaller than his father's—the same depth, but narrower. It was also considerably brighter, mainly due to there being fewer dark bookcases, and the walls had several large, colorful paintings. There were no drapes on the window.

Peter Bernadine himself was, I noticed as he stood up to greet me, pretty much a physical carbon copy of his father, though more casually dressed. And whereas the elder Bernadine had pure white hair, his son's was pitch black and slicked down to the point of almost glistening. He also sported a small moustache that reminded me of Adolph Hitler's.

I reached his desk and we shook hands. "Have a seat, please," he said. His deep voice seemed somehow incongruous with the rest of him.

"My father tells me you're looking for information on an 'associate' of Tony Tunderew's?" he asked as I sat down.

He and his father must have talked while I was waiting in the reception area.

"Uh, yes," I said. "Larry Fletcher. Do you know anything about him?"

Bernadine smiled. "Not really, other than the fact that I gather he's Tony's…uh, shall we say 'special friend'?" he said.

Now that one caught me a little by surprise. "What makes you think that?" I asked.

Bernadine sat back in his chair and reached into his shirt pocket for a pack of cigarettes. He made a gesturing offer to me, and I shook my head. He waited until he had lit up and blew a long stream of smoke into the room before continuing:

"I only spoke with him twice, I think," he said, "but he made it pretty obvious. All he talked about was how excited he was for Tony, writing a real book that was sure to make him famous. And the last time he was in, he was telling me about how Tony had given him the money to get a new apartment."

"So you think Tunderew is gay?" I asked.

Bernadine shrugged and took another long drag from his cigarette. "It doesn't matter to me whether he is or isn't," he said, "but I wouldn't put anything past him. I'm sure if he saw some benefit in it, he'd probably screw a dead baby." He flicked his cigarette over the almost full ashtray on the corner of his desk, and smiled. "As you may gather, he's not one of my favorite people."

"But you published his book," I observed. "Why?"

He kept the smile as he said: "You're working for him, aren't you? Why?" Then he made a quick nod to indicate he didn't expect an answer. "Money is a pretty strong incentive for doing things we might prefer not to do. I knew when he came to me with *Dirty Little Minds* that it could be a runaway best seller. I knew, too, that he wouldn't have come to Bernadine Press unless he'd been turned down by every other mainstream publisher first. I must say his timing was perfect. The Governor Keene scandal—not that there is any direct relationship between it and *Dirty Little Minds*, of course—was just breaking. He was obviously desperate, and when he said he was already working on another book which would be even more explosive than *Dirty Little Minds*, I decided to get him to commit to a multiple-book deal. If *Dirty Little Minds* tanked, we wouldn't be out anything. If it caught on, which it did, we had every right to demand something in return for our having taken the chance with him. He agreed."

"I was a bit curious about that," I said. "Why three books?"

Bernadine stared at the end of his cigarette for a moment before answering. "A little unusual, perhaps," he said, "but just as my instinct told me *Dirty Little Minds* would be a goldmine, it also told me Tunderew couldn't be trusted any further than I could throw him. We're a small house, and we can't afford to offer six-figure advances. I knew if *Dirty Little Minds* was as big a hit as I expected it to be, other publishers would be throwing money at him for his next book. Our having refusal rights only on a second book would encourage him to dash off some piece of crap—not that *Dirty Little Minds* is exactly 'War and Peace'—just to meet the terms of the contract. Then he'd be free to peddle the big one to somebody else—which, it turns out, is exactly what he did. He was apparently stupid enough, or arrogant enough, not to think we'd get wind of it. So by writing in first refusal rights on the next *two* books, we were covering our ass."

"And now he wants to back out of the entire contract," I said.

Bernadine nodded, took a last drag on his cigarette and stubbed it out on the pile of other butts in the ashtray.

"He does," he said, "and he's not going to."

"How often are you in contact with him?" I asked.

He pushed the ashtray aside and sat back in his chair. "I'm

pleased to say we aren't. One of the first things he did when *Dirty Little Minds* started to take off was to hire an agent—Sal Armata, one of the best. Everything goes through him now."

"Did you know someone is blackmailing Tunderew?" I asked, watching for his response.

"Really?" he said without even looking up from the ashtray. "Good for them. I hope they get every cent he has."

"Well, he's going to do everything he can to see that they don't, and he's surely not going to just sit back and write out a check. I'm trying to find who's behind it before it goes too far."

Before he could leap to the accurate conclusion that I might be referring to him, I hastened to add: "It occurred to me that it might be tied in with the book he's working on. What do you know about it?" I asked.

"Enough to be sure that what he submits to us will be the one he roughly outlined for me. As I said, we're not stupid. Since he said he'd started on the second book when he convinced me to go with *Dirty Little Minds*, I asked him for an outline before we signed the contract. There are enough basics in there to guarantee he won't be able to foist something else off on us."

"So you know who the subject of the next book is?" I asked.

He smiled yet again. "Well, his books are all completely fiction, of course..." *Uh huh* "...but I think any third grader could figure it out. But of course I'm not going to say anything further than that. I'm sure you understand."

I did, though I really, *really* wanted to know. Whoever it was just might be the blackmailer.

* * *

On the way back to my office, I had a serious little talk with myself. I was increasingly aware that I really didn't care who was blackmailing Tony T. Tunderew. And I felt guilty about it because it was my job to care—or at least find out who was behind the blackmail—and that I would do my best to do. I hadn't had a chance to try to find Judith Francini yet, but of the people I'd contacted—Larry Fletcher, Catherine Tunderew, and the

Bernadines—any one of them had a pretty good reason, and I could empathize with them all. But if I had to place any bets, I realized that Peter Bernadine had edged ahead of Catherine Tunderew. He had to know Glen O'Banyon was defending Tunderew in the suit, and he also had to know that O'Banyon won the majority of his cases.

Tunderew had mentioned that the blackmailer wanted the money on a specific date—the 15th—and that that date was two days after his next royalty check was due. It could well be coincidence, but if it wasn't, it was unlikely that anyone other than somebody at Bernadine Press would know when royalty checks went out.

Yeah, but the blackmail demand was for only $10,000—a small fraction of what Bernadine Press stood to lose if Tunderew broke the contract. Of course, perhaps the blackmailer intended the $10,000 to be only the first installment.

I debated on whether I should try to contact his new agent, Sal Armata, but decided to hold off on that. Armata was new to the picture and probably couldn't provide any constructive information. Still, I'd keep him in mind.

Tunderew would be back in town Thursday, and I hoped to be able to talk to him then. I still wasn't sure how he was going to take the news that Larry Fletcher probably wasn't the blackmailer: Tunderew was so sure he was. Again, he might well think I was covering up for a fellow fag—everyone knows how we stick together, after all. If that's what he wanted to think, let him.

* * *

I was surprised, upon returning to the office, to find a message from Jonathan asking me to call him. Since, as I've said, he almost never called me at work, except maybe on his lunch hour, I immediately returned the call.

"Evergreens," said a voice I recognized as one of Jonathan's co-workers.

"Is Jonathan around?" I asked.

"Sure. Hold a second."

A very long "second" later, I heard the phone being picked up, and Jonathan's voice.

"Hi, Dick," he said without my saying anything. "Thanks for calling back."

"What's up?" I asked, sensing something in his voice.

"I've got a favor to ask," he said. "A *really* big favor and I'll understand if you say 'no.'"

"Randy wants you to pick him up again and bring him into town?"

There was a pause, then: "Uh, yeah…well, no, not exactly, but…uh…"

"'But uh what?" I asked, pretty sure I wasn't going to like what came next.

"But can he stay with us for a few days? He got kicked out of New Eden."

Oh, joy! I thought.

"Only for a few days," Jonathan added, his words picking up speed in an attempt to forestall my anticipated interruption. "I was going to tell him about Haven House, but he's too old to stay there. He's pretty sure he knows someplace he can stay after a couple of days, but right now he hasn't got anywhere and he let me stay with him when I didn't have anywhere and I really owe him, and I don't want him to have to just be out on the street with no place to go and…"

"Okay, Jonathan, okay," I said, trying to get him to let up on the accelerator. "He can stay with us a few days if you want…but it can't be forever."

I could almost hear him exhale in relief. "No, it won't. I promise. Just a few days."

"What time are you supposed to pick him up?" I asked.

"I'm not," he said. "He's here now."

Great! I thought. I wondered what Randy had done to get kicked out of New Eden on little or no advance notice. Whatever it was, it couldn't be anything good. And I was more than a little concerned for Jonathan. I didn't want Randy to start influencing him in the wrong direction.

"Okay," I said, "I'll pick you up right after work." I didn't ask what Randy would be doing in the meantime, but I hoped his showing up wouldn't get Jonathan in any trouble with his boss.

I had a few minor time-filler projects, including a trip to the Hall of Records to trace previous ownership on a parcel of land for one of the straight attorneys for whom I did occasional jobs. Hey, if I'd wanted a life of glamour I'd have gone to beauty school.

Even though I deliberately took my time, I was in the car and on my way to the nursery half an hour early. When I pulled up in front of the main building, I saw Randy sitting on a bench, leaning forward, elbows on knees and hands clasped between them, apparently lost in thought. An Army-Navy Surplus duffle bag was propped against the edge of the bench. He didn't even look up as I got out of the car and walked toward him. Finally he noticed me and sat up. "Hi, Dick," he said, not smiling.

"Randy," I acknowledged, then gave a head nod toward the duffle bag. "You want to put your bag in the trunk?"

He got up quickly. "Sure," he said, picking up the bag and slinging it over his shoulder. He followed me to the car and, when I opened the trunk, tossed the bag in.

"Thanks for letting me stay with you guys," he said casually. I was struck by the realization that this was how Randy lived his life—one place to the next, never long in any one of them, everything he owned in a duffle bag. It was not a happy realization.

"No problem," I said. I was not about to ask him what had happened that had made him leave New Eden. I figured if he wanted to tell me, he would. Or Jonathan would, later…if he knew. We moved around to the sidewalk-side of the car. Not knowing how long Jonathan might be, I didn't want to get in. I felt a little awkward, not really knowing what to say, and there was about a minute of silence until Randy looked toward the nursery entrance gate and gave a small heads-up nod.

"Jonathan likes it here," he said. "He's doing pretty good." I read into the last sentence that he didn't mean just the job.

"Yeah," I said. "I'm really proud of him."

Randy said nothing, but nodded.

At that moment, luckily, Jonathan emerged from the gate and, grinning, came over.

I went around to the driver's side as Jonathan and Randy got in.

Jonathan, never at a loss for words, kept things from being too quiet on the way home by telling us of his day's adventures, which included having gone with a landscaping crew to the suburbs to dig up a perfectly good front lawn, lay down fresh sod, and then discover they'd gone to the wrong house. Since his boss had written up the order and put down the wrong address, nobody got blamed for the mistake.

* * *

The evening went fairly smoothly. We picked up a bucket of fried chicken and trimmings on the way home, put Randy up in the guest bedroom, and spent most of the evening watching TV. Jonathan tried to do a little studying for his Thursday night class, but apparently didn't want Randy to feel neglected. Randy himself didn't have much to say, though he didn't seem too concerned over his current situation. He in fact made a couple oblique references to a pretty solid future not too far off. Hustler talk? I couldn't tell, but as with the previous times he'd done it, there seemed to be an air of conviction that went somehow beyond fantasy.

Jonathan and I went to bed around eleven, Randy opting to stay up and watch TV. Jonathan stayed in the living room with him until I was in bed, then came in a few minutes later.

"You'd better watch out," he said as we assumed our pre-sleep front-to-back "spoon" position, Jonathan's back to me and my arm over his shoulder.

"For what?" I asked.

"Randy thinks you're hot," he said. "He asked if we ever did three-ways."

"And what did you tell him?" I asked.

"I told him 'sure!' He'll be in in a minute."

I slid my hand rapidly down his side, open palm, grabbed his ass and squeezed so hard he yelped. "Okay, okay," he said in a stage whisper. "So I didn't." There was a pause and then: "You want me to?"

I squeezed again, and he buried his head in the pillow to muffle a still-audible "Owwwww!"

When I moved my arm back over his shoulder, I said: "So did you find out why he left New Eden?"

He nodded, but said nothing.

"A secret?" I asked, and he flipped over so we were face-to-face, belly-to-belly.

"Barbara Dinsmore came home early last night from a trip and found her husband sitting spread-legged behind his desk in his office. He wasn't wearing any pants and Randy was there, too, on his knees between Mr. Dinsmore's legs. She wasn't happy."

"Had she known her husband liked guys?"

He shook his head. "If she didn't, she sure does now. Randy got right up, hitched up his pants, and left while the Dinsmores had a little talk. This morning, Mrs. Dinsmore called him into the office and told him he had exactly 15 minutes to get off the property or she'd call the police. He said she was very calm, but he could see the fires of hell behind her eyes. He said he just hoped her brother didn't find out about it, for Mr. Dinsmore's sake."

"Her brother?" I asked.

"Yeah, her brother is Administrative Director for the place, and apparently very protective of his little sister."

"Interesting," I said. "And how is Randy taking all this?"

Jonathan shrugged. "He's okay with it. He said he was getting ready to leave New Eden anyway. He's got big plans. He wouldn't tell me what they are, but he's got 'em." He was quiet a moment, then said, rather softly: "I hope they work out for him."

"Me too," I said, and we went to sleep.

* * *

The first thing I did when I got to the office Thursday morning...well, after making coffee and reading the paper and doing the crossword puzzle, of course...was to dial Tunderew's number and ask that he call me as soon as he could. I had no idea if he was already back in town or if he'd be in later that day, but I wanted to talk with him before I went any further on the case.

Not twenty minutes later, the phone rang.

"Hardesty Investigations," I said as I picked up the phone.

"Tony Tunderew here," the voice said. "I'm at the airport, and I'm leaving immediately for my cabin up north. I'll be back in town tomorrow morning. Did you talk to Larry Fletcher?"

"Yes, I did," I said. "I also talked with your ex-wife and the Bernadines, and…"

"I didn't hire you to talk to my ex-wife and the Bernadines," he said curtly. "I hired you to talk to Larry Fletcher. Why did you go any further than him?"

Control, Hardesty, control! my mind voice cautioned. "I thought you hired me to find the blackmailer," I said.

"I did," he said. "I told you Larry Fletcher is the blackmailer."

"I don't think he is," I said.

He sighed dramatically. "Well, I was afraid you'd say that, but then you girls always do stick together, don't you?"

"I'll send you my bill," I said, and slammed the phone back onto the receiver.

That rotten sonofabitch! I thought, infinitely grateful—as he damned sure should be—that he wasn't standing in front of me at that moment.

Chapter 5

God! I hate getting that angry! I was so furious I was really glad no one else was around —especially not Tony T. Tunderew. Even thinking about *that* was scary. And my mood did not materially improve when I realized he didn't want me to find out who the blackmailer was if it wasn't Larry Fletcher. Fletcher was a real threat to him not because of being gay but because of what he probably didn't even realize he knew about where Tunderew had gotten the material for *Dirty Little Minds* . I wondered how Tunderew was getting the dirt for his new book, since he was no longer working for a company whose files he could steal.

I managed to get through the day, somehow, and by the time I left the office for home, I had myself pretty much under control. I'd hardly thought of Randy all day, or of the fact that this was Jonathan's school night, which meant that Randy and I would be alone together for a couple of hours. I wasn't particularly looking forward to that aspect of the evening—not because I was tempted to pursue the possibilities of Jonathan's revelation that Randy thought I was hot, but simply because I didn't have a clue as to what we would find to talk about.

I needn't have worried. By the time I got home, after stopping at the store to pick up items on the grocery list Jonathan had made up that morning, Jonathan was already there, sitting in the kitchen talking with Randy.

Jonathan got up from the table to give me a hug as I put the groceries down on the counter, then took a step back and looked at me, head cocked.

"Everything okay?" he asked.

"Fine," I said. "Just a rough day at work."

"Ah," he said, sensing I didn't want to say anything more with Randy present—he wouldn't have known what I was talking about anyway.

Jonathan rummaged through the bags for things that had to

be refrigerated and while he had the freezer door open, he took out a tray of ice cubes while I exchanged greetings with Randy.

"You want a Manhattan too, Randy?" Jonathan asked.

"Nah, I'd better pass," Randy replied. "I don't want to smell of booze. But thanks anyway."

I wondered what that was all about, but didn't say anything.

As long as I was by the cabinets, I got out a glass for my Manhattan. Jonathan reached for the bourbon bottle, but I waved him off. "I can get it, babe, thanks. You grab your coke."

"I figured we could just have hamburgers tonight," Jonathan said, "since it's school night. And Randy wants me to drop him off downtown, so we'll have to leave a little earlier than usual."

Hamburgers explained the package of buns, the large bag of chips and the cottage cheese that had been on the grocery list.

As was becoming another custom, on school nights I had my Manhattan at the kitchen table to keep Jonathan company while he fixed dinner. I reacted to hearing of Randy's plans to go into town—I didn't have to ask what he planned to do there—with slightly mixed feelings: mild relief in not having to worry what we'd find to talk about, and a slight sense of annoyance if he was expecting us—or Jonathan—to go in to town at 11 o'clock to pick him up at Hughie's again.

Jonathan, who was getting pretty good at reading my mind even when he was standing at the stove with his back to me, said: "Randy says he'll take the bus home. I'll give him my key in case he comes in late."

"Okay," I said, for want of anything better to say.

"Yeah, I've gotta pick up a little spending money," Randy said.

"I'm curious," I said. "Doesn't New Eden pay the residents for their work, above and beyond the room and board?"

Randy nodded. "We get $100 a week, on paper," he said. "But they automatically deduct $75.00 for the room and board. It's some sort of legal, bookkeeping thing. We get $25.00 a week spending money, but hell, I spend that much on the vending machines. I'll be doing a lot better than that pretty soon, though. I think I've got a really good job lined up, but I need some cash to hold me over."

Again I wondered how much of the job talk was bravado and how much reality. Obviously, it wouldn't be a job through New Eden's placement center.

"I had to make a couple of long distance calls to set it all up," he said. "Just let me know when the phone bill comes in, and I'll pay you back."

"No problem," I said, hoping he had not spent the entire day calling old friends in Timbuktu.

After helping me set the table, Randy went to the bathroom, which gave Jonathan a chance to ask me about work, and I gave him a brief version of my talk with Tunderew.

"Well, good riddance to him," Jonathan said. "You shouldn't be working for people like him anyway."

* * *

Although Jonathan had been taking the car on school nights for some time now, I always felt a little lost without it. I hadn't planned to go anywhere, but it was just the sense of being…well, restricted, somehow.

Randy and Jonathan left a little after six. Though I tried not to think of him, Tunderew kept bubbling to the surface of my consciousness like a fart in a swimming pool. I forced myself to do the dishes, figuring that concentrating on not breaking anything would get my mind off it, but it didn't work. I don't like being used, and Tunderew had used me. What really pissed me off was the fact that he didn't trust me to follow through on the case. It was the first time in my life that I had encountered homophobia on such a personal level, and I didn't like it one bit.

Okay, okay…relax, my mind-voice said, but I couldn't.

A phone call from our friend Jared Martinson, a former beer-delivery man now teaching Russian Literature at a college about an hour north of the city (a long story), did provide some needed distraction. Jared said he was making one of his not-frequent-enough trips to town for the weekend for a little recreation at the Male Call, his favorite leather bar. I invited him, as always, to stay with us, knowing that, as always, he'd refuse since he'd be too busy tricking. I allowed myself a small erotic fantasy of him accepting the invitation and having to spend the night sharing a bed with Randy; something I'm sure both of them would enjoy.

Also as usual when Jared came to town, we arranged to have brunch at Calypso's on Sunday before he headed back north. He said he'd call our mutual friends, Tim and Phil (after whom Jonathan's goldfish were named) to see if they'd like to join us.

Jonathan got home at the regular time, and we watched some TV and talked a while—though by unspoken mutual agreement, *not* about Tunderew. He was looking forward to getting together with Jared, Tim and Phil, and it struck me, as it often did, how strangely gay life frequently works. All three guys had entered my life as tricks and evolved into close friends. Though Jonathan obviously knew that I'd slept with all of them—a lot more than once—he never said a word about it, and accepted them all as his friends, too.

I asked him if he'd learned anything else about Randy's mysterious job prospects and/or anticipated financial windfall.

"Not really," he said, rubbing his hand idly back and forth on my thigh. "Apparently he does have something going on, though. He said he was going to meet some rich guy tomorrow night and might be going away with him for the weekend. Maybe he found himself a sugar daddy. It would be nice if he could settle down for awhile."

Though I somehow doubted that would ever happen unless he got out of hustling for good, I just nodded and said: "Yeah, it would."

* * *

The guest bedroom door was closed when we got up in the morning and I was a little surprised that I hadn't heard Randy come in, whatever time it might have been. He wasn't up by the time Jonathan and I left for work. And while Randy's being there had not really been all that much of an inconvenience, I was rather hoping he'd be moving on soon.

The very first thing I did upon arriving at the office—after making coffee, but before reading the paper and doing the crossword puzzle—was to prepare a very detailed bill for Mr. Tony T. Tunderew, former client, best selling author, and all-around jerk.

As soon as I'd sealed the envelope, I walked it down the hall to the mail slot and dropped it in. I didn't want to waste one additional minute in severing all ties with him.

When I returned to the office, I got on with the important parts of my morning ritual: drinking my coffee, reading the paper and doing the puzzle. I then called Glen O'Banyon's office to give him the news of my parting of the ways with Tunderew. I was quite surprised, after I'd been put through to O'Banyon's secretary, Donna, to have her say: "Mr. O'Banyon is here, Mr. Hardesty. Would you like to talk with him?" It was a rare thing for him to be in the office at this hour, and more rare still that he'd be available to talk.

There was a brief pause, then O'Banyon's voice: "Good morning, Dick."

"'Morning, Glen," I said. "I just wanted to call to tell you…"

"I know," he interrupted. "I just got off the phone with him. That man is a true piece of work, and I don't think he has any idea how close I am to telling him to find another attorney. I apologize for having dragged you into this in the first place."

"Hey," I said, "*I* should be apologizing to *you*. I'd never want to jeopardize your position with a client, or to have him blame you for having referred me."

"Oh, no worry about that. He's far from stupid, and he knows full well that, with any other lawyer, his chances of breaking the contract with Bernadine would be next to impossible. I'm not even sure I'll be able to do it. Strictly between the two of us, I feel sorry for Bernadine, but I'm obliged to do everything I can for my client, like it or not."

"I understand," I said. "I just didn't want you to feel I'd put you in a bad position."

He laughed. "Don't give it another thought. I'll be seeing him at 4 today, as a matter of fact, on the contract matter. He's driving down from his place up north for it, and I think he'll be on his best behavior."

* * *

I felt a little better after talking with O'Banyon and spent the rest of the morning organizing the materials I'd gathered from my earlier trip to the Hall of Records. I'd promised the attorney for whom I'd done the job that I'd bring it by that afternoon.

I was just getting ready to leave the office when the phone rang. It was Jonathan.

"Sorry to bother you at work, Dick," he said, "but I've got another favor to ask."

"Yeah?" I said, hoping it was not a request that Randy move in permanently.

"Randy just called, and he found out he left his new pair of sneakers at New Eden and he wondered if we could run out there tonight and pick them up before he goes to meet his friend. I thought maybe we could do that and then you and I could go out to dinner—my treat. Would that be okay? We can go someplace nice, and…"

Despite being mildly annoyed at the thought of being Randy's limousine service again, I found Jonathan's all-too transparent efforts to try to appease me kind of sweet.

"Well, okay," I said, trying to sound stern, "but I'm going to be expecting more than just dinner out of this."

I could almost see him grinning. "Anything you want, sir," he said. "Anything at all!"

"Remember that," I said. "See you at home."

* * *

Randy was in the living room, watching TV, when I got home. His hair looked still wet from the shower, but for someone who had a big date with some rich guy lined up, he apparently hadn't gone to any extra trouble to dress any differently than he normally did.

We exchanged greetings and he accepted my offer for a

Manhattan. Since he'd refused a drink the night before, when he was going out to hustle, I wondered what the difference was—obviously because he knew whoever he was seeing tonight and either knew a drink wouldn't bother the guy, or he didn't care. He got up and followed me into the kitchen. I could see into the guest bedroom and was favorably impressed to see that he'd carefully made the bed, on one corner of which, at the foot, was a large dopp kit—probably big enough for a change of underwear and maybe an extra tee shirt, but not much else. Again I found that odd, but then realized I had never fully understood how hustlers led their day-to-day lives.

He noticed me looking.

"I'll stash that in a locker at the bus station," he said, indicating the dopp kit. "I'm not sure if I'll be needing it yet, and I never just carry it around with me."

Hardesty, the Saver of Lost Souls, bobbed briefly to the surface, and I found myself feeling oddly sad to think how totally unpredictable Randy's life was. He couldn't even be sure enough to know if his big weekend plan would happen or not, or, probably, not even if his rich date would show up. What a way to live.

I fixed our Manhattans and we were just walking back into the living room when Jonathan came in, carrying a bag from the fast-food place about two blocks away. He came over for our usual hug, and gestured the bag toward Randy.

"I hope you don't mind, Randy, but since we've got to leave so early and Dick and I have to shower, I picked you up a couple burgers and some fries. We'll grab something later. Oh, and some coleslaw, too. And a chocolate shake."

Randy smiled—something I realized he did not do very often. "Thanks, Jonathan."

Noticing our drinks, Jonathan said: "I'll just take this in the kitchen until you're ready for it. I'll put the shake and the slaw in the fridge, and we can pop the other stuff in the microwave if it gets cold."

The TV was still on, and the news was just beginning, so Randy and I sat down to watch and drink our Manhattans.

Jonathan came back from the kitchen just long enough to say: "I think I'll hop in the shower if that's okay." Without waiting for a reply, he moved off toward the bathroom.

Randy took a couple sips of his Manhattan then said: "Do you mind if I eat now? I'm kind of hungry. I'll put the Manhattan in the fridge for later."

"Sure," I said. "Grab a TV tray there alongside the refrigerator."

He looked at me a little strangely. "It's okay if I eat in here?"

"Of course," I said. "We do it all the time."

"Thanks," he said, and went into the kitchen.

Though my eyes remained on the TV screen, my mind was elsewhere. I thought about how mildly uncomfortable I always felt when visiting other people's homes for any length of time—not knowing the hosts' routine, or if they had any little unspoken rules. This was how Randy lived his life: in other people's houses, in other people's worlds.

God!

I'd just about finished my Manhattan, and Randy's straw was making sucking sounds as it hit the bottom of the shake when Jonathan came back into the room, looking scrubbed and wholesome and sexy as all hell. He gave me a spread-armed-open-palmed "ta-da!" approval seeking gesture, and I grinned at him.

"Yes, you're gorgeous," I said, then got out of my chair, gulping the last bit of my Manhattan as I rose. "My turn."

* * *

Randy was supposed to meet his whatever/whoever-he-was at the bus station at 7:15. That would give us just enough time to get to New Eden, pick up his sneakers, and get to the station. He'd called during the day, as soon as he'd found his sneakers were missing, to see if they were still in his room. He talked to his roommate, who said they were there.

When we pulled through the open gates of New Eden, the first thing I noticed, to the left set atop a small rise and surrounded by obviously young trees, was what I assumed to be the Dinsmores' new home. Jonathan had been right. It was a very nice house, but hardly palatial.

I'd never been to New Eden, but was duly impressed. At the end of the road in the distance were several large barns, complete with silos, near a cluster of what appeared to be storage sheds and animal pens. Halfway down the road, on the right, was a neat white two story building that looked like what I found out it was: an administration building. Beyond it, on both sides of the road, was a row of equally neat, southern colonial style buildings that reminded me very much of the dorms at my old college.

Randy directed me to the second building on the right, and we pulled up in front.

"Be right back," he said, as he got out of the car and moved quickly to the front entrance.

"I'm impressed," I told Jonathan. "This is really a nice place."

Jonathan nodded. "Isn't it?" he said. "Did you see the trees I helped plant, by the house?"

"I did," I said. "They look very nice."

"I like trees," Jonathan said, more to himself than to me.

Randy emerged empty handed from the dorm and hurried to the car.

"Damn it!" he said as he got in. "She's got them up at the house! I sure as hell don't want to face her *or* her brother!"

"We can just go," I said.

I looked into the rear view mirror to see Randy shaking his head vigorously. "No way! Those are *my* sneakers and I paid a lot of money for them, and they're *mine!*" I realized there were not many things in this world that Randy could say that about.

"I can go in and get them for you if you'd like," I said. I knew at once my offer was based far more on curiosity than on altruism. I saw Randy plop backwards into the seat.

"That'd be great," he said.

I turned up the narrow lane that led up to the house, and parked in the small parking area about fifty feet from the side. There were no other cars in the area, though a two-car garage with the doors closed was just to the rear of the house. A walkway led up to the middle of the house, then split off, one arm going toward the back door, the other toward the front. I chose the front.

I rang the bell and waited for perhaps fifteen seconds until the door opened and I found myself face to face with Barbara Dinsmore. A very attractive woman in her late 30s, medium-long light-brown hair, an understated but perfectly tailored cream-colored woman's business suit, subtle but perfectly applied makeup, and the hint of a very pleasant perfume. She was perhaps five feet five inches tall, but perfectly proportioned: what used to be called "petite."

She looked me over calmly, politely. "Can I help you?" she asked with what I determined to be professional pleasantry. I caught a glimpse through the open door of a man crossing my field of vision at the far end of the room and wondered if it were Jeffrey Dinsmore or the brother.

"I've come to pick up a pair of sneakers Randy…" *Jeezus, I had to think!* "…Jacobs left in his room. I understand you have them here."

There wasn't a quiver, a blink of reaction.

"You are…" a pause no longer than a heartbeat but wide enough to drive a truck through "…a friend of Randy's?" It was amazing how, without any stressing or emphasis, there was not the slightest doubt of what she meant by the word "friend".

"Yes," I said. "As you know, he doesn't drive, so I told him I would come by to get them."

I knew perfectly well that all she had to do was look out one of the windows overlooking the parking area to see Randy in the back seat. And I was quite sure she had done exactly that when we drove up. But I hadn't lied.

"Of course," she said. "Would you excuse me for a moment?" She closed the door, leaving me standing there.

Less than a minute later, the door opened and she handed me a brown paper bag. "Here you are," she said, again professionally pleasant.

"Thank you, Mrs. Dinsmore," I said.

She smiled warmly. "You're very welcome. Good day." And she closed the door again.

Now, for a woman who recently found her husband being serviced by some kid who now wanted his shoes back, I thought as I walked to the car, *that is one very <u>cool</u> lady!*

* * *

We dropped Randy, who'd changed shoes on the way, off at the bus station at 7:12. It had started to rain, and I hoped he wouldn't have to stand outside in it too long. I was really tempted to stick around to see who picked him up, but realized that wouldn't be exactly ethical, somehow, so we just went on to dinner at Napoleon.

Although Randy had only been with us a few days and, as I've said, never really got too much in the way, it was really nice that it was just to be the two of us. Dinner was, as always, very nice, with Jonathan insisting on splurging for a Chateaubriand. The meal probably took a big chunk out of his paycheck, but I set aside my "Me Tarzan! Tarzan pay!" tendency because I knew he wanted to do it and it was important for him.

After dinner we drove out to Ramón's for a drink. Our friend Bob Allen, the owner, was there, but his lover, Mario, was working at another bar, Venture, where he'd recently become manager. It was a fairly busy night, so we only had a chance to exchange a few words between customers, but it was good to see him. Jimmy, the other bartender, made a special point, as he always did, of flirting with Jonathan shamelessly, but I knew it was just a game he played because Jonathan always got so flustered by it.

On the way home, we stopped at Griff's to hear Guy Prentiss do a set, then called it a night.

* * *

Jonathan was up first on Saturday morning, and though I woke up when he did, I just lay there making the slow transition from sleeping to waking, and enjoying an odd sense of mild decadence.

I heard him in the kitchen, starting the coffee, then the sound of the TV in the living room. Comfortable sounds.

You're a lucky man, Hardesty, my mind voice said.

I was just agreeing when Jonathan called: "Dick! You better come in here! Quick!"

I threw aside the covers and hurried into the living room, naked.

On the TV screen, the camera moved from a police car with strobes flashing to a reporter standing in the night rain with a microphone, to a broken guardrail, then over the edge to the bottom of a ravine where lay the mangled remains of a car, upside down with its wheels in the air and its front end submerged in a rushing stream.

It took a second for my mind to process what the reporter was saying, and when I did, I heard "…identified as best selling author Tony T. Tunderew. The identity of the passenger has not yet been released."

* * *

By switching back and forth between channels through the morning, we were able to determine that the accident had taken place on a winding stretch of the foothills on the road to Neeleyville, about ten miles north of the city, at around 8 or 8:30 Friday night. I assumed he must have been on his way back to his cabin after his meeting with Glen O'Banyon. From what Catherine Tunderew had said about her ex-husband's various conquests, his passenger was probably going to be the latest notch on his bedpost.

I felt a little guilty that one of my first thoughts was that the bill I'd sent him would not be paid. Of course I always weep for the fallen sparrow but I really couldn't dredge up too very much sympathy for Tony T. Tunderew as a human being. Being sorry anyone had to die is about as far as I could take it.

I made a mental note to call Glen O'Banyon on Monday to express my regret over his losing a client, but I suspect his reaction to Tunderew's passing would be pretty much what mine was.

We then got on with our day.

Apparently Randy's big date had worked out, since he hadn't come back or called, but he had pretty much indicated it would be a weekend-long thing.

We were just getting ready to go to the laundry and do the week's grocery shopping when the phone rang.

"I got it," Jonathan said and hurried over to pick it up.

I was busy tossing clothes into the laundry bag, but I heard him say "Yes, it is." A very long pause and then: "No, he's just staying with us for a few days." He had my full attention at this point. Another pause then: "No, I don't." Followed by the longest pause of all, and finally a little boy's voice saying, "Thank you."

The sound of that "Thank you" was like a bucket of ice water being thrown on the back of my neck. I hurried into the living room to see Jonathan staring down at the phone, which he'd put back on the cradle.

"You know who was in the car with Mr. Tunderew?" he asked.

I knew.

Chapter 6

Jeezus!

My first concern was Jonathan. His face was ashen and he looked as though he were in shock—which I suppose he was. I hurried over to him and put my arms around him, and he just stood there, his arms at his side, like some softer version of a department store manikin. He didn't cry, and that, knowing that Jonathan could cry over just about anything sad, really got to me. I led him over to the couch and sat him down.

"What was Randy…" he started to ask, looking at the coffee table, then stopped. I'm sure he started to ask what Randy was doing in a car with Tony Tunderew, but he knew why. That's what hustlers do; they get in cars with people. But this wasn't just a street corner pickup. Randy had gone to meet someone specific, and it was obvious to me, at least, that it had to have been Tony Tunderew whom he was meeting. The blackmail threats had a solid base—Tony T. Tunderew, world class homophobe, liked guys. Ironic as all hell that he should be found dead in a car with a hustler.

I immediately felt ashamed of myself. It wasn't "a hustler"—it was Randy Jacobs, someone I knew.

There was the very outside possibility that Tunderew wasn't the guy Randy was supposed to meet. Maybe that guy didn't show up. Tunderew struck me as the kind of closeted anal retentive who would cruise the bus station for young guys just arrived in town.

The timing, though…Randy was supposed to meet the guy at 7:15. Would it take about 45 minutes to get to the area the accident took place? It could. It was raining. Maybe Tunderew stopped for gas along the way. Maybe Tunderew was running late in picking Randy up.

That Randy Jacobs would somehow have known Tony Tunderew, though…that just didn't make much sense.

But Tunderew was on the road headed for his cabin. Neeley-ville's a hell of a long ride just for a quick trick. If Randy was just a street corner pickup, they could just as well have taken care of business in the car.

Well, there would be one way to know for sure if Tunderew were the one Randy had been waiting for: if he was, Randy would have had his dopp kit with him. If it was just a quick pickup, it would be in a locker in the bus terminal.

Brilliant line of thinking, Sherlock, my mind voice said. *But what the hell difference does it make one way or the other? Randy's dead. Tunderew's dead. Whatever they were doing in that car is totally moot. They're dead.*

All of this took place in my brain as I sat beside Jonathan on the couch, silent.

"Did Randy have any relatives you know of?" I asked, figuring the silence had gone on long enough, and reaching out to take his hand.

Jonathan shook his head. "The policeman on the phone asked me that," he said, "but Randy never said anything about his family, if he had one. As I told you, he'd been in foster care most of his life until he ran away." He sighed and turned his hand over so we could intertwine fingers.

I didn't ask how the police had had our number. Obviously Jonathan had given it to Randy or Randy had copied it down while he was here.

"It's scary," Jonathan said, talking more to himself than to me, "and sad. Really sad. To think that all Randy had was me...I mean us. And I really didn't know him all that well. Not really. I didn't even know him well enough to know if we were really friends." He looked at me and shook his head slowly. "Funny the things that make people friends. Sometimes it isn't so much that you have things in common as it is that you don't have anything else."

I could sense that the shock of hearing of Randy's death was fading into the reality of it.

He looked at me and I could see his eyes start to water. "I've got you," he said, "and I've got Bob and Mario and Tim and Phil and Jared and my fish and my plants and the people I work with and school and…and Randy didn't have anybody. Or anything. Just a new pair of sneakers. And now he never will."

A tear ran down the side of his nose signaling the cloudburst to come. I put my arm around him, and pulled him toward me just in time.

* * *

Needless to say, the rest of Saturday was pretty much shot. We did go out, later in the day, to drop the laundry off and to make a quick run through the grocery store, just for essentials.

There was a message on the machine from Tim and Phil when we got home, saying they'd talked to Jared and would be joining us for brunch Sunday.

"I'll call them back and cancel," I said, but Jonathan shook his head.

"No, I'd like to go if you would," he said. "I can't just sit around moping."

"Well," I said, "you want to go out to dinner tonight, then?"

He gave me a small smile. "Not really," he said. "I think I'll just concentrate on getting my moping out of the way. I hope you don't mind."

I walked over and hugged him. "You're entitled," I said. "I'll leave you alone, but I'll be here if you need me."

"Thanks," he said, then wandered off to the kitchen to feed his fish.

I called Tim and Phil back. I was typically-me nosy about whether Tim, as an assistant medical examiner at the coroner's office, might be assigned to work on either Tunderew or Randy. I had no reason to suspect that anything unusual—other than sufficient trauma from the accident to cause death—would be found, but if by chance it was, I'd like to know about it.

Phil answered the phone; we talked for a few minutes and verified the time and place for Sunday's brunch. I told him briefly about the accident and Randy, though not about my short and unpleasant relationship with Tony T. Tunderew, and said not to think it unusual if Jonathan were not his usual talkative self. He understood. He, Jonathan, and Randy all shared a hustling background, but Phil and Jonathan were among the lucky ones who had gotten out of it alive and relatively unscathed.

Telling me to give Jonathan a hug for him, Phil turned the phone over to Tim. I explained again about the accident and asked him if he could let me know in the rare event that anything peculiar were to show up in the autopsies. He said he would and, like Phil, told me to let Jonathan know they were thinking of him.

Jonathan had returned to the living room with a watering can and began watering his plants, plants that he'd managed to accumulate by bringing home throwaways from his work and nursing them back to health.

On my way to the bathroom, I went quickly into the guest bedroom and moved Randy's battered duffle bag from beside the bed into the closet and closed the door. I smoothed out the bedspread to get rid of the still visible indentation where Randy'd set his dopp kit. We could figure out what to do with his things later; Jonathan didn't need any more reminders right now.

We had a quiet dinner—emphasis on the "quiet"—watched TV with me on the couch and Jonathan sitting on the floor, leaning back against me, and went to bed fairly early.

* * *

Sunday went better than I'd expected. Jonathan was quiet, for him, but by the time we left to meet Jared, Phil, and Tim at Calypso's, he apparently had put his moping behind him. Randy was gone and nothing could bring him back, and I think Jonathan realized it.

We were the first to arrive at Calypso's. Jared had said he would order a table on the patio, but after letting the maitre d' know we were there, we decided to wait for the others at the bar. I ordered a Bloody Mary for me and a Virgin Mary for Jonathan, and we moved to a clear area near the patio end of the bar to wait. As always on a Sunday the place was crowded, and I was debating on whether we should ask the maitre d' to be seated now lest he be tempted to give our table to someone else if the others took too long to arrive.

A moment or two later, though, I glanced to the entrance to see Jared—you couldn't miss a body and face as spectacular as Jared Martinsen's at 60 paces—moving through the crowd, followed by an equally spectacular hunk I did not recognize. It took me a minute to realize they were apparently together, which struck me as a real first. Jared had never brought anyone to any of our get-togethers.

Interesting, I thought.

"Dick. Jonathan," Jared said as we exchanged handshakes. He turned to the guy beside him. "This is Jake."

Oh, indeed it is, my crotch said appreciatively. While Jake, Jonathan, and I shook hands—a really strong, natural grip, I noted—I took stock of Jared's new friend and was struck by how well they complimented each other. They could have been cast from the same body mold—the incredibly but naturally-muscled one very rarely used, I might add—but whereas Jared had dark hair and dark eyes, Jake was true Nordic blue-eyed blond. If just looking at Jared switched on every gay boy's fantasy of the ultimate leather man, Jake was without a doubt a gay Paul Bunyon. That image wasn't hurt by the fact that he was wearing a plaid flannel shirt with the sleeves rolled up and tight Levi's that amply demonstrated that he and Jared shared other attributes.

"Hope you don't mind my coming along," Jake said, "but Jared wanted me to meet you all."

Do we mind, boys and girls? my mind asked.

No, we don't mind at all. Not a bit, it answered.

"We hooked up Friday night at Venture," Jared said, which again struck me as being of more than passing interest. It implied that he had spent the entire weekend with the same guy, which surely had to be a first.

Jared moved to the bar to order their drinks, and Jake turned to Jonathan. "I've seen you before, haven't I, Jonathan?" he asked.

Scorpio Alert!

Cool it, Hardesty.

"I don't think so," Jonathan said, glancing quickly at me to see if I might be reacting to the idea, then added, looking at him a second time: "Oh, yeah, at New Eden! You were working on the garage!" He paused long enough to give me an evil-kid grin before turning back to Jake and adding, "I didn't recognize you with your shirt on!"

"Thanks, I think," he said, smiling. "But that's right. You were with the landscapers."

"You're in construction?" I asked in what surely had to be the most idiotically redundant question of the year.

"Yeah," he said as Jared returned, handing him his drink. "I've got a contracting outfit. We build houses, mostly. We've done a couple of things out at New Eden, including the Dinsmore's new place."

I noticed that, as he talked, he put his free arm around Jared's waist, casually.

"Sorry we're late," Tim's voice said from behind me, startling me. I'd been concentrating on the Jared/Jake dynamics so intently I didn't even know they'd come in.

Handshakes all around, introductions made, and Tim and Phil's drinks ordered, Jared caught the maitre d's eye and indicated we were ready to sit down.

* * *

Have I mentioned—probably any fewer than two dozen times—that I really enjoy brunch? This one was particularly nice on several levels. First, I could see it had taken Jonathan's mind off Randy for the moment; secondly because I was fairly well awed by the Jared/Jake thing, whatever it might be. As I said, this is the first time Jared had *ever* brought someone to our gatherings. His weekend trips to town were usually trick marathons, with as many as four different guys coming and going in the course of two days. At the risk of being redundant again, Jake was obviously something special.

And Tim had a bit of news we all found pretty impressive: Phil had been contacted by a New York talent agent who had seen his ads as official underwear model for Spartan Briefs, and wanted him to come to New York to try out for a part on one of the biggest soap operas on TV.

"And?" Jonathan and I echoed at the same time.

Phil, who had sat there looking mildly embarrassed while Tim told of it, said: "And I turned it down, of course."

"Why?" Jonathan asked, wide-eyed.

"Well," Phil said, first finishing his drink and signaling the waiter for another round for the table, "for one thing I'm not an actor. For another thing, I'm away from home too much of the time as it is, and since we've both got good jobs here, I couldn't ask Tim to give up his, and there's no way in hell I'd move to New York alone." He reached over and punched Tim lightly on the shoulder. "Besides, it took me long enough to find this guy. I'm not going to lose him."

Tim grinned. "I told him he could go if he wanted to," he said. "But I didn't mean it."

* * *

I was surprised when I got to the office Monday morning to find a message from Lieutenant Mark Richman of the City Police. While I'd developed a very comfortable working arrangement with him over the course of several cases, and we'd even had a couple of beers together, I knew this wasn't a social call. I was afraid I *did* know what it was about, though, and I was not happy.

I called the City Building Annex and asked for Lieutenant Richman's extension.

"Lieutenant," I said when I heard his familiar voice, "it's Dick Hardesty. I got your message."

"Thanks for returning it so quickly," he said. "Do you have any plans for lunch today?" Richman never was one to waste much time on idle chit-chat.

"Uh, no," I said, then did a little cutting-to-the-chase myself and said: "Where and when do you want to meet?"

"Sandler's? Quarter after?" he asked.

"Okay, I'll see you there."

We'd met at the same place and at the same time so often now, and always in relation to a case, that we'd developed almost a verbal shorthand. I knew he wanted to talk to me about Tunderew, but how he possibly could have known I'd had anything at all to do with the late unlamented, I couldn't imagine. Richman was sharp, but...*that* sharp?

After I'd hung up with Richman, I called Glen O'Banyon's office and left a message for him to call me when he had a chance.

* * *

The waiter had just poured my second cup of coffee when I saw Lieutenant Richman enter. It never ceases to amaze me how the mind digs its own little ruts and refuses to let you get out of them. I'd seen Mark Richman too many times to count, yet every single time I did I thought of what a shame it was that he was straight. Oh, well.

"Dick," he said by way of greeting, reaching across the table to shake hands before sliding into the bench across from me.

"Lieutenant," I said.

The waiter hurried over with his coffee and we placed our usual order—we'd done this so often neither of us needed to look at a menu. When the waiter left, Richman poured his usual third-of-a-cup of sugar into his coffee, stirred it, and said: "How do you know Randy Jacobs?"

Randy? Not Tunderew?

"He, uh, was a friend of Jonathan's. He was staying with us for a few days," I said. "How did you know I knew him?"

Richman took a sip of his coffee. "He had your phone number in his pocket, for one thing," he said. "I went through both his and Tunderew's personal effects. I went through Jacobs' things first—there weren't many—and I recognized your number the minute I saw it."

Well, that would have been very flattering if you were gay, I thought, *but a little disconcerting since you're not.*

"I'm curious," I said: "Was his dopp kit in the car?"

He nodded. "We assumed that's who it belonged to," he said. "Why do you ask?"

Because that pretty much proves that Tunderew was the guy Randy planned to meet, and not some casual pickup, I thought. But I didn't say that to Richman. I wanted to see where all this was going, first.

"Just curious," I said. "He took it with him when he left the apartment."

The waiter arrived with our food and, as usual, Richman dug right in. He paused after a few forkfuls and said: "And then we come to Tunderew," he said.

Here it comes. "Tunderew?" I asked.

He looked at me with a raised eyebrow as if to say: "Don't play games."

"Tunderew," he said. "It was a pretty messy wreck, and they found Tunderew's briefcase smashed open, with papers all over the ground. Apparently, it had not been locked. If it had been, we couldn't have opened it. He kept an address book, and your name was in it. From what little I know of the man, I doubted you and he were golfing buddies."

"Hardly," I said, "though I would have been happy to use a nine iron on him. Do you have any reason to think the accident wasn't accidental?"

"Not really," he said. "They did find skid marks and some broken glass, possibly from one of Tunderew's headlights. It appears as though he had braked to avoid something…maybe a deer…but hit it, lost control and swerved through the guardrail."

"Did they find a dead deer?" I asked.

"No, though it might possibly have not been killed outright and wandered off into the woods; we're checking on that. No blood, either, though."

"So maybe he hit another car? Rear ended it?"

He shrugged. "Possibly. We'll know more when we examine the glass found on the road. But if he'd hit another car, chances are he'd at least have broken the tail lights, and I didn't see anything about them having found any red glass."

He speared the last piece of his meatloaf, mopped up the remaining gravy with it, and transferred it to his mouth. When he'd chewed and swallowed, he said: "But as to the question of whether it might not have been an accident, maybe it's just my copying your famous tendency to follow your gut reactions, but let's see… There's a dead famous writer who has your name in his address book, a dead young male passenger whose relationship to the writer is unknown, and your phone number in the young man's pocket. Why do I smell the vague aroma of fish?"

I wasn't quite sure what to say, so he broke the silence. "So let me ask you—do *you* have any reason to suspect that the accident might not have been an accident? Exactly who is—or rather, was—Randall Jacobs, and what was his relationship to Tunderew?"

Now it was my turn to take the last bite of my BLT, chew, and swallow before answering.

"Okay," I began, "it's like this…"

I told him everything I knew: about Tunderew's being blackmailed and the alleged reason for it, about my having contacted the prime suspects in the blackmail, about Randy being a hustler—which gave a solid basis for the blackmail, and how Randy ended up in the car with Tunderew. There was a link between Tunderew and me, Randy and me (well, Jonathan), and obviously between Randy and Tunderew. But they weren't the same links. That it had been Randy in the car rather than some other hustler or one of Tunderew's woman conquests —assuming his ex-wife was not totally wrong about his sexual preferences, and I had no reason to believe she was—was purely one of those unfortunate coincidences that seem to crop up far too often in life.

"Well," Richman said when I'd finished, "the blackmail angle is an interesting one. But blackmail is one thing, murder something quite different. And why would a blackmailer commit murder if the blackmail was working? Who did you decide—if you did—was doing the blackmailing?"

I sighed. "Well, I wasn't really on the case long enough to be sure. My bet at the moment would be leaning heavily towards Bernadine Press. They were suing him for breach of contract because he was trying to back out of his deal to give them the rights to publish his second book. They stood to lose a *lot* of money if the contract were broken—blackmail would be a way to get at least some of it back. With Tunderew dead, and not around to fight the lawsuit, they might have a better chance of keeping the contract in force. But that'd be only *if* he'd finished it, yet, and I have no idea as to whether he did or not. If he hadn't… I can well understand their wishing he was dead—I get the feeling that a lot of people felt that way about him, but to actually do it, I don't know."

The waiter came by with refills for our coffee, and as usual Richman waited until he was gone before saying: "We're putting the cart way ahead of the horse here in assuming the accident was anything but an accident. But if it turns out it wasn't, how about the subject of the second book? If it *hadn't* been finished yet, somebody might have a pretty good motive to make sure it never was."

I nodded. "I agree," I said. "But I have no idea who the new book was supposed to be about. And from what I know of Tunderew's devious methods of getting information, it's quite likely the subject might not even know about it."

Richman finished his coffee and looked at his watch. "I'd better be heading back," he said.

"So where does that leave us?" I asked. "Are the police going to hold a full investigation?"

He shrugged, and motioned to the waiter to bring the check. "That'll depend a lot on what the final report on the accident shows," he said. "The preliminary autopsy results should be on my desk when I get back to the office, and if they don't show anything unusual like a gunshot wound, and if there's no further indication of another car being involved, there's not too much to go on. Do you know if he'd paid the blackmailer anything?"

I shook my head. "I doubt it. The payment was to be made by the 15th of this month."

Richman pursed his lips and knit his brow. "Hmm," he said. "I was going to say that we could look into the blackmail angle, since blackmailing is a criminal activity. But with no money having been paid, and Tunderew dead, I'm not sure what pursuing it would get us." I reached for the check, but he got to it first. "My turn," he said, hoisting his rear end off the seat to reach into his back pocket for his wallet. "As to where we go from here on this whole Tunderew thing, let's wait until we see what develops first, okay?"

* * *

No message from O'Banyon when I returned to the office, but I knew he was probably in court all day. There was one from Tim, though. He said he had some information and would call me back on his afternoon coffee break.

Information? Damn! What kind of information? About what? Well, the deaths, obviously. But…

They say patience is a virtue, but you certainly couldn't prove it by me: I've never had so much as an atom of it. So waiting for Tim's call was about 30 seconds longer than eternity.

Finally, at 2:30, the phone rang.

"Hardesty Investigations," I said as usual, though I didn't wait for the second ring before picking up the receiver.

"Hi, handsome," Tim's voice said. From the sounds of traffic in the background, I gathered he was using one of the pay phones in front of the building.

"What's the 'information'?" I asked, a little abruptly. (Hey, a lot of impatience can build up in an eternity and 30 seconds.)

"Both Tunderew and Randy died from massive trauma suffered in the crash itself," he said. "No evidence whatever of any foul play. But the interesting thing is that Tunderew must have been high as a kite when the car went through the railing."

??? I thought. "Drunk?" I asked.

"Cocaine. High levels. It's a wonder he could even drive."

Well, well.

"And Randy?" I asked. I was almost certain Randy had been clean when we dropped him off at the bus station. Jonathan had never indicated anything about Randy being a user.

"No drugs," Tim said.

He told me that Catherine Tunderew had claimed her ex-husband's body; no one had claimed Randy, and the thought that perhaps no one would made me incredibly sad. I wanted to ask about what might happen to Randy if no one did claim him, but Tim had to get back to work, so we hung up with the promise to talk after I got home.

So Tunderew was coked up, eh? That made a pretty strong case for the strictly-an-accident theory. But…my mind went back to the TV report I'd first seen on the accident…the reporter standing in the rain, the camera panning past him, down from the broken guardrail to the bottom of the ravine. There was something…what?…something that caught my attention in that scene. What in hell was it? I only saw the report once, and I certainly do not have what I'd consider a photographic memory. But I do have a knack for knowing when something isn't right.

I looked at my watch and saw it was only 2:45. The reporter standing in the road in the rain. What was I getting at?

Come on, Hardesty! Stop playing these stupid games with yourself!

I tried to ignore it and do some paperwork I'd been putting off far too long, but I couldn't get my mind off that image of the reporter…and the road. It had something to do with the road.

As Oscar Wilde said, "I can resist anything but temptation." I'd gotten myself going on this accident scene thing, and I knew I wouldn't let it go until I did something about it. With a deep weltschmerz sigh, I got up and left the office.

* * *

It was a nice day for a drive, and it was good just to get out and do something a little different. It would have helped had I not had to be thinking every second about Tunderew, Randy, the accident that killed them, and what had led them to that particular spot at that particular time.

I took the Neeleyville turnoff toward the range of hills that made a sweeping semi-circle north of the city. I wasn't sure exactly where the accident had taken place, but didn't think it would be hard to find. The road crossed a small stream and began its winding climb up the first of several hills, each one steeper and taller than the one before. The slope of the hill between the stream and the car became steeper until the stream was lost from sight. The edge of a ravine appeared about a block to the left of the car, then slowly edged ever closer, as if hoping no one would notice, until it paralleled the road with only a guardrail between the pavement and a sharp drop-off.

Luckily there was little traffic, and most of what there was was headed toward the city. I was able to keep a watch on the guardrail ahead. And then I saw it...a 20 foot section of obviously new rail, about 100 feet before a curve to the right, which took the road out of the line of sight past the steep upward slope of the hill. Making sure there was no one coming up behind me, I pulled as far off the road as I could get—the shoulder was just wide enough to allow cars to pass from behind without having to swerve over into the other lane.

I got out of the car and walked over to the rail, looking down, as the camera had done, to the stream at the bottom of the ravine, probably 90 feet below. The car had been removed, of course, and I could see broken small trees and shrubs where it had either been hauled up, or damaged on the way down. It was an odd feeling to realize that two people I had known, even slightly, had died right here. I backed away from the edge, and looked up the road toward the curve.

And it hit me! What my mind had seen and I had not. There was a good 100 feet of straight, relatively level road leading to the curve! Why would the accident have happened *here*, and not closer to the curve? Well, sure, if Tunderew were stoned, it could have happened anywhere...but he *hit* something before he went over! If some idiot had come speeding around the curve and into the uphill lane, Tunderew might have suddenly swerved to avoid it. A head-on collision would have been catastrophic for both cars; if they'd missed each other, where had the broken glass come from?

I looked carefully at the road. There were maybe six feet of skid marks, swerving from the right lane—my lane—sharply over the center line. Then there was a faint, broken circle of smudges as if the car had spun around in a circle heading for the guard rail, but obviously from only one set of tires. Why would there be skid marks if he hadn't thought he was going to hit something? A deer? The upward slope of the hill to the right was pretty steep—hard to imagine what a deer would be doing on the road in the first place or how, if one was there and been hit with enough force to break a light and make a car lose control, would it have been able to run up that steep an incline and disappear.

What the hell had happened? I didn't know. But my instinct was telling me that Tunderew's being high or not, it was no accident.

I got back in the car, drove about a mile further up the road until I could find a safe place to turn around, and headed back to the city.

* * *

I made it back with enough time to swing by and pick Jonathan up from work so he wouldn't have to take the bus home. He'd been saving every penny he could so that he could buy a car of his own. We'd talked about my getting a new car myself—a "family" car, if you would—and letting him have this one for back and forth to work and school, but he insisted on buying it from me, and at the Blue Book value.

He was uncharacteristically quiet on the ride home, looking out the window. I knew he was thinking of Randy, and so was I. I was also increasingly aware of the fact that since Randy had most likely died only because he was with someone a lot of people had reason to want dead, that meant that I was probably going to find myself trying to find out who had killed Tony T. Tunderew. To be brutally honest, I didn't really *care* who had killed Tunderew but I owed it to Randy as a human being to find out what had happened to him.

My thoughts were interrupted when Jonathan, still looking out the window, asked: "What happens if nobody claims Randy? He doesn't have any family."

"I'm going to call Tim when we get home to ask him," I said, and Jonathan just nodded and lapsed again into silence. I didn't even bring up the subject of drugs. Randy had been clean; there wasn't any point.

* * *

After a quiet—in more ways than one—dinner, I helped Jonathan with the dishes and then went into the living room to call Tim. Jonathan got out his textbook and sat down on the floor in his customary cross-legged pose, the book open on the carpet between his knees.

"Tell Tim 'hi,'" he said without looking up.

It was Phil who answered the phone, and we talked for a few minutes, mostly about Sunday's brunch and Jared's friend Jake, who had made quite an impression on us all.

"It'd be nice if Jared finally settled down," he said, and I laughed, then felt a little guilty for Jonathan's sake.

"Yeah, it would," I said, "But don't count on it. Jared's not the settling down kind."

"Well, stranger things have happened," he said. "How's Jonathan doing?"

I glanced down at him as he turned a page in his textbook, apparently fully absorbed in it.

"He'll be fine," I said. "Oh, and is Tim around?"

"Sure," he said. "Just a sec."

When Tim came on, I asked him what the procedures were for dealing with someone like Randy, who apparently had no family at all.

Tim sighed. "I was afraid that might be the case," he said. "When no one steps in to claim a body, tracking down relatives is usually up to the police. I'm sure they'll do everything they can to find *somebody*. He had some sort of ID card from New Eden," he said, "so they'll start there. And he had a bank book with his name on it, I understand. When no one can be found to claim a body, we keep it for ten days, and if no one has claimed it by then, it's cremated at the county's expense and buried in Rosevine Cemetery. That's where the county has its Potter's Field." He paused for a moment, then said: "I never knew the kid, but I'd sure feel bad to think that he'd end up there."

I couldn't agree more. But I'd found the reference to the bank book both surprising and interesting.

"Did you see the bankbook?" I asked.

"No, but it was in the bag with his personal effects. I just noticed it listed on the inventory form they keep with the bag."

"Is there some way you could get a look at it?" I asked. Not many hustlers have bankbooks, and I remembered Randy's boasts about some expected windfall.

"I suppose I could," he said. "Totally against policy, of course, but I'll see what I can do."

"Thanks, Tim," I said. "Jonathan sends you both his best. Talk with you later."

When we hung up, I told Jonathan what Tim had said.

"I'll bury him," Jonathan said softly, outwardly concentrating on his textbook.

"Uh…" I said, watching him closely, "that's really sweet of you, but…"

"I'll use my car money," he said. "I'm not going to have Randy buried in some Potter's Field like some throw-away nobody cared about."

"Well," I said, really touched by his naturally generous nature, "let's wait and see what happens first, okay? They might be able to find a relative somewhere."

"Okay," he said, still without looking up from his book.

* * *

And just how do you ever expect to make a living if you spend all your time working on cases you're not being paid to solve? one of my mind voices—the one responsible for my finances, and which I'd always pictured decked out in a green eyeshade and a celluloid collar—demanded huffily.

It was right, of course, but I just couldn't turn my back on Randy and finding out why he'd died—which, in order to do, I had to find out why, specifically, Tunderew had died.

I was sitting at my desk, drinking my umpteenth cup of coffee, lost in my thoughts, when the phone rang.

"Hardesty Investigations," I said, as always.

"Dick, it's Glen. Sorry I didn't get back to you yesterday. I was out of town until this morning. Quite a surprise about Tunderew, eh?"

"I don't know if 'surprise' is quite the right word," I said. "I'm sorry you lost a client, though."

"Not to worry," he said. "I've got a couple others to keep me busy. But do I detect a note of skepticism in that reference to a surprise?"

Sharp guy, O'Banyon, I thought. But of course he was sharp or he wouldn't be one of the richest lawyers in the city.

"If you mean do I suspect the accident may not have been an accident, the answer's yes," I said. "It's not absolutely certain, but my money's on murder."

"Well, that *is* interesting," he said. "Especially in light of..." he trailed off.

I waited all of three seconds for him to continue, and when he didn't, I prompted: "In light of...?"

"In addition to representing him in this breach of contract matter," O'Banyon said, "I was also drawing up a new will for him. He was supposed to be in tomorrow to sign it."

"Can I assume somebody was being cut out of the old will?"

"You can assume it, if you wish, but I can't give you any details, of course."

"Catherine Tunderew?"

I took the pointed silence that followed as confirmation.

"Well," I said, "as *you* said, 'interesting!'"

"You're not thinking of getting involved in all this, are you?" he asked. "As I recall, you weren't planning on starting a Tony T. Tunderew fan club."

"I don't give a shit about Tunderew," I said, "but I knew the kid who was in the car with him."

"Ah?" he said, obviously curious.

"Randy Jacobs, a friend of Jonathan's. A hustler, by the way, which brings us back to the blackmail issue that got me into this whole thing. I owe it to Randy and Jonathan to find out who was responsible, and I can't do that without finding out who killed Tunderew. *If* it wasn't an accident," I hastened to add.

There was another moment of silence, then O'Banyon's voice.: "Well, keep me posted, will you? And if there's anything you need from me…"

"I'll let you know for sure," I said. "Thanks, Glen. I'll talk to you soon."

We hung up and I heard myself sigh.

How do you manage to get yourself into these things? one of my mind voices asked innocently, obviously referring to me.

It's a gift, another replied, with just the slightest hint of sarcasm.

I ignored them both and got to work.

Chapter 7

Okay. Catherine Tunderew. Did she know she was being cut out of her ex-husband's will? Did she even know she'd ever been *in* it? If the answer to both those questions was 'yes,' that would move her ahead of the Bernadines on the suspects list. I'd call her.

The second book. Had it been finished? If so, where was it? If not, who was it's subject, and where was it? Check with Tunderew's agent...uh...Sal Armata.

If the book was finished, Bernadine Press' claim on it, with the contract still in force and Tunderew dead, would probably be honored. A lot of money was involved, and money has been known to be a good motive for murder. And Catherine Tunderew, if she was indeed in the still-in-effect old will, would be a very wealthy woman. If it hadn't been finished then the focus would shift to anyone who had an interest in keeping Tunderew from finishing it. Neither the Bernadines nor Catherine Tunderew would come out very far ahead if the book wasn't completed.

Randy's bank book. What was a hustler—who had to have Jonathan drop him off near Hughie's so he could make "some spending money"—be doing with a bank book? How much was in it, and where had the money come from?

Was Tunderew secretly gay, or bi? If not, how would Randy ever even have met him in the first place?

My thoughts, fueled by the caffeine of countless cups of coffee, were moving faster and faster and getting me not one inch closer to any answers.

Uh, excuse me, one of my mind voices somehow not affected by the caffeine interrupted, *but before you leap on your horse and go galloping off in all directions, mightn't it be a good idea to see what the police found out first? It might have been an accident!*

Well, it might. But I still doubted it.

After debating whether or not I should bother Lieutenant Richman at police headquarters, I decided it was worth a try. I picked up the phone and dialed the City Building Annex.

"Lieutenant Richman," the voice answered when I was put through to his extension.

"Lieutenant," I said without feeling the need to identify myself—we knew each other well enough by now to recognize each other's voice. "Sorry to bother you, but I was wondering if they'd found out anything more about Tunderew's accident?"

"I am just now looking over the report," he said, "and, aside from the fact that the toxicology report from the autopsy showed that Tunderew had high levels of cocaine in his body when he died, apparently the answer is 'no.' The broken glass was from the passenger's side headlight and turn signal. Obviously, he hit something, but we haven't a clue what it might have been. If it had been another car, we might have expected there to be bits of it's paint found on the passenger's side fender or bumper. But there wasn't. Of course, the car was so badly mangled, it would be hard to tell how much damage the initial impact caused."

I suddenly recalled a case I'd had some time before, where another car had gone off a cliff in what the police ruled an accident until I went scrounging around the wreck in the junk yard to which it had been taken and found a spent bullet in the shredded passenger's side front tire—it had been shot out, causing the car to lose control. I reminded Richman of that case and wondered if, however unlikely it might be, perhaps something similar might have happened to Tunderew—the first shot breaking the headlight, the second causing the tire to blow.

"I remember that one," Richman said, "and we do try to learn from our mistakes. Blown tires are routinely checked on all fatal accidents now. In Tunderew's case, despite the damage to the rest of the car, the tires were all intact."

"So will there be any further investigation into this, or will it just be ruled an accident?" I asked.

Richman sighed. "Dick," he said patiently, "seventeen people died in one-car traffic accidents in this county alone last year. We just don't have the time or the manpower to treat every one as a potential homicide if there isn't more compelling evidence to indicate it than is the case here, especially since Tunderew was under the influence of drugs at the time of the accident. I'm sorry, but that's just the way it is."

"I understand," I said, and I did. But...

He paused, then said: "But that's not going to keep you from looking further into it, is it?"

As I said, he did know me pretty well by that time.

"I owe it to Randy," I said.

"Yeah," he said, "I can see where you'd think that. So just keep me posted *if* you dig up anything, okay?"

"I will, Lieutenant," I said. "I promise." An out-of-nowhere thought popped into my head. "One more thing, Lieutenant," I said. "You mentioned Randy's having a bank book. Did you find it in his dopp kit?"

There was a slight pause, then: "No, now that you mention it; as I recall the report said the kit was zipped up when it was found, so they couldn't open it. But there were a lot of papers scattered around, mostly from the open briefcase."

My mind grabbed that one and ran with it. "A lot of papers?" I asked. "Like maybe enough for a book manuscript?"

Richman paused only a moment. "No, I don't think so. Apparently just mostly receipts, a couple of past due bill notices, stuff like that. A date book that was almost totally illegible because he had used a pen and the ink had been pretty much blurred by the rain. There might have been more stuff, but it probably landed in the stream and floated away."

A considerably longer pause while we both absorbed the implications of that bit of information. "I'll check the photos taken at the scene. An interesting point."

Very interesting, I'd say.

"Thanks, Lieutenant," I said. "I'd appreciate that."

He said he'd get back to me, and we exchanged our goodbyes and hung up.

What would Randy's bank book be doing in Tunderew's briefcase?

I think I knew.

* * *

I'd read in the morning paper that Tunderew's funeral would be held on Thursday at the McGinnis & Morbey Funeral Home, with burial at—and I found this part both ironic and sad—Rosevine Cemetery, the same place where Randy may very well end up, but in a far different part of the grounds. McGinnis & Morbey was a pretty fancy place, and I wondered who had made the arrangements. Catherine Tunderew, no doubt, which was pretty nice of her, considering how she'd been treated by the dearly departed.

There were quite a few questions I had for her, and I took a chance on calling her number. I'd never have done it if I felt I might be intruding on her grief, but she'd made it pretty clear that any love she might have had for Tunderew had faded long ago.

The phone rang three times, and then her answering machine kicked in: "Hello, this is Catherine Tunderew. I'm obviously unavailable at the moment, but please leave a message."

I did so.

I next looked up the number of Sal Armata. There was no listing in the white pages, but I found it under "Literary Agents" in the Yellow Pages. I dialed the number and heard the phone being picked up on the second ring.

"Sal Armata," the voice said. I was a little surprised that he'd be answering the phone himself.

"Mr. Armata," I said, "my name is Dick Hardesty. I'm a private investigator, and I was doing some work for Mr. Tunderew. I wonder if, as Mr. Tunderew's agent, you could answer a few questions for me?"

"I'm afraid not," he said. "I ceased being his agent upon his death."

"But aren't you handling the negotiations for his second book?"

"There *is* no second book," he said. "A book isn't a book until it's finished. He hadn't finished it at the time of his death."

Aha, I thought.

"Do you have any idea how close he was to finishing?" I asked. "Do you have any part of the manuscript?"

"I know he was close to the end," he said. "But he never gave me any part of the manuscript."

"But you do know who it was about, then?" I asked.

There was a pause, then a cautious: "It wasn't *about* anyone," he said defensively. "The book was a work of fiction."

"Like *Dirty Little Minds*?" I asked.

"Exactly," he said. "Some people may have seen some vague similarity to certain well known individuals, but that would only be a testament to Mr. Tunderew's ability to create lifelike characters."

Uh huh.

"And you can't tell me which actual person the 'lifelike character' this book might resemble?"

"No," he said. "I don't engage in speculation. As I say, it's a work of fiction."

"Well, thank you very much for your time, Mr. Armata," I said. "I'm sorry that you lost a client—especially one with such great potential for you."

"Win some, lose some," he said. "Now if you'll excuse me..."

"Certainly," I said. "Thanks again." And I heard the click of his hanging up.

* * *

I assumed Armata must have been in the business quite a while to be able to take the loss of his potential share of the profits from an all-but-guaranteed blockbuster in stride. From what I'd gathered from the Bernadines, I assumed Tunderew had only taken Armata on as an agent for the second book, and he got nothing from *Dirty Little Minds*. But I also suspected he probably knew more about the second book and how close to completion it was than he let on. Still, he seemed a little more casual about the whole thing than I'd have thought.

I'd just called downstairs to the diner in the lobby for a turkey club, a small salad (hey, I was trying to eat healthier), and a chocolate shake (okay, so I wasn't totally succeeding), and had just headed for the door to go down to get it when the phone rang.

"Hardesty Investigations," I said as I leaned across the desk to pick up the phone.

"Mr. Hardesty, it's Catherine Tunderew. You wanted to talk to me?"

"Yes, as a matter of fact I did," I said, walking back around my desk to sit down. "First, I'd like to express my condolences on Mr. Tunderew's death."

I could almost hear a small smile in her voice when she said: "That's very kind of you, Mr. Hardesty, but as I think you know, condolences are hardly necessary."

"I understand," I said. "But several questions have come up and…"

She interrupted. "Are you still working on this blackmail thing?" She asked. "I'd have thought that issue would have become moot with Tony's death."

"Well, that part of it, yes. But the passenger in the car with Mr. Tunderew was an acquaintance of mine, and…"

She interrupted again. "Oh, my, this is all beginning to sound very complicated. Why don't we talk in person over a cup of tea? Would you like to come by around 2:00 again?"

"Uh, yes, that would be nice. If you're sure I won't be intruding."

She gave a small laugh. "On what?" she asked. "Certainly not my grief, and I've just finished work on my last commissioned book, so I have all the time in the world. Do come over and we'll talk."

"That's fine," I said. "I'll see you at 2:00."

As I hung up I wondered why Franz Lehar suddenly popped into my mind, and then the thought was immediately followed by the title music from his operetta: "The Merry Widow."

Where do you come up with these things, Hardesty? my mind asked.

* * *

I went downstairs to pick up lunch, then returned to my office and ate it while pretty much staring off into space, thinking. I had no doubt that Tunderew had been killed, and I rather suspected that the people I knew about with good reason to want him dead were almost assuredly not the only ones. He had profited, in *Dirty Little Minds*, from a lot of influential people's misery, and in large part contributed to and perpetuated it. The Governor Keene scandal, which might eventually have just faded away, was forever immortalized in print. The subject of the next book had every right—if he/she even knew they were the target—to be sufficiently unhappy to be willing to go to great lengths to prevent its publication.

I'd just about put Larry Fletcher out of my mind as far as any involvement with the blackmail was concerned, and I'd never so much as considered him as a factor in Tunderew's death. But the more I thought about it…could he really be as naive as he came across? Never turn your back on the quiet ones. What if he had somehow found out that it was Tunderew who'd gotten him fired, and realized that Tunderew had been using him as a doormat and made a ton of money off what Fletcher had done for him because he thought Tunderew liked him? I know I might have been more than a tad miffed if it had happened to me.

And then there was Bernadine Press…

I pulled myself out of my reverie and looked at my watch. Time to head out for tea with Catherine Tunderew.

* * *

The work area of her living room was, I noticed when I entered, a lot less cluttered than the last time I'd been there. Well, she said she'd just finished a commission. She greeted me wearing a tent-like Hawaiian mumu with a pleasantly muted floral pattern. Her greying hair was in a rubber-banded pony-tail. Again, she wore no makeup. She might not have been awaiting the photographers from Vogue, but she did look comfortable.

She showed me to a seat, then went into the kitchen for the tea.

When we were both settled in, she said: "Now tell me what you're about, Mr. Hardesty."

I explained to her that her ex and I had had a parting of the ways over the blackmail issue when I told him I thought the person he was positive was responsible was, in my opinion, in fact not.

"Someone gay, of course," Mrs. Tunderew said, taking a sip of her tea. "How very like Tony—he always was rabidly homophobic. Some people see Jews behind everything that's wrong with the world. Some see Republicans." She gave a small smile. "For Tony, it was homosexuals. Which is why, when you originally mentioned he was being blackmailed for possibly being gay himself, it struck me as rather unlikely. And which, perversely enough, is probably why he hired you—to keep it all 'in the family' as it were."

Odd. I didn't think I'd ever mentioned to her that I was gay.

Like it matters? my mind-voice asked.

She looked at me with slightly knit brows. "Though I am curious as to why you would ever have consented to work for him."

I shrugged. "Because he pushed the right buttons by implying that if I didn't, I'd be as big a bigot as he was."

She smiled again and took another sip of tea. "Tony was a very good button-pusher," she said. "He'd have made a wonderful elevator operator."

"Well, the fact that my acq...my friend...Randy was gay and was in the car with him lends a good deal of credence to the blackmail claim. I can't imagine any other reason the two of them would have been together, or how they would ever have met." I was lying, of course, but she didn't have to know that.

I reached for the small round tin of butter cookies she had brought in with the tea.

"It's quite possible," she said as I took a bite of cookie and washed it down with a sip of tea, "that they met while Tony was doing that article."

I swallowed. "Which article was that?" I asked.

"Tony had a good-old-boy buddy on the staff of the Journal-

Sentinal, our answer to the Washington Post." She smiled again.
The Journal-Sentinal was to journalism what pond scum is to
Albert Einstein. "Several months ago he asked Tony to write a
bottom-of-the-shoe report on local prostitution. It was a two part
series, one dealing with female prostitutes, and into which I'm
sure he poured his heart among other things. The other was on
male prostitutes, which he approached with complete revulsion.
But of course Tony would never let revulsion get in the way of
making money. He interviewed several men for the article. Was
your friend by chance a prostitute? No offense to either you or
your friend, of course."

"None taken," I said. "And yes, he was a hustler. But again I
don't see the connection between his possibly having been
interviewed for an article several months ago and his being in the
car with your ex-husband when he was killed." I was hoping my
naivety might spark some sort of response or reaction. It didn't.

She nodded, slowly. "Just a thought," she said.

I decided it was time to change the subject.

"Did your ex-husband have a drug problem?" I asked.

She raised an eyebrow slightly and accompanied it with a
small smile.

"You might say that," she said, "though I understand that it
was only after his finding fame and fortune that he's been able to
afford to indulge it to the fullest."

Okay. Next question: "Are you the beneficiary of your
husband's...your ex's'...will?"

She looked at me over the rim of her tea cup, from which she
had just taken another sip.

"I was," she said. "I very much doubt that I am now. I suppose
I should check with the lawyer who drew up both our wills."

"I strongly recommend you do that," I said, thinking of the
fact that Glen O'Banyon had been in the process of drawing up
a new will for Tunderew—and it was unlikely that Tunderew
would have written one excluding his wife and then another one
after that. I had another question.

"And if I may ask—who is paying Mr. Tunderew's funeral
expenses?"

She shook her head and set her now empty cup on the tray with the plate of cookies. "Bernadine Press," she said.

Bernadine Press? my mind asked.

"Bernadine Press?" I echoed.

She sat back in her chair. "Yes, interestingly, I got a call from Peter Bernadine asking me the same thing as you did about whether I was beneficiary of the will. When I told them I wasn't sure, he asked if I were planning on a service for him as his ex-wife. I told them that as far as I was concerned, they could put him in a cardboard box and leave him out by the curb on garbage day. And I certainly would never have had enough money to afford a funeral through McGinnis & Morbrey. More tea?"

"I'm fine, thanks," I said.

"They offered to pay for the entire thing," she continued, "if I would agree that if I discovered I am in the will, they could deduct half of the funeral cost from future royalties from *Dirty Little Minds*. I told them that if they were willing to take that gamble, it would be fine with me, but if I wasn't in the will, it would be totally at their expense.

"I gather they're planning to make a big media event of it. I wouldn't be surprised if there were a Ferris wheel and a tilt-a-whirl. And pony rides for the kiddies."

On thinking it over, I realized that a big, lavish funeral probably would be to Bernadine Press' ultimate advantage. The cost of the funeral could easily be offset by additional book sales. Still, something in that scenario didn't ring quite true. It was all just a little bit *too* generous an offer.

"Do you have any idea where the manuscript for the second book might be? Or how far along he might have gotten?" I asked, changing the subject yet again.

She shook her head. "I haven't a clue," she said. "I would imagine it's up at the cabin somewhere, but I wouldn't know. He got the cabin in the divorce and insisted I give him my key. I'm sure he'd have had me prosecuted for trespassing if I'd tried to go up there after the divorce."

I finished my tea and decided it was time to leave. I thanked her for her time and wished her the best.

* * *

Nope. *Something's* not right. I debated on whether or not to return to the office—it was close to time to go home, and I could drive out and pick Jonathan up. I decided to make a quick stop at the office for a phone call. For some reason, I wanted to talk to Peter Bernadine.

* * *

"Bernadine Press," the receptionist answered.

"Is Peter Bernadine in?" I asked.

There was only a slight pause, then: "May I tell him who's calling?"

"Dick Hardesty," I said.

"One moment, please."

Another pause, then Peter Bernadine's voice. "Mr. Hardesty. What can I do for you?"

"I understand Bernadine Press is paying Mr. Tunderew's funeral expenses," I said. "That's extremely generous of you."

"Well," he said, "he did bring quite a bit of money into the company. We figured we owed him."

"I was just talking with Mrs. Tunderew," I said, "and she told me of your agreement."

I could almost hear the smile in his voice. "To be brutally honest with you, Mr. Hardesty," he said, "we would never in a million years have even considered paying a cent toward with his funeral, but when she contacted us to suggest the arrangement, it made good sense."

"She contacted you?" I asked.

"Yes," he replied. "She pointed out that by paying half of the expense ourselves and taking her half out of future royalties, we could recoup our half in increased sales. We were still hesitant, but when she agreed not to contest our rights to the new book as part of the deal, we leapt at it. If the manuscript is as far along as she indicates it is, a ghost writer should be able to finish it off in no time."

!!! I <u>knew</u> it!!! I thought.

"So everybody comes out ahead," I said.

"Yes," he said. "All we were interested in from the start was having the two book contract honored. So we're happy."

"Well, I wish you all the success in the world."

"Thank you, Mr. Hardesty. It may be immodest of me to say so, but we've earned it."

* * *

"If the manuscript is as far along as she indicates it is, a ghost writer should be able to finish it off in no time"! How did she know how far along the manuscript was? She told me she knew nothing at all about it. Just what kind of games was Catherine Tunderew playing?

I'd had the feeling all along that she was just a little too casual about her entire relationship with her ex-husband. He'd used her all the years he'd been struggling to make it, dumped her the minute he did, cheated on her for thirteen years, and was about to cut her out of his will so she couldn't get anything even after he was dead. And she just sits there and accepts it all? Not likely.

Well, she didn't have to worry about the will part now, anyway. Which led to several other questions. Did she know Tunderew was planning to change his will? Was she just stringing Bernadine along by implying she knew more about the second book than she did—and that she'd have legal control of both books? And why tell me she didn't care if they left Tunderew's body out on the curb and then con Bernadine into footing the bill for an expensive funeral? And from what Bernadine had said, *she* had called *them* with the funeral idea, they hadn't called her.

Was it possible she still loved Tunderew after all the crap he'd pulled on her? She'd stayed in the marriage for 13 years, after all, and it was Tunderew who had walked out on it. What a piece of work! (Well, 'work' wasn't exactly the first word that came into my head, but...)

To my great dismay and growing frustration I realized that I was, as I have an almost magical knack for doing, getting into something *way* over my head. If somebody had killed Tunderew, they had also killed Randy, and if I wanted to know who killed Randy I had to find out who killed Tunderew. And it <u>still</u> might have been an accident!

* * *

Mark Richman called to tell me that he'd looked at the accident scene photos and that Randy's bankbook had been among the materials around Tunderew's open briefcase. Randy's dopp kit was, as he'd said, found still zipped shut. The pieces of the puzzle were starting to come together.

I had to put everything on hold for a few days when I got a need-it-yesterday assignment from Glen O'Banyon. One of his paralegals had had a family emergency, and another was working on another urgent case, so I had to make two one day out-of-town trips to file legal papers, pick up a brief from another lawyer, and do a preliminary interview of a couple of prospective witnesses. Fortunately, they weren't over-nighters, and I made it home in time for dinner both days.

Tunderew's death was noted in both Time and Newsweek, though no mention was made of plans for a second book.

Jared called Wednesday, saying he was coming into town Friday to spend the weekend with Jake—something of an eyebrow-raiser—and wanting to know if we'd like to join them for dinner Friday night.

They had found no-one to claim Randy's body, and time was running out. When Tim called to tell me he'd had a look at Randy's bankbook and found it contained $1200—which I'm sure Randy would have considered a small fortune—hell, I'd consider it a small fortune!—I found it significant that there had been 12 weekly deposits of $100 each.

Randy had said everybody at New Eden got paid $100 a week, but that $75.00 of it was taken off the top for room and board, and that he spent most of his remaining $25.00 on vending machines.

Phil had told me that when he was hustling, he'd set aside half of everything he made, but I don't think he kept it in a bank account, and even if Randy did—though he never struck me as a bank account kind of guy—exactly $100 every week? And that still didn't explain why Tunderew would have had Randy's bankbook. No, there was something else going on there, and I was increasingly sure I knew what it was.

"Oh, one odd thing about the bankbook," Tim said. "The name of the bank was taped over."

Well, that was indeed a little odd. Why would he tape over the bank's name? I filed that question away for future reference, and forced myself back to the reason for my call.

I asked Tim to find out, if he would, just how we might go about preventing Randy's having to be buried in Potter's Field—whether Jonathan could claim the body if no one else did. I was concerned about the cost that might be involved: Jonathan had been very good about saving every penny he could toward a car, but he really didn't have all that much. He insisted on paying half of our groceries and some toward the rent and utilities, and that didn't leave much of what those who have it call "discretionary income."

"I think I might know a way," he said. "Let me check with a guy I know, and I'll get back to you."

It wasn't an hour later that Tim called back. "It'll take a little juggling," he said, "but here's what we've worked out: if he's not claimed by Monday, the body will be taken to the crematorium. They usually cremate on Friday—sometimes Thursday and Friday, depending on how busy they are. If you'll reimburse the county for the cremation, they'll be willing to turn the ashes over to you: it will save them the cost of interment."

"Thanks, Tim," I said. "I know Jonathan will be relieved, and I'm sure he can manage the cremation cost."

"He's a good kid," Tim, who was still this side of 30 himself, said.

"Tell me," I replied.

There was a possibility that somehow the money in Randy's account could be applied toward his funeral expense, and I'd check that out, but even so it would probably take longer to arrange than we had time for at the moment.

* * *

We met Jared and Jake Friday night for dinner at Napoleon. Jake was there when we arrived. Dinner hour was just getting into full swing and the place was filling up fast. Like Jared, though, Jake was pretty hard to miss in any crowd. We made our way to him, exchanged greetings, and ordered our drinks. We'd no sooner paid for them than Jared appeared.

I found it interesting and took a perverse little delight in noting that while Jonathan and Jared and I and Jared exchanged hugs, Jared and Jake gripped shoulders. They acted—and looked—like two out-of-uniform NFL linebackers meeting at a Kiwanis dinner. But I wasn't fooled for a minute: I could almost hear the "*bzzzzzzUPP!*" of electricity between them.

Nice try, though, guys, I thought.

It was as expected a pleasant, relaxing evening, and I was pretty proud of myself—I made it almost all the way through the salad before I said: "So tell me, Jake—you do a lot of work at New Eden?"

Jonathan gave me a quick glance out of the corner of his eye.

"Yeah, quite a bit," he said. "We did the house, and a couple of the utility sheds, framed out the new cow barn."

"How are the Dinsmores to work for?" I asked.

Jake took a sip of his wine, then shook his head. "I haven't had all that much direct contact with them," he said. "They're gone quite a bit of the time, Mrs. Dinsmore particularly. I deal mostly with Mel Hooper. He's the administrator."

"And he's also Mrs. Dinsmore's brother, I understand," I said.

Jake gave a quick laugh. "Oh, yeah!" he said. "He's her big brother in more ways than one, and everyone there knows it. Have you ever seen her?"

I nodded. "Once," I said.

"Well, then, you know she's really a good looking woman—if you're into women," he added with a grin. "A lot of the guys out there are, of course, but it's really interesting. She could walk around the entire complex naked and there wouldn't be so much as a wolf whistle when she walked by. They all know better. One guy did it one time, and Mel had him thrown off the property within five minutes."

"Have you ever spent any time with the Dinsmores themselves?" I asked casually (I hoped). "I was wondering how they get along together."

He speared the last tomato slice on his salad plate. "Usually I'll just see one or the other, but whenever I've seen them together, they seem to be the perfect couple," he said. "Nice people, really devoted to each other. She worships the ground he walks on, from what I hear."

"And what about him?" I asked.

Jake looked at me and gave me a small smile. "The rumors, you mean?"

"Rumors?" Jared asked.

The busboy came to remove our salad plates as the waiter arrived with our entrees. We were all quiet until everyone had everything and the waiter moved off.

"As far as I know they're just that—rumors. But I have heard about Jeff's having a soft spot for the occasional male hustler," he said. "All the kids at New Eden—well, they range up to the early 20s—come from the streets. A lot of the girls were hookers, a lot of the guys hustlers. Story goes that Jeff may be partial to the hustlers—but apparently *only* hustlers. And he's apparently *very* discreet about it."

"Does his wife know?" Jared asked.

Jonathan and I looked at one another, but neither said anything.

"No idea," Jake said, "but I'd sure hope not, for his sake. If she were ever to sic her brother on him, Jeffy-boy'd be a goner. I haven't got a doubt in the world about that. Mel and Jeffrey aren't exactly the best of buddies as it is, from what I understand."

Since I'd recently seen a photo in the paper of the Dinsmores at a fund-raiser of some sort and Mr. Dinsmore didn't look any the worse for wear, I'd assume Mrs. Dinsmore had kept her husband's little dalliance with Randy strictly between the two of them.

* * *

The weekend flew by, as weekends have a nasty habit of doing. After dinner on Friday we'd dropped out to Ramón's for a nightcap—it was obvious that Jake and Jared had other things on their agenda that they were anxious to get to. Bob Allen was working the bar, so we didn't have too much time to talk with him. He seemed favorably impressed by Jake, though, and invited us all over to his and Mario's place for a barbecue on Sunday afternoon. He said he'd be calling Tim and Phil to ask them, and I was once again struck by how nice it is to have friends.

Saturday was Saturday. Jonathan didn't say much about it, but I could tell, as we went about our usual Saturday morning around-the-house chores, that he was still thinking about Randy a lot. Around noon, while Jonathan was making what was becoming our traditional Saturday lunch of grilled cheese sandwiches and cream of tomato soup, we did talk a little about what we would do with Randy's ashes.

"I don't want to bury him," Jonathan said. "He would hate to be put in some hole somewhere. He should be somewhere he can be free."

I told him I knew just the place, and I'd take him there when he thought it was time.

"Okay," he said, and opened the cupboard to get out the soup bowls.

The phone bill arrived in Saturday's mail and as usual I glanced over the long distance charges. There was a call to my ex, Chris, and his lover Max in New York, a couple of calls to Jonathan's brother, Samuel, in Wisconsin, and two to a number I didn't recognize. Randy had said he'd made a couple long distance calls about his prospective new job. I did recognize the area code, though: Neeleyville, and I instinctively knew to whom the calls had been made: Tony T. Tunderew at his cabin.

To verify, I went to the phone and dialed the number. I'm not exactly sure what I thought that would accomplish. If it was the number for Tunderew's "cabin" he certainly wouldn't be around to answer it. There might be a machine, though, and I knew I would recognize his voice.

I heard two rings, then a click, and: "The number you have reached has been disconnected and is no longer in service."

Disconnected, eh? Tunderew had only been dead a little over a week—it wasn't likely it was disconnected for not paying his bill. The only obvious explanation was that someone had had it disconnected, and I could think of only one person that might have been: Catherine Tunderew.

Chapter 8

Two things that attempted call had made crystal clear: First, that Catherine Tunderew was a lot more complex a character than she ever let on, and one who needed a lot closer looking into. Secondly, that Randy's relationship with Tunderew went considerably beyond being a casual trick, as I had been increasingly suspecting. If Randy had the phone number to Tunderew's cabin, given Tunderew's notorious love of secrecy, there had to be a damned good reason. Randy said he expected to get a job—obviously from Tunderew, somehow. And then there was that bank account with the 12 regular $100 deposits. If they came from Tunderew, I was pretty sure I knew why.

Obviously, Tunderew's next book had something—well, I'd wager a lot more than "something"—to do with the Dinsmores, New Eden, and the Eternal Light Foundation! Randy had been a plant: Tunderew's spy. He was using Randy to get dirt for his new book just as he'd used Larry Fletcher for *Dirty Little Minds*. Chances are that Tunderew had opened the account in Randy's name and made the deposits—I'd be willing to bet in the form of money orders—into the account. He'd probably send the bankbook in with each deposit and have it returned to a P.O. box—probably a separate one. And that answered the question of why the name of the bank had been taped over. That way he could show Randy that deposits were being made in his name but, not knowing which bank the account was in, he couldn't access the money until Tunderew was through with him.

I was more convinced than ever that Tunderew's—and Randy's—deaths had been no accident.

The Dinsmore's moved onto and toward the top of the suspects list. If they had found out that their little empire was the target of Tunderew's next book, they would understandably do whatever they could to keep it from being published. Including murder? Anything is possible, of course, but "possible" and "likely" are far from being synonyms.

One thing was for sure…I wouldn't run out of leads to follow for quite a while.

* * *

Sunday's barbecue at Bob and Mario's went very well, and I did my subtle best to find out if there might be anything more Jake could tell me about New Eden in general and the Dinsmores in particular. There wasn't. They were apparently everything that Mom, apple pie, and the American flag stood for. All of which, of course, meant that any juicy scandal that Tunderew might have dredged up couldn't help but be a runaway best seller.

But first things first, and the first thing on my agenda when I got to the office Monday morning was Catherine Tunderew. *Had* she known she was being cut out of Tunderew's will? How did she know how far along the new manuscript was? Or was she just trying to con the Bernadines into footing the bill for Tunderew's funeral by saying she did?

One way to find out. I picked up the phone.

* * *

Since I'd been to Catherine Tunderew's twice, I decided to invite her to join me for lunch. She didn't seem particularly surprised to hear from me again, and readily agreed to meet me at The Broken Drum, a pleasant little café (as opposed to "restaurant") not too far from her apartment. It was the kind of small-town-charm, curtained-window, hanging-plants-every-where, small, tableclothed tables with wooden, round-topped chairs, that for some reason simply does not exist in the gay community. Maybe a little too comfy-cosy for most gays.

I could see by looking in the window—there were only about ten tables in the place, only six of which were occupied—that Catherine had not yet arrived, so I took a short walk to the end of the block and returned. As I did so, I saw Catherine Tunderew emerging from a cab in front of the café.

We met at the door, which I opened for her, and we took one of the vacant tables. A young woman, probably a college student, dressed in an attractive old-fashioned blouse with frills at the collar and wrists and a long granny skirt, came over and asked if we would like coffee. I said yes; Catherine opted for peppermint tea. The girl pointed out to us a large easel near the door on which a blackboard announced the day's offerings in a variety of colored chalk.

When she'd gone to get our coffee, Catherine smiled warmly. "It was very nice of you to invite me to lunch," she said. "I really should get out more."

"I'm glad you could come," I said.

She was looking at me closely, still smiling. "And should I guess the reason behind the invitation...other than your natural kindness, of course?" The smile hadn't changed, so I assumed she wasn't being sarcastic.

I'd thought about how I was going to approach all the questions I had, and had decided the direct route was the best.

"I have reason to believe," I began, then paused as the waitress brought our coffee and tea and left without asking if we were ready to order—which we weren't. When she left, I continued: "I have reason to believe that your ex-husband's death may have been something other than an accident."

Her expression did not change by so much as the furrowing of her brows. "Really?" she said. "I'm really sorry to hear that."

"But not surprised," I said.

She gave a small shrug. "Some people collect matchbooks," she said, removing the tea bag from her cup and setting in on the saucer. "Tony had a knack for collecting enemies. I'm sure several people wished him dead, but I can't imagine anyone actually doing it. And that that unfortunate...young man...had to have been with him."

The waitress returned to take our order and we quickly looked at the blackboard. We both chose the spinach quiche and, smiling, the waitress headed for the kitchen.(I know, real men don't eat quiche....Sue me.)

Catherine was looking at me again. "May I ask exactly why

you care about all this, Mr. Hardesty? I believe you'd said your professional association with Tony had ended."

I took a sip of coffee and nodded. "It had," I said. "And, if you'll excuse me for saying so, had it not been for the fact of Randy Jacobs having been in the car with him, I'd have absolutely no incentive to find out what had happened. But if someone did murder your ex-husband, he or she also murdered Randy, and I owe it to him to find out who was responsible and why."

She nodded. "I see," she said. "And I gather I am included on your list of possible murderers?"

I got the definite impression she rather enjoyed trying to provoke a reaction, so I tried very hard not to give her one.

"Well, let's just say at this stage I'm mainly trying to *eliminate* possibilities. I'm curious as to why, when I asked if you were in your ex-husband's will, you said that you had been, but didn't imagine you were now. You did know he was having a new will drawn up at the time of his death, didn't you? And that he died before it could go into effect?"

Our quiche arrived, and she picked a large strawberry out of the small side dish of fresh fruit. "Yes," she said. "My lawyer…I call him 'my' because he had been my family's lawyer for some time before Tony and I ever met. He drew up the original will…had called me from Chicago to say that Attorney O'Banyon had requested a copy. He didn't say why he wanted it, but two plus two, you know. So I knew I would soon be out. But as you say, the new will was not fully executed before Tony's death. Pure serendipity."

She carefully ate the strawberry, closing her eyes in mock ecstacy at the taste. Then she opened her eyes and looked at me with a bemused expression. "Oh, my, that did give me an excellent reason to kill him, didn't it? Too bad I never thought of it. Am I at the top of your list, now?"

You're getting there, lady, I thought.

"As I say, I'm not making a list yet," I lied.

"And what else would you like to know? The fact that none of it is—no rudeness intended— really any of your business shouldn't keep me from answering. If Tony's death—and your friend's, of course—was, as you so delicately put it, 'something other than an accident', I'd be as interested as you—possibly more, considering I was married to the man for thirteen years—to find out who was responsible. I have nothing at all to hide."

Now, why do I doubt that? I thought. Still, she had opened the door, so I might as well barge right in.

I waited long enough to have another forkful of quiche —which was delicious—and a small slice of cantaloupe before speaking.

"I was also curious as to how you might know how far along the second book is if, as you said, he was apparently working on it at the cabin, to which you had returned the key."

She paused, fork halfway to her lips, and pulled her head back slightly, giving me a look of feigned surprise. "Why Mr. Hardesty," she said in a tone which reminded me for some reason of Scarlett O'Hara, "I am truly impressed. It must be exciting to be a private investigator!"

She conveyed the forkful of quiche to her mouth, chewed discretely, swallowed and said: "I told you I had returned Tony's key. I did not say I didn't have another one. The day after Tony's death, I took a drive. I suppose I wanted to see where he had died, for some perverse reason. When I passed by the spot, I kept on driving until I found myself at the cabin. I felt the urge to go inside…to see it for what might be the last time. It was just as Tony had left it, which is to say a shambles. I don't think Tony had ever picked up after himself in his life. That's what I, his wife, was for."

She gave a small smile. "Anyway, I couldn't help but notice that beside his typewriter there was a stack of papers which, when I glanced at it, I saw to be a novel. I'll share the title with you, if you promise not to make it public knowledge."

Despite myself, I had to admit I found Catherine Tunderew somehow spellbinding. I was perfectly aware she was playing me like a fiddle, but I rather enjoyed the music.

"Please," I said.

"The title he had given it was *No Door to Heaven*. It was a very thick stack of paper. I merely thumbed through it quickly, but enough to see that he had completed 322 pages. From that I gathered that he must have been fairly close to completion."

"And did you happen to recognize who the book might be loosely based on?"

She shook her head. "No," she said, taking the last piece of quiche from her plate, "I only glanced at a paragraph here and a paragraph there. It is, I did note, however, very much in the style of *Dirty Little Minds*. I didn't really recognize anyone specifically. There was something there, though, in one paragraph, about a murder."

I definitely had the feeling I was part of a puppet show, and I wasn't the one pulling the strings. She *was* good.

A murder, eh? my mind asked.

"Is there any way I might be able to look at the manuscript?" I asked. "It might give me some solid clue as to who is responsible for his death."

She smiled at me sweetly. "Why, Mr. Hardesty!" she said in that Scarlett O'Hara tone. "Of course not! I've placed it in a safe deposit box where it will remain until all the details of its disposition can be resolved."

"And you have not read it?" I asked.

She looked at me steadily. "No," she said calmly, "I have not. I never was a fan of Tony's writing. I don't really care who it may be...loosely...based on."

She took another sip of her tea. "But don't worry," she said, consolingly, and I almost expected her to reach across the table and pat my hand. "I'm sure that whoever may have served as the...inspiration, shall we say...for *No Door to Heaven* has no idea whatsoever that he is about to be immortalized. Tony was very good about keeping his own secrets." She smiled again and then added: "And of course it *is* completely a work of fiction."

Of course.

As the waitress came to clear away our dishes and bring me the check, Catherine said: "If you'll excuse me a moment, I'd better go call for a cab," and started to get up from the table.

"Please," I said, "...I'll be glad to give you a ride home."

"I wouldn't want to put you to the trouble," she said, though

I noticed she was settling back in her chair even as she said it.

"It's no trouble at all," I said. "Is something wrong with your car?"

She sighed and nodded. "I made the mistake of leaving it parked on the street when I returned from the cabin Saturday evening, rather than putting it in the garage, and some idiot smashed into it. Of course they didn't even have the courtesy to leave a note. I didn't find out about it until I went out Sunday morning to put it in the garage. I'm not sure exactly when it happened, but the entire rear end was smashed in. I can't tell you how angry I was—and still am."

There they were: my little sirens and bells sounding in the back of my mind.

"Did you report it to the police?" I asked.

She shook her head. "I didn't see any point, really. There was nothing they could do at that point. Luckily, it was driveable and I have insurance."

"So it's in the shop now?" I said/asked.

She nodded again. "Oh, yes. Fortunately, there is a body shop I've dealt with before very near me, so I just drove it over there and left it in their lot. I put the key and a note in their mail slot. They do excellent work, but they take forever. I called yesterday and they said they're still waiting for parts. I should have known better than to have bought a foreign car."

* * *

I drove her home, exchanged thanks with her—hers for lunch, mine for her information—and headed back toward the office.

Almost.

The street to the south of Catherine Tunderew's was Harker Blvd., mostly commercial. Since body shops are seldom found on strictly residential streets, I turned at the first corner past Catherine's apartment building and went down to Harker. Turning left, I drove for three or four blocks looking for an auto repair shop, and found none. I circled around the block back to Harker and headed back in the opposite direction.

Sure enough, less than two blocks from Catherine Tunderew's apartment was All-Pro Auto Body. I parked the car and walked over to the chain link fence which surrounded the entire lot. The repair shop itself was rather small—two service bays and a small office. Both service bays were open, and I could see a yellow Cadillac in one and a Dodge station wagon in the other. About four cars, in various stages of obvious distress, stood in a row between the building and the street. One was a late model Ford with the driver's side front end pushed in almost to the windshield; one a Buick with a smashed passenger's side door and buckled roof; one an older model, silver Jaguar with missing front bumper, a broken passenger's side headlight with a missing rim, and a long red-smudged sideswipe scar along the passenger's side from just behind the front bumper to past the door...*aha!* ...; the fourth, a small brown Renault with nothing visibly wrong with it.

If a car had been coming down the hill toward Tunderew, made too sharp a correction on the curve and been in Tunderew's lane...Tunderew might have swerved to avoid it, clipped it long and hard enough to make the scrape, then lost control and gone through the guardrail.

Good thinking, Hardesty! my mind said admiringly, then had to go and add: <u>*But*</u>... God, I hate "buts". *But* I had no idea if this was Catherine Tunderew's car; *but* the car the Jag had tangled with had obviously been red and I didn't know what color Tunderew's car was; *but* the Jag had a broken front headlight with a missing rim *and* a missing bumper, which almost certainly would have been found on or near the road and weren't. So even if this was Catherine Tunderew's car, it was extremely unlikely it could have been the one involved in Tunderew's death. I'd check on the color of Tunderew's car, though, just to be certain.

I noticed a fast-food place directly next to the body shop and decided to walk over and get a Coke. As I was walking down the driveway to the door, I checked out the chain link fence behind the row of damaged cars, and noted that the little brown Renault, which seemed to be unscathed when viewed from the front, had a badly damaged rear-end; the bumper pushed into an inward V, popping the trunk open and crinkling the lid. Both taillights were intact and nothing seemed to have broken off. I walked over for a closer look.

Now *this*, I'd wager, was Catherine Tunderew's car. She didn't strike me as being the Jaguar type. A Renault, now…

*But…*my mind said.

Sigh.

A Renault's a pretty small car; I hadn't been able to make out either the color or what kind of car Tunderew's was from the brief shot I'd seen of it on TV, upside down in the creek, but it looked like at least a full-sized sedan. I'd imagine Tunderew would favor something that came close to reflecting his ego, even though they really don't make cars that big. The accident took place on a straightaway; the skid marks—there was only one set—clearly indicated Tunderew's car was the one that had done the hitting. A big car hitting a smaller car from behind? Chances are it would have been the smaller car that would have gone out of control. And the bumper's inverted V-shaped dent suggested it had been hit at an angle rather than straight on. It's possible Tunderew might have tried to swerve at the last minute, but to be at the angle indicated was a little hard to picture. And how could he have not seen a small car directly ahead of him? Not to mention what would Catherine Tunderew have been doing on that stretch of road at that specific time? Coincidence? Uh…I don't think so.

She admitted she'd been to the cabin, but would she have risked going up there if she thought Tunderew might be there? She could have been on her way up there at the time of the accident. But again, I didn't think so. Catherine Tunderew was a complex lady, but to have been the cause of a fatal accident, then just keep right on driving…? Anything's possible, but not every-thing's likely.

I went into the fast food place, ordered a Coke to go, then returned to my car for a pen I kept clipped to the sun visor.

Going back to the fence, I wrote the license numbers of both the Jag and the Renault on the napkin I'd grabbed with my Coke. I'd check 'em out.

* * *

All the way back to my office, I couldn't get my mind off Catherine Tunderew and her late husband's new book.

No Door to Heaven, eh? Well, if I hadn't already been pretty sure who the subject of the book was, that title all but telegraphed it. Interesting enough in its own right, but add to that Catherine's casual observation…what was it?…ah, yes: *There was something there, though, in one paragraph, about a murder.* A murder? God, I wanted to get my hands on that manuscript! But Catherine Tunderew had admitted she had the manuscript safely under lock and key somewhere.

A murder! Where? Here? Or at one of the other New Eden locations? When? Who? Why? How many angels can dance on the head of a pin? How high is up?

Jeezus!

I had the distinct impression that I was standing at the end of a hallway that stretched away nearly to infinity, lined with doors on both sides, and that I had to open every single one of them to find what I was looking for.

* * *

I had a message from Tim waiting on the machine when I returned to the office. He'd made arrangements with his contact at the crematory. Randy would be cremated at the end of the week, and Tim left a number to call to make the arrangements to pick up the ashes. I jotted it down, but thought I'd let Jonathan do the calling. I felt he'd want to.

Next, I checked my calendar to see if I had anything scheduled for the next day (surprise—I didn't). I wanted to spend as much of the day as possible at the public library to find out every-thing I possibly could about the Dinsmores and their various enterprises. I wasn't even sure how many New Edens there were. I'd read the Time article on the Dinsmores when they'd made the cover, but I hadn't paid all that much attention to it at the time.

I realized, too, that if I set off at a full gallop in pursuit of a possible/probable Dinsmore connection, I would also have to try to juggle the involvement of the other possible suspects on my list. For some reason, Larry Fletcher came back into my head. What if he *was* stalking Tunderew as Tunderew had claimed? What if he had somehow seen Tunderew pick up Randy at the bus station? Guys in their forties do not commonly pick up guys in their 20s at the bus station unless they're a relative in from out of town. Jealousy and betrayal are nasty emotions individually. In combination, they can be deadly. Take it from a Scorpio.

So I decided to keep Larry on the list.

Just above Larry Fletcher, I'd put the Bernadines...most especially Peter Bernadine, who stood to either inherit the family business or watch it go down the tubes. From all I could gather, Bernadine Press had been hanging on by its fingernails, and *Dirty Little Minds* had all but kept the company from bankruptcy. It needed another blockbuster to put it back on solid footing. I hadn't thought much about it at the time, but the elder Bernadine had mentioned something about being in negotiations with their bank—which meant they'd applied for a loan. And I'd bet that they were using the fact of having a solid contract for Tunderew's second book as a form of implied collateral. They'd given Tunderew his big break and had every right to expect something in return. Tunderew, being the jerk that he was, of course had neither a sense of loyalty nor any discernable scruples about biting the hand that had fed him. No second blockbuster, perhaps no loan. Murder is admittedly a pretty drastic solution to any problem, but the very existence of Bernadine Press was at stake.

And then we come to Catherine Tunderew who, despite her feigned indifference to her ex-husband, had everything to gain and nothing to lose by his death. Hell hath no fury, etc. (Wasn't someone just talking about there being truth within cliches? Oh, yeah: me.)

I certainly wouldn't have to worry about running out of clues to follow up on. Now, if somebody were just paying me for all this...

* * *

Over the years, I'd managed to cultivate a number of friends and acquaintances in various governmental offices who were able to provide me with information I might otherwise have found it difficult to come by. There was our good friend Tim Jackson at the coroner's office, Mark Richman and Marty Gresham at the police department, Mollie Marino at the City Clerk's office, and Bil (that's the way he spelled it, for some reason) Dunham at the D.M.V. I called on them as infrequently as possible so as not to make a pest of myself, but it was nice to know they were there when I needed them. Some, like Mollie Marino, had been satisfied clients who helped me out of gratitude. And while it might sound a little calculated on my part, I have to admit I wasn't above going out of my way for a client in one way or another specifically because I knew I might be able to use their services in the future. Bil Dunham at the D.M.V. was one of the latter. I'd handled a fairly simple case for him some time before and because he'd been pretty financially strapped, I'd made a direct deal with him—I'd cut my rate in half if he'd do some occasional license information checking for me. He agreed, and it worked out well for both of us.

I picked up the phone, called Bil to give him the plate numbers I'd copied from the body shop lot, and asked him to check them for me. The next part was a little more tricky. I wanted to call Marty Gresham, my latest "close" contact at the police department. I'd first come into contact with Marty when he was a rookie working in Missing Persons Records. He'd been really helpful to me on the case I was working on at the time and partly because of it, he'd caught the eye of Lieutenant Richman and some of the other higher-ranking officers on the force. He was quite obviously being fast-tracked toward his goal of becoming a detective and he somehow gave me undue credit for helping him along. After his stint in Missing Persons, he'd done a short tour as a patrol officer and was currently, from what I'd heard, assigned to Administration under Lieutenant Richman's watchful eye. Marty had also just gotten married, so I didn't know how much of his off-hours free time he might be able to devote to helping me on this matter.

I'd made it a definite rule not to ask favors of the police unless it was really necessary, and never in any case that they might not eventually become involved at some point down the line. And while the police didn't have any solid evidence upon which to base an investigation into Tunderew's death, a lack of solid evidence never stood in my way. I was positive that Tunderew had been murdered, and once I could prove it, the police could step in and take it from there. I rationalized my asking for a couple of favors on the basis that I was in effect once again doing part of their job for them.

There were two things I wanted from Marty: the color of Tunderew's car, and a quick check for any problems New Eden, the Dinsmores, or the Eternal Light Foundation might have gotten themselves into locally.

Even so, I didn't want to bring him into it without asking Richman's okay first (plus the fact that I didn't know how to reach Marty directly). I placed another phone call.

"Lieutenant Richman," the familiar voice answered.

"Lieutenant, Dick. Sorry to bother you, but I was wondering if I could ask Marty Gresham to check on a couple little details for me? I understand he's been assigned to Administration. So if you could spare a few minutes of his time…"

"You're still on the Tunderew thing, obviously," he said.

"Yeah," I admitted. "And I'm more convinced than ever that it was no accident."

"Anything specific yet?" he asked.

"No," I said, "but I feel I'm getting there."

I was rather expecting a pause while he thought it over, but there was none. "Okay," he said. "I'll ask Officer Gresham to call you."

"Thanks, Lieutenant," I said, and we hung up shortly after my usual promise to keep him posted if I found anything the police might need to know.

It was getting pretty late in the day, and it was unlikely that Marty'd be calling. I'd not heard from Bil at the D.M.V. either, so I decided to wrap it up. I'd stop by the office in the morning to check for messages before going to the library.

* * *

I arrived home to find an excited Jonathan waiting for me in the kitchen. He usually got home shortly before I did, but since I'd left work a few minutes early, I was rather surprised to see him there already. I assumed he'd gotten a ride home from one of his co-workers.

"Dick," he called as soon as I opened the door, "Come look! Luke and John had babies!"

I went into the kitchen to join him. After our usual greeting-hug, he turned quickly back to the fish tank and pointed to the clump of artificial grass in one corner. "Look!" he said. "See them?"

It took me a moment before I could see, moving in and out among the leaves, several very tiny black fish. Since Jonathan had two of each kind of three varieties and only two (Luke and John) were black, the process of elimination fairly well established parenthood.

"They weren't there this morning," he said. "Isn't it great? I'll call Tim and Phil as soon as they get home to find out if baby fish need anything special."

"Like formula?" I asked, as usual tickled by his enthusiasm.

He looked at me quickly before realizing I was teasing him.

"Yeah," he said. "And whether we should burp them when they get done eating."

"Well," I said, "you get to change the diapers. Don't expect me to get up at three in the morning to do it."

We exchanged grins, and he put his arm around my waist.

"You know," he said, "if Luke and John can make babies, I can't see any reason why we can't, too. Ya wanna go try?"

"Oh, yeah!" I said, taking him by the hand and heading

toward the bedroom.

* * *

We'd just come out of the bedroom when the phone rang. "You want to get that?" Jonathan said. "I'll go get your Manhattan and think about starting dinner."

I moved to the phone as he headed for the kitchen.

"Hello?" I said. I had made a concerted effort, after umpteen years of answering the phone with "Dick Hardesty" to try to fit in with the rest of the world. It still seemed odd, but I did it.

"Dick?" the familiar voice said. "It's Marty. Lieutenant Richman told me you'd called. What can I do for you?"

Considering that he'd just gotten married, I was a little surprised that he'd take time away from his new wife to call me. But what did I know?

"Thanks for calling, Marty," I said. "And congratulations on your marriage. How do you like it so far?"

He laughed. "Great!" he said. "Cindy's at a baby shower for her sister, so I thought I'd call."

I quickly filled him in on what I needed, and told him that I might well have a couple of other things for him to check after I'd done the library research.

"No problem," he said. "I should be able to get the info on the car first thing in the morning. Checking on the other stuff might take a little bit longer, but I can hopefully have it all for you by tomorrow afternoon."

"I really appreciate it, Marty," I said.

"I owe you," he said.

We small-talked for a minute or so more, then hung up just as Jonathan came back into the living room with my Manhattan and his coke. I joined him on the sofa. He looked puzzled.

"Odd," he said. "I checked on the babies, and there aren't as many of them as I thought there were."

I knew why, but didn't want to alarm him. I was sure he'd figure it out for himself, or Tim and Phil—from whom he'd gotten his first two fish, which he of course named "Tim" and "Phil," in their honor—would clue him in. I could have told him, of course, but really didn't want us to be as overrun with fish as we were with plants.

In an effort to take his mind off the missing babies, I told him what I'd learned from Tim about Randy's ashes, and how much it would cost. Again, I did not offer to pay part of it. I knew this was something he wanted and needed to do by himself. I knew, too, it would take a very large chunk out of his savings, but held out hope that the money in Randy's bank account could somehow be used to reimburse him.

After we'd finished our drinks, Jonathan went into the kitchen to check on dinner. A moment later, I heard a very loud "*Damn it!*" I got up quickly and went in to see what was wrong.

"Phil just ate one of the babies!" Jonathan said. "I *saw* him! How could he do that? It was a *baby!*" Then he looked at me and a quick look of embarrassment crossed his face. "Well, it was a baby *fish*, but it was still a baby."

"And Phil is a big fish and big fish eat little fish," I said gently.

Jonathan shook his head sadly and stared into the tank. "Yeah, you're right, of course. But I should have realized that! Stupid, Jonathan! Stupid!"

I put my arm around his shoulder. "Not stupid," I said. "Sweet."

He gave a very large sigh. "Yeah," he said disgustedly. "Sweet."

He quickly reached into the silverware drawer and took out the tea strainer, then opened a cupboard under the sink to take out his original fish bowl—the one Phil and Tim had given him before we got the larger aquarium. He filled the bowl with water, then took the strainer and began attempting to catch whatever of the smaller fish remained in the grass. It wasn't easy, and he kept having to shoo the bigger fish out of the way.

"Phil," he muttered, staring threateningly at the offender, "if you don't want to spend the rest of your life in solitary confinement in the toilet tank, you'd better get the hell out of the way!"

He managed to rescue four of the tiny fish and transport them to the other bowl. It took another five minutes of futilely searching the grass for survivors before he sighed and gave up. He made another quick check of dinner, turned down the flame under the pans, and said: "You want to set the table while I go call Phil and Tim? Dinner's almost ready."

Chapter 9

There were no messages waiting when I arrived at the office Tuesday morning. I was tempted to make a pot of coffee and do the crossword puzzle before leaving for the library, but decided against it. Instead, I didn't even sit down, but left the office and headed for the main library.

I'd always had a fascination for libraries. As a kid I was an avid reader, and as a result of my spending so much time at my local library, I got my very first job there, while still in high school, as what they called a "page"—I loved that title, considering. It mainly entailed putting books back on the shelves, going down to the archives for back issues of newspapers and magazines. The very first love of my life, a classmate in school, would meet me at work and I would sneak him down to the archives where we would spend an intense and testosterone-filled five minutes before rushing back upstairs. Looking back, I'm amazed we were never caught.

The first thing I did was look up the Time Magazine with the Dinsmores on the cover. I remembered it had been sometime the preceding February, so that helped cut down the search time. As I said, I'd read it when it came out, but didn't remember much about it.

It was a pretty good article, actually, with more information than I'd expected. Jeffrey was heir to a Texas oil fortune. Barbara Dinsmore's father was a circuit court judge. They'd met at the small religious college they'd both attended, married right after graduation and gone off to do missionary work in Peru. Shortly after they returned to the U.S., Jeffrey Dinsmore's father died. Jeffrey sold his interest in his father's company and started the Eternal Light Foundation, which began by doing outreach programs for disadvantaged teens. From that beginning, the first New Eden was opened outside Atlanta, followed shortly by another near Dallas, and then the one here. Both Dinsmores were very skilled and professional fund raisers. They didn't resort to blubbering, teary-eyed Sunday morning TV show appeals to the lonely and naive, promising eternal salvation in exchange for a "love offering." The bulk of their outside funding came from large companies and corporations, to whom they appealed on the basis of the social benefits of their projects rather than the religious. Undoubtedly, a lot of their success could be traced in part to their family connections, but they were very persuasive in their own right.

The article, probably not surprisingly, gave no hint that there might be an apple tree or two in New Eden. It did mention in passing that the couple was childless by choice, which made me wonder momentarily, knowing Jeffrey Dinsmore's apparent attraction to male hustlers, if the choice were mutual or one-sided.

I was able to find any number of newspaper and magazine articles on the Dinsmores and their good works and awards, but again with no indication of things being less than idyllic at New Eden. No complaints, which I might have expected, from the residents at the various facilities alleging exploitation by the Dinsmores; no indication whatsoever of misappropriated funds or a lavish lifestyle. I did manage to find a couple of tabloid articles (our library had reference copies of even these birdcage liners, though I suspected they had to keep them submerged in vats of disinfectant to keep the stench away from the other archived materials) claiming satanic rituals were conducted at each New Eden, involving the sacrifice of virgins, small children, or illegal immigrants, depending on the tabloid in which the story appeared (they were all pretty much word-for-word copies of one another). One article hinted darkly of routine mysterious disappearances of residents and the existence of mass graves somewhere on each New Eden property. That last one I paid a little attention to, wondering if it might in any way be related to the "murder" Catherine Tunderew mentioned being referred to in the new book. But I made a note to check on any more-reliably-reported disappearances at any of the New Edens.

Of course the built-in problem with alleged disappearances

was that by the very nature of a New Eden, the turnover rate of residents must be relatively high. Compound that by the fact that New Eden served "throwaway kids"—those who either had no families, or none who knew or cared where they were. It would be pretty hard to tell who had just left and who might have gone unwillingly. In short, if there were "disappearances," who would have reported them? Who would even know?

Having read everything I could find on the Dinsmores and the Eternal Light Foundation and the local New Eden—I'd have to go to Dallas and Atlanta if I wanted to check the papers there for any other information—I decided to just head back to the office. It hadn't been a wild goose chase, but it hadn't exactly pointed the way to where any skeletons were kept, either. In fact, I came away with the impression that for all intents and purposes, the Dinsmores were pretty admirable people.

I had two messages waiting at the office and I hit the "Play" button as I circled my desk to sit down. The first call was Bil Dunham, identifying the owners of the plate numbers I'd given him—as I'd suspected, the Renault was Catherine Tunderew's; so much for the red-paint-smeared Jag. The second was from Marty Gresham who left his City Annex extension and asked me to call, which I did immediately.

"Administration, Officer Gresham," the voice said.

I didn't want to keep him away from his work any longer than I had to, so I got right to the point. "Marty: it's Dick. Did you find out anything?"

"Not much," he said. "Tunderew's car was gunmetal grey, by the way. An El Dorado. But as far as any run-ins with the law involving New Eden or the Dinsmores, nothing. They're squeaky clean."

"Have there been any reports of missing residents?" I asked.

There was a long pause, then: "I was going to say 'no,'" he said. "But I seem to recall when I was in Missing Persons Records something about a teenage boy…filed by his parents…from someplace out of town, I think, but…" Another long pause. "Are you going to be around for a while? Let me make a quick check to get the facts straight, then I'll call you right back. I remember

New Eden came into it somewhere along the line, but it was quite a while ago."

"Sure," I said. "I'll be here. But it's almost time for your shift to end, isn't it? I don't want to incur your wife's wrath by keeping you after work."

He laughed. "She'll live," he said. "I just have to run downstairs, and it will only take me a minute. I'll call you right back."

"Thanks, Marty; I appreciate it."

I hung up and reached for the newspaper and a pen.

I was just putting in the "d" in "brigand" ("Freebooter": 7 letters) when the phone rang.

"Hardesty Investigations," I said, not waiting for the usual second ring before picking up the phone.

"Dick, Marty. The kid's name is Denny Rechter, 17 years old. Reported missing last July 6th by his parents. They'd come into town from Bayonne, New Jersey, looking for him. Someone had tipped them that he was at New Eden, but when they got there, he was gone. Whether he got wind they were coming and just took off, or why else he might have left no one seemed to know. His folks filed the report in hopes he was still in the area and someone might spot him. They made three long-distance phone call inquiries after that over the next couple of months, then nothing. No idea if they ever found him or not. They never got back to us."

Now it was my turn for a long pause. "Marty," I finally said, "I know this is a stretch, but would it be possible to check with the Dallas and Atlanta police and sheriffs departments to see if they have anything on any problems at the New Edens in their jurisdictions?"

"I'll have to okay it with Lieutenant Richman," he said, "but I'm pretty sure he'll go along. But can I ask what all this has to do with that writer's death? I assume that's what you're following up on, right?"

"Yeah," I said. "And I hope it's got nothing to do with it. But something tells me it might have *everything* to do with it."

"Hmmm," he said. "Okay, I'll check it out, if the Lieutenant okays it. I'll get back to you either way."

"Thanks, Marty," I said, looking at my watch. "Now you'd better get home to your ball and chain."

"And you to yours," he said lightly.

* * *

Okay, my mind voice mused as I drove home: *one missing kid report in two years does not exactly a block-busting, best-selling expose make. And this was probably a kid who'd run away from home in the first place. Most likely, he just ran again.*

But it was also quite possible that as a runaway, if he'd gone to New Eden it was because he was living on the streets. And he wouldn't have been the first runaway kid living on the streets to turn to hustling to survive. And Jeffrey Dinsmore has an eye for hustlers. And...

And a square peg will fit into a round hole if you hit it hard enough with a hammer, another mind voice chimed in.

They both had valid points, but the missing kid and everything else aside, I'd bet my bottom dollar that the Dinsmores and New Eden were, for whatever reason, the subject of Tunderew's next book. I mean, *No Door to Heaven?* Come on! There are a lot of other religious organizations and preachers and ministers and cults out there. But only one close enough for Tunderew to have direct access. No, I'd have to go with the Dinsmores. And I suspected, too, that it had something more lurid than just Jeffrey Dinsmore' sexual ambiguity. As to whether Tunderew had died as a direct result of it remained to be seen.

Four suspects, four motives, my mind went on. *Larry Fletcher: jealousy and betrayal; Bernadine Press: company survival; Catherine Tunderew: revenge and a fortune; the Dinsmores: to keep their skeletons (whatever they might be) in the closet.* Again, there might very well be several other prime candidates out there, knowing Tunderew as little as I did, but these four would keep me more than busy for a while.

The only ones on my list that I'd not yet spoken to were the Dinsmores, and it was time I remedied that. How to do it I wasn't quite sure yet, but I'd figure it out.

* * *

I must say that one of the benefits of a being in a relationship was that it kept me from spending as much time as I normally would have dwelling on whatever case(s) I happened to be working on at the time. And even though Jonathan spent a lot of time studying every night after dinner, there was still enough interaction between us to keep my mind from getting bogged down.

I got home to find Jonathan busy in the kitchen. I noticed he'd taken the fake grass out of the bigger aquarium and put it in the smaller bowl, apparently to give the four surviving smallest fish somewhere to hide—though what they'd need to hide from in there wasn't clear. He was in the process of sprinkling fish food on the surface of the water in the larger tank, talking as always to each one by name as they came up to grab the small flakes—except for Phil, the one who had started all the trouble, but quite probably hadn't been the only offender. Phil was still obviously on Jonathan's shit list. He didn't seem to mind.

Well, just having said that I didn't spend all my time worrying about cases anymore, I spent most of the night worrying about this one—mostly about how to approach the Dinsmores. I finally figured it would be best if I could talk to them separately, if I would be able to talk to them at all. One of the most recent newspaper articles I had read at the library had mentioned something about Mrs. Dinsmore having an upcoming speaking engagement in Philadelphia at a conference on teen runaways. This coming Friday? It didn't say if Mr. Dinsmore would be in attendance, but from what Randy and I think Jake had said, the couple didn't do everything as a team, and that Mrs. Dinsmore was gone frequently. I'd have to take a chance that Mr. Dinsmore would be in town, though there was no guarantee on that. One way to find out.

* * *

I was mildly pleased with myself that I was actually able to finish reading the paper and do the crossword puzzle Wednesday morning before reaching for the phone.

"New Eden," a young female voice answered after three rings. "Can you hold, please?"

I love questions like that, since you are inevitably and instantly put on hold whether you can or can't. Luckily, in this instance I could. A moment later a click and "Thank you for waiting. How can I help you?"

"Is Mr. Dinsmore in, please?" I asked.

"I'm sorry, sir, he's not available at the moment. Can I take a message?"

Obviously, and logically, the Dinsmores screened their calls.

"Yes," I said, "My name is Dick Hardesty, and I would like to speak to Reverend Dinsmore about a former New Eden resident, Randy Jacobs."

There was no indication of recognition of the name when she replied: "Can I have your phone number, Mr. Hardesty?"

I gave it to her and asked if she knew when the Reverend might be available.

"I really can't say," she said, "but I'll see to it that he gets your message."

"I'd appreciate that, thank you," I said, and hung up.

I'd decided the night before, while trying not to think of the case, to see if I could get a closer look at Tunderew's car, wherever it might be. Not much chance of finding anything given the severity of the wreck and the fact that it had ended up partly in a creek, but...

I also wanted to go back to take a closer look at Catherine Tunderew's Renault in the repair shop's parking lot. I figured that paint transferred in the accident would be pretty hard to find on Tunderew's car after everything it had gone through, but some might have been transferred from Tunderew's gun-metal grey car to whatever it hit. It was worth a look.

I called the police impound lot to ask if there was any specific salvage yard to which wrecks were taken, and was told that the city had a contract with Marv's Salvage to take wrecks not specifically requested to be taken elsewhere.

I remembered Marv's Salvage from that earlier case I'd mentioned, where a car had gone off a bluff and I'd found a bullet in the tire.

Not really expecting a quick response from Dinsmore—if he'd bother to call back at all—I left the office and headed for Marv's Salvage.

* * *

Marv's Salvage was just as I'd remembered it: same chain link fence beside the open gate, the same small parking area in front of the glorified shed of an office, beyond which stretched row upon row of smashed cars, pickups, busses, and trucks: huge piles of fenders and bumpers and twisted frames. All still both mildly depressing and mildly fascinating. I parked the car and went into the office, which still smelled of rust and old oil. The same battered desk piled high with papers, same battered adding machine. But nobody there.

Going back outside, I could hear the grinding of gears and the diesel cough of some sort of heavy machinery. Looking down the main aisle in front of me, I could see puffs of black smoke. Leaving my car where it was, I walked toward it.

An old end-loader was scooping up small piles of whatever and dropping them onto a larger pile. I couldn't identify anything specific: just pieces of jumbled metal. I stood there for a full two minutes before the driver, who I recognized as the same guy I'd talked to last time I was there, saw me and shut off the engine.

"Help you?" he called down, without getting out of his seat.

"Yeah," I said, "I'm looking for a gunmetal grey El Dorado brought in recently. It went over a cliff on the road to Neeleyville a couple Friday's ago."

"What do you want with it?" he asked.

I was pretty sure he'd never remember me, so I took out my billfold and pulled out my automobile club membership card. "I'm an insurance investigator," I lied, flashing the card at him, assuming he couldn't identify it from that distance and wasn't likely to get down from the end loader to check it out, "and I just need to take a look at it."

Apparently satisfied, he nodded. "Yeah, I remember that one. It's down there…" he pointed back in the direction from which I'd come, "…next aisle over, toward the front."

"Thanks," I said, as he turned the ignition key and the end loader roared back to life.

I found it—or what was left of it—with no problem. It looked like it had been made of tinfoil rather than aluminum and steel. The entire frame was twisted, the entire top squashed to about half it's normal height, as if a giant had stepped on it. Only the rear end was relatively undamaged. The engine had been forced into the passenger compartment and it was pretty obvious that the occupants hadn't had much of a chance for survival. The whole front of the car reminded me of a Pug dog.

I examined the front passenger's side and noticed something very odd. At an overall glance of the front end, it was hardly noticeable, but up close…I swore there was a…well, an oddly *flat* section, as if the front of the right fender to just a couple inches from what remained of the grill had been stamped by something. The area was wrinkled but not crumpled as was the rest of the front and everything from about a foot behind the smashed headlight back toward the passenger door. As I say, it would have been easy to miss when just looking at the overall effect.

Catherine Tunderew's Renault had a deep, V-shaped indentation in the trunk. I found it hard to picture the flat area relating in any way with the angled denting of the trunk. I crouched down and examined the flattened area very carefully looking for any traces at all of paint the cops might have missed. There was nothing.

Odd, indeed.

* * *

I'd been afraid, on the drive to the body shop, that the repair parts might have come in, and Catherine Tunderew's car would either be in the service area or gone. But luck was with me, and it was still where I'd last seen it, backed up to the chain link fence bordering the fast food joint's parking lot. I parked on the street and walked over to the fence. The rear end was about three feet from the fence itself, but close enough so I could get a pretty close look. Nothing. Deep V-shaped indentation in the bumper and back of the trunk and even in the popped trunk lid. But all neat. No noticeable scrapes or scratches. Like some giant (maybe the same one who stepped on the top of Tunderew's car?) had picked up the Renault and pushed in the center of the rear end with his thumbs. But absolutely no sign of gunmetal grey paint, or anything that might have caused the flattened area on Tunderew's front fender.

Oh, well. Nice try.

* * *

On my way back to the office, I stopped at the diner in the lobby for a Caesar Salad and two cartons of milk to take with me. And I thought again, as I waited by the register, how strange it still seemed not to see Eudora and Evolla, the identical twin waitresses who had finally retired after what must have been 90 years behind the counter.

I'd just sat down at my desk, pried the lid off the styrofoam container, and unwrapped the plastic fork when the phone rang.

"Hardesty Investigations," I said, picking up after the second ring.

"Hardesty Investigations?" the very masculine voice asked. "Do I have the right number? I'm returning a call from a Dick Hardesty."

"Ah, Reverend Dinsmore," I said, demonstrating the brilliant deductive reasoning for which I have become famous. "Thank you for returning my call."

"And you are a...?" he asked.

Well, I'm a lot of things, of course, but I knew what he meant.

"I'm a private investigator, yes," I said.

"And what is it you are investigating?" he asked, his voice a mixture of caution and suspicion.

"Actually," I said, "I was hoping you might be able to give me some information that might help me determine who was responsible for Randy Jacobs' death."

There was a long pause, then: "Randy died in a car crash. I would assume the driver would be the one responsible. But why would you think I would have any information that could help you? You really should be talking with Mel Hooper, our Resident Administrator. He knows far more about our residents than I."

"But Randy Jacobs worked in the office in your home, I understand."

There was a pause, then a cautious: "Yes, he did," he said. "What relevance might that have?"

I let that one pass for the moment. "And you know who the driver of the car was, I assume?" I asked.

"That writer...Tunderew? The one who wrote that muckraking expose on...Governor Keene, I believe it was?"

"So everyone assumes," I said. "Have you read it by chance?"

He gave a short, dismissive laugh. "Good heavens, no! I prefer to focus on the positive aspects of life."

"May I ask how you heard of Randy's death?" I asked. "His name never appeared in the papers."

"The police contacted Mel Hooper, who told me. The police had found a New Eden identification card on Randy's body. I still find it hard to believe he's dead."

"Were you aware Mr. Tunderew was writing another book?" I asked.

He sounded a bit puzzled when he said: "I suppose that's what authors do, isn't it...write another book? But I can't imagine that I'd have any interest in reading *it*, either. But what does that have to do with Randy, and just what is it you think I might be able to tell you about Randy?" he asked. "I was truly sorry to hear of his death, but I really don't know what you're looking for." A slight but definite shift in the tone of his voice told me he knew quite well.

"If you'll excuse me, Reverend," I said, "I'm just a little curious as to why you didn't ask what Randy might have been doing in Mr. Tunderew's car?"

There was a long pause, then a sigh. "I assume by your

question you are referring to the fact that Randy was a hus...a male prostitute. If that is indeed what he was doing in the car with Mr. Tunderew, I am deeply sorry to hear it. I had thought Randy had put his street life behind him."

Uh-huh.

It was my turn for a slight pause. "Well, actually that was one of the things I rather hoped to be able to discuss with you...in person," I said. "Would it be possible for us to meet sometime within the next couple of days?"

A much longer pause, then: "I really don't know, Mr. Hardesty," he said. "I'm still a bit skeptical of what you're expecting me to tell you."

"I'm not expecting anything," I said, realizing it was more or less the truth, "but perhaps I should mention, for what it's worth, that I am gay, and therefore the subject of...Randy's... homosexuality is not something I care to investigate or exploit."

Apparently he got that one, since he said: "Well, perhaps we might meet. Today is out of the question, I'm afraid. Tomorrow I have meetings most of the day, and then I must see my wife off to an out of town speaking engagement. Would Friday be all right? I have to be in town for a lunch meeting, but I could perhaps come to your office right after that—2:30, say?"

"That'd be fine, Reverend. I appreciate it."

I gave him my address, and we hung up.

*   *   *

A typical Wednesday evening at home: Jonathan sitting cross-legged on the floor studying, me watching TV. A phone call from Tim and Phil just after dinner, Tim verifying that Randy's body would be cremated Thursday, and that we could pick up the ashes on Friday, and Phil suggesting that we come over to their place afterwards for dinner, if Jonathan thought he'd be up to it. As an added inducement, he said they'd just gotten a few new fish that Jonathan might be interested in meeting. I passed the invitation on to Jonathan, who looked just a little uncertain until I mentioned the fish, at which point he brightened considerably and said "Sure!"

Shortly after we hung up, the phone rang again—it was my ex, Chris, calling from New York on one of our frequent call exchanges. As usual the phone passed back and forth between Jonathan and me as each of us talked first to Chris, then to Max. The big news from their end of the line was that Max had agreed to be stage manager for a gay theater group run by a friend of his, and Chris was going to design the sets for the first production of the next season. They were both excited about it and Jonathan, of course, was immediately gas fumes to their lighted match. And when Max told us they fully expected us to be there on opening night, I thought Jonathan was going to run into the bedroom and start packing.

We'd talked about a visit to New York while Chris and Max were here for a visit not too long before, and Jonathan had, in his inimitably subtle way, been mentioning it every couple of days since. He'd never been to New York and was really looking forward to going, as was I, actually.

They promised to keep us posted, and we assured them we'd be there.

Of course, that shot the rest of the evening as far as Jonathan was concerned. The only way to calm him down was for me to suggest we might play a little impromptu game of "The Casting Director and the Chorus Boy."

* * *

Marty Gresham called just after I got back to the office from lunch on Thursday.

"Hi, Marty," I said. "Any news?"

"Maybe," he said. "I just heard from the DeKalb County Sheriff's office in Georgia. They said New Eden's squeaky-clean; never any trouble. But interestingly and probably coincidentally, though, they recently found the skeleton of a male between 18 and 20 in a wooded area along the banks of the Chattahoochie river about halfway between New Eden and the city. Most likely the body had been dumped in the river somewhere upstream and gotten snagged in the brush. He had been dead probably three years. Forensics determined the cause of death as an apparent skull fracture, and dental records matched those of a missing kid named James Temple. His last known address was New Eden, but no one there seems to remember when he left or under what circumstances. He had to have been one of the original residents, though, because the Atlanta New Eden has only been open about three and a half years. The kid had apparently been working the streets in Atlanta before he went out there. Maybe he went back to hustling and met the wrong..." he hesitated, looking for the word, then apparently gave up "...what do you call them?"

"Johns," I said. "Same as with the female hookers."

"Ah, thanks," Marty replied. "Maybe he met the wrong John. According to the Sheriff's office, Atlanta had a string of hustler murders at about that same time. None of the others linked to New Eden, though. I haven't heard yet from Dallas. Just thought I'd let you know what I'd found. I don't know if it helps at all, but..."

"Oh, it all helps," I said. "And thanks again."

* * *

It occurred to me that if conclusion jumping were to be made an Olympic event, I could probably easily go for the gold. But I really had to try to hold myself back. Okay, so they found a body, and the kid... *name? Name, damn it!*...James. James...Temple! had spent some time at New Eden. So had a lot of street kids. And he was a hustler. A lot of street kids hustle to survive. I wrote Temple's name on a notepad, and I added the missing kid...Denny Rechter. I'd be curious as to what Dinsmore might have to say about them, if he knew them at all. With as many kids as come and go at every New Eden he could hardly be expected to know every one of them personally. I might just be on a butterfly hunt, but it was worth a try.

Now, if something showed up from Dallas...

* * *

Thursday night being Jonathan's class night, I thought I might take the opportunity to run out to Ramón's and talk to Bob Allen. It was kind of a weak excuse not to stay home alone, and while Bob probably couldn't provide any information on the case, he did know an awful lot about what was going on in the community. If there were any rumors floating around out there about New Eden or the Dinsmores, Bob would be the one to know it. I called to make sure Bob would be there, and was told he would.

I drove Jonathan to class, then headed to Ramón's.

It was only about 7:15 when I got there, and the place was pretty quiet—just a few leftovers from Happy Hour, most of them I recognized as regulars. We exchanged nods and waves of greeting, and I sat down near the office end of the bar. Jimmy, who had merely nodded when I came in, walked over.

"Hi," he said, extending his hand. "I'm Jimmy. This your first time here?"

"Go ahead, rub it in," I said, as I took his hand.

"Ah, well I remember the days when we were thinking of putting a 'reserved' sign on that stool for you. But then you get married and moved on, and forget all us little people…"

"I'll have an Old Fashioned, if you don't mind," I interrupted pointedly.

"Yes," he continued, his face a mask of martyrdom, "many's the time I offered you my shoulder to console you in your hour of need…" he popped quickly back into his regular-Jimmy mode long enough to grin and say: "How come we never did make it, by the way?"

"Maybe because you never brought it up," I suggested.

"Maybe it was," he said, then lapsed back into his melodrama. "Well, too late now, I suppose. My loss is Jonathan's gain…"

"May I have an Old Fashioned, please?" I asked again, and he looked at me sharply.

"Hey, I'm on a roll, here," he said brightly.

Luckily, I knew he was kidding.

"And you'll have my vote at Oscar time," I said. "Now, about that Old Fashioned…"

He shook his head, then the grin returned. "Comin' up," he said, and turned toward the back bar for a bottle of bourbon.

We exchanged drink for money, and Jimmy nodded toward the office. "Bob's expecting you," he said.

"Thanks, Jimmy," I said, picking up my drink and napkin and heading for the office door.

* * *

Probably not surprisingly, Bob didn't really know much at all about New Eden. Ramón's didn't get many hustlers in—they mainly hung out downtown, along Arnwood, and on a two-block stretch of Ash just off Beech, the main artery of The Central. Bob didn't know anything about the Dinsmores other than what he read in Time and various newspaper articles. Other than the fact that gays and lesbians were welcome at New Eden, they were very much in the minority, and there were no direct or official links with the gay community at all.

Still, I always enjoyed just shooting the breeze with Bob, and we seldom had a chance for just the two of us to get together. As always, he asked what I'd heard from Chris, and I told him about his and Max's pending excursion into the world of the theater, and that Jonathan and I were planning a visit for the opening of their first production. Bob thought it was a great idea all around.

As also happens when we get to talking, I nearly forgot about the time, and Bob had to remind me that I had to pick Jonathan up at school.

* * *

At 10:30 Friday morning, the phone rang. It was Marty Gresham.

"Very interesting report from Dallas," he said, getting right to the point. "Actually, Dallas County referred me to Kaufman County, which is where New Eden is located. They did have an incident there—one of the New Eden residents was found murdered near a little town called Scurry. A guy named Mike Barber, 22. The Dallas police have a record on him for hustling. Apparently he was busted so often some of the cops got to know him personally. One of them was the one to get him into New

Eden, as a matter of fact." He stopped to take a breath.

"Anyway, Barber was found beaten to death on a dirt road just outside Scurry—obviously, he'd been dumped there. It's about 15 to 20 miles from New Eden, but he was last seen at the bus station in Kaufman the night before his body was found. He'd gotten into a fight with two other residents—two straight buddies who claimed Barber came on to them. Fighting is strictly forbidden by New Eden rules, and they were all three kicked out that same night."

"So the two guys he was fighting with killed him?" I asked. "How in hell could New Eden have been so stupid to kick all three off the property at the same time? That was all but setting up a killing!"

"Yeah, it seems that way, but according to the police investigation report, the New Eden administrator drove the two straight guys into the town of Kaufman and bought them each a bus ticket to Dallas. He waited with them until the bus came, then he left. Jeffrey Dinsmore himself drove Barber in a separate car to Kaufman about an hour later, where Barber said he was afraid the two guys would be waiting for him at the bus station in Dallas and said he wanted to go to San Antonio instead, so Dinsmore bought him a ticket for San Antonio. Dinsmore said he watched Barber get on the bus, then drove off. The bus driver remembers a guy fitting Barber's description getting on the bus, then getting right back off again. Apparently he got off the bus as soon as he saw Dinsmore leave and cashed in his ticket for the money. They theorize he decided to pocket the money and hitchhike, which is how he probably ended up in Scurry, which would have been on his way to San Antonio. They think he just got picked up by the wrong guy."

I didn't buy it. "Did the administrator actually *see* the two guys get on the bus to Dallas?" I asked.

"No, he didn't. He was parked on the other side of the street. He sat in the car with them until the bus pulled up, the guys got out of the car and crossed the street and he lost sight of them on the other side of the bus. He naturally assumed they got on."

Jeezus! I thought. *They could just as easily have not gotten on and waited for Dinsmore to drop Barber off at the station, then killed him.*

Yeah, but then how would they have gotten Barber's body to Scurry? my mind asked. *They didn't have a car.*

No, said another voice, *but Dinsmore did.*

Chapter 10

"So Dinsmore did wait to see Barber actually get on the bus." I asked.

"Yeah, he said Barber waved at him just as he climbed on, and Dinsmore drove away. He assumed the other two were well on their way to Dallas, so he didn't think there would be a problem."

"Even though he didn't know for sure that they might not still be in Kaufman waiting for Barber?"

Gresham sighed. "Apparently not," he said.

"And did the police subsequently try to track down the other two guys? To even see if they ever got on the bus?"

"Well, they checked with the bus driver. Six people got on in Kaufman, and two guys did get on , but the driver was having a problem with one of the other passengers and couldn't give an accurate description, so whether they were the same two, I don't know." There was a pause, then: "But they couldn't have done it, anyway. How would they have gotten Barber's body from Kaufman to Scurry? They didn't have a car."

"I was thinking the same thing," I said. He apparently didn't make the same Dinsmore connection as I had, and I didn't mention it. But I'd be sure to ask Dinsmore about that when he came in.

"*Did* the police ever try to track the guys down to question them?" I asked again.

"Yeah," he said. "The Dallas police managed to find them both—it took a while, since they'd gone their separate ways when they got back to Dallas—and both of them swore they'd gotten on the bus and never saw Barber after the fight."

Interesting, I thought.

"Interesting," I said.

Marty was quiet a moment, then said: "You don't think there's anything funny going on at New Eden, do you? Two New Eden residents being murdered is a little suspicious, but I mean, Barber was in Dallas and Temple in Atlanta. That's quite a stretch."

"I'm not sure yet," I said, half-truthfully. "But I intend to find out."

* * *

And here you go again! my mind voice said, scornfully. *Bring on those windmills!*

I sat back in my chair, and listened to the conversation going on in my mind.

Just what *did* I think I was doing? I started out with Randy being in a car with Tony Tunderew and here I am trying to figure out what happened to some poor dead kid on a dirt road in Scurry, Texas. Or one beside the Chattahoochee River in Georgia.

What were they to me?

Well, I realized that last question was raised by my cynical side, which showed up from time to time in spite of myself. The answer to that question was that they were both Randys, and all three were real people with real lives cut far too short. And if I didn't care who they were or what had happened to them, who would?

Ah, Hardesty, one of my mind voices sighed softly. *Do you have any idea of how many Randys there are in this world? How many kids there are, dead and alive, who nobody knows, or misses, or cares about? What about them? You can't save the world, Dick, no matter how hard you try.*

True, I couldn't. But I could do my best for those I *did* know about. And it wasn't totally about me chasing windmills. All of these deaths were, however loosely, tied in with Tony T. Tunderew. I'll bet he had somehow found out about these kids—how I had no idea—and their links to New Eden and by extension to the Dinsmores. What else he had found out I couldn't say, but I was more certain than ever that *No Door to Heaven* was going to lay it all out, and that he had died because of it.

I thought again of the irony of how Randy's incredibly bad luck to be in the car with Tunderew when he died had put me in the spot I was in. If Randy hadn't been there, I wouldn't have given a hoot in hell how Tunderew died or who might have been responsible for it. But I did now.

As lunch time approached, I began looking far too frequently at my watch. Would Dinsmore even show up? What if he didn't? What could I do about it? Not much.

I wasn't particularly hungry, and tried to distract myself by typing up a couple reports and paying some bills. I gave some thought to trying to balance my checkbook but decided that that particular exercise in futility wouldn't do much to improve my mood.

At 12:15 the phone rang.

Dinsmore canceling, I'll bet, one of my mind voices volunteered.

"Hardesty Investigations," I said, picking up the phone and hoping the voice was wrong.

"Hi, Dick. It's Jonathan."

Like I didn't know? I wondered. I resisted the temptation to ask "Jonathan who?"

"Hi, Tiger," I said. "What's up?"

"I'm sorry to bother you at work," he said, "but I wanted to remind you that we have to go pick Randy up this afternoon."

I knew, of course. But it was his way of dealing with something he dreaded, and of being reassured that I was there with him.

"I know, Tiger," I said. "We've got until 4:30, and I'll call you when I'm on my way to pick you up. I've got someone coming in around 2:30, but I'll make it over there as close to 3:30 as I can. That'll still give us time."

"Okay," he said. "I'll be waiting. I asked the boss if I could work in the yard today instead of going out on delivery and installation, so I'll be here."

"Good," I said. "Did you have your lunch yet?"

"Sort of," he said. "I'm not really very hungry."

"I know," I said. "Well I'll see you later, then."

We exchanged goodbyes and hung up.

* * *

At 2:15 there was a knock at the door, and I got up hastily from my desk and went to open it. It was my first look at the real-life Jeffrey Dinsmore, and I was duly impressed. Just about six feet tall, short dark brown hair with just a touch of grey at the temples, a very handsome, masculine face. "Reverend Dinsmore," I said by way of greeting. "Please, come in."

We waited for our handshake until I'd closed the door behind him. His grip, like everything else about him, all but exuded confidence and self-assurance. He was dressed and groomed impeccably, but not ostentatiously. No jewelry other than the requisite wedding band.

I showed him to a seat and asked if he'd like some coffee, which he declined.

When we'd both been seated, he glanced around the office. "I've never been in a private investigator's office before," he said with a small smile. "As a matter of fact, I don't think I've ever met anyone in your line of work before, though I was a great fan of Mickey Spillane when I was in my teens." Then his eyes moved slowly but deliberately to mine and the smile faded.

Ingratiation period over, my mind observed.

"Tell me about Randy Jacobs," he said.

Well, since he wanted to get straight to the point, so did I.

"So you think Randy was hustling when Tunderew picked him up?" I asked, watching him closely but, I hoped, not too obviously.

He looked at me with a slightly puzzled expression. "Isn't that what you said?" he asked.

"Not exactly," I replied, and his puzzled look remained. "How much do you know about Tony Tunderew?" I asked.

He gave an almost imperceptible shrug. "Almost nothing other than what I said when we talked on the phone."

"You didn't read his book, then?" I asked. He'd already told me he hadn't, but I wanted to watch his reaction when he told me again.

"No," he said, "as I told you, it's not the type of reading I think I'd enjoy."

He paused, his expression still fully controlled but reflecting a hint of puzzlement. "I'm still not sure what all this has to do with Randy's death," he said.

"I mentioned that Mr. Tunderew was writing another book?" I could see his mind working in the narrowing of his eyes.

"Yes," he said, slowly.

"Did you know it was about New Eden?" I was taking a real chance here, since I didn't know positively that it was.

"You can't be serious!" he said, and I could sense a slight cracking of his facade of composure.

"I'm afraid I am," I said.

He sat there silently for a moment as the cracks repaired themselves.

"Then you're saying that Randy was not in his car by accident," he said.

I overlooked the unintentional pun. "I don't think so," I replied. "I think Randy had been supplying Tunderew with information on New Eden, the Eternal Light Foundation, and..." I hesitated only briefly, "...you."

That one got to him, I could tell. He did his best to hide it, but failed.

"I don't believe it," he said. "It's impossible." For an instant there, his entire body sagged as he realized that it was indeed possible.

He cleared his throat before speaking. "Who else knows?" he asked. "And for whom are you working?"

"I'm not working for anyone," I said. "Randy was a friend of...a friend. By total coincidence, Tunderew had hired me to find out who was trying to blackmail him for allegedly being gay. It wasn't really until Randy had left New Eden and I found out about your...relationship...with him that I really started putting two and two together. I don't believe Tunderew's death was an accident. I think someone killed him...and Randy had the incredibly bad luck to be in the wrong place at the wrong time. It's because of Randy that I'm doing whatever I can to find out exactly what happened."

"And you actually believe New Eden...*I*...am involved

somehow? That's preposterous!"

I noticed that his face did not reflect the same certainty as his voice.

"I'm not ruling anyone or anything either in or out," I said. "There are other leads I'm following, but there are just too many arrows pointing in the direction of New Eden to ignore."

I could read the suspicion in his eyes, and I suppose I couldn't really blame him. He had no way of knowing I wasn't out to screw him (which I'm sure my crotch would have thought was a great idea). In an effort to reassure him that was not the case, I said: "My only concern in all this is to find out who is responsible for Randy's death. I share your sentiments on muckrakers, and I found Tony Tunderew to be a thoroughly despicable human being."

We sat for another moment in silence as he was lost in his own thoughts and I tried to sort out mine. Finally, in an attempt to satisfy myself on the point, I asked:

"You're sure, then, that you had no idea Tunderew was targeting you and New Eden?"

I turned my vibes detection systems on full and zeroed all my attention on his face and body language.

Zilch.

His head moved slowly back and forth. "None," he said. "I swear. I admit that I had a moment of weakness with Randy, but I can't see how just one unfortunate incident of moral lapse on my part could be fuel for an entire book."

Well, now there's an interesting comment on several levels, I thought. *'One unfortunate incident'? Not the way I hear it.*

I doubled the intensity of my alertness to his reactions when I said: "Well, there were the other deaths…"

He looked at me sharply. "*Deaths?*" he asked. "If you're referring to Michael Barber, I take full responsibility for my failure to prevent what happened to him. But I watched him get on the bus! And though there was no possible way I could have anticipated what happened to him, there has not been a single day since that I have not wished I had waited until the bus drove off to be absolutely sure…"

"You can't blame yourself," I said, wondering if that was a true statement.

Again the shake of the head. "But I do," he said. "I do."

"And what about James Temple?" I asked.

He looked puzzled again. "Who?" he asked.

"James Temple," I repeated. "One of the early residents of the Atlanta New Eden."

His eyes narrowed slightly, whether in suspicion or in thought I couldn't tell.

"James Temple. Ja...*Jim* Temple..." he said after a moment. "What about him? How do you know Jim?"

"He's dead, too. He was murdered, just about the time he left New Eden."

Either Jeffrey Dinsmore was one of the world's greatest actors or what I was telling him was coming as a complete surprise and an almost physical shock. His facade of ministerial control collapsed totally...only for a moment, and then the walls were back up.

"You're wrong," he said, again firmly. "Jim's not dead. He left. All our residents leave eventually; that's part of New Eden's purpose, to give them a fresh start in life. Surely I'd have known if something had happened to him."

"His body wasn't discovered until just recently, on the banks of the Chattahoochee about halfway between Atlanta and New Eden," I said.

I think "lost" best sums up the look on Dinsmore's face. "No," he said, as if saying it would bring James Temple back to life. "No. He..."

Watching someone in total control of himself lose that control is not a pleasant sight. In order to prevent him from swirling more quickly into total confusion, I tried to arrest it with another question.

"Do you have any idea why Temple left?"

He shook his head. "None. I thought he really liked it at New Eden, and he seemed to be doing well. Then we—my wife and I—returned from a religious conference, and he was gone. It's not at all unusual for a resident to simply leave without notice, but that Jim would do it was a real surprise."

"And you never heard from him again?" I asked.

He looked quickly away and said, "No."

"I'm sorry?" I said, staring at him. He looked at me and again I saw a lightning-quick flush.

"I mean, yes, I did. About six weeks after he left I got a small package from him."

"May I ask what was in it?"

And again the flush, longer this time. "It was...it was a small bible I'd given him...in gratitude for his being such a good worker," he hastily added. He paused, and I knew there was something else.

"And?" I prompted.

"And it was torn into shreds," he said. He shook his head. "I have no idea why he would have done such a thing. There was no note of explanation, nothing. It's a total mystery."

Why didn't I think so? But rather than pursue it further at the moment, I decided to move on. "Temple worked in the residence office, is that right?"

He gathered himself together and looked at me. "Yes, that's right. All our residents have specific work assignments."

"And did Barber by any chance also work in the residence office?"

"We have several offices at each facility," he said, but I could sense both a realization on his part and an effort to evade it. "There's the administration office, the farm office, and the residence office."

"But like Randy, they all worked in the residence office, didn't they?" I asked.

I could swear I saw him pale. "Well, yes," he said finally.

"And what about a Denny Rechter. Did he work in the residence office, too?"

"Denny?" he asked, then his eyes widened noticeably. "Are you saying Denny's dead, too? That's impossible! Totally impossible!"

"I hope you're right," I said. "So far, Denny Rechter has only officially been reported as missing. But did he work in the residence office?"

"For a brief while, yes," Dinsmore admitted. "But one morning he didn't show up for work and Mel Hooper, our Residents' Administrator, said the police had contacted him in regards to Denny's parents being in town looking for him. Apparently he'd been a runaway, and he ran again when he somehow heard his folks were coming to take him home." He shrugged. I could clearly sense there was a lot going on inside that he didn't want to let out.

I did want to know more about exactly how New Eden operated, but not right now. I had more pressing matters on my mind. "May I ask if you were...involved...with all four at some point?"

"Involved? What are you implying?" He tried to sound shocked, but I could see he knew it wouldn't work. "No! Of course not!" he said adamantly—but as far as I was concerned, certainly not convincingly. "I love my wife..."

I held up my hand to forestall the anticipated outpouring of denial.

"I'm sure you do," I said. "But that really isn't relevant to whether or not you were...if 'involved' isn't accurate, let's substitute 'sexually active'...with James Temple, Michael Barber, and Denny Rechter as well as with Randy Jacobs."

I think if he thought anger might do him any good, he'd have registered it more visibly. I could see it was there, but he also knew there wasn't much point in displaying it. And while there was also little point in denying he'd had sex with Randy—and I questioned as to whether it may not have been more than once—he wasn't about to admit to any more than he had to.

"No! Absolutely not!" he said. "Randy was...well...he pretty much seduced me, that's what he did. I'm only human, and my wife was traveling much of the time, and..."

I held up my hand again. "Please, Reverend," I said, "your sexual orientation would be none of my business except for the fact that as a 100 percent gay man, I tend to get extremely defensive when other gay men end up dead for whatever reason." He simply stared at me.

"What does your wife think about your being…only human?" I asked.

He dropped his glance to the floor. "I assume Randy told you she…she…"

"Caught you in the act?" I said.

"Exactly. It was terrible. You have no idea how shocked and horrified she was. But my wife is about as close to being a saint as it is possible for a human being to be. I explained exactly what had happened and why, and she forgave me. I swore to her that it would never happen again."

I'm sure you did, I thought. *And I'm sure she believed you.*

"Well," I said, getting back to who might have killed Tony Tunderew, "you're right that a one-time experience with a single male hustler wouldn't be enough on which to build a best-selling expose. But the disappearance of one and the verifiable deaths of two—" I wasn't counting Randy's peripheral death— "male hustlers who all worked in the residence office of a respected and well known religious conservative would understandably run up red flags. Especially for someone like Tunderew. I wouldn't even rule out the possibility that Tunderew used Randy to set you up. But if that was the case, he just set the trap—you took the bait. And the fact of the matter is that there's nothing like a juicy sex scandal—with hints of murder—to sell a very large number of books."

Dinsmore's was looking more and more distressed. "*Is* there a second book?" he asked. "I mean, was this Tunderew fellow just in the *process* of writing it, or did he finish it? A book like that could destroy everything my wife and I have worked for all these years! Everything! We can't let that happen."

Luckily for him, I don't think he realized he'd just voiced a very probable motive for Tony T. Tunderew's murder. But I figured he deserved to know what he was up against.

"As far as I know," I said, "the book was close to completion, but I don't think he'd actually finished it. But that doesn't mean someone else won't. You might be wise to talk to your lawyers."

I could tell that we'd gone just about as far in one conversation as I could logically expect to go. Dinsmore's cage had been rattled thoroughly, and I wasn't sure if that was a good thing or a bad thing. As we got out of our chairs, I tried to think of a way to approach the possibility of our talking again after he—and I—had had a chance to digest everything we'd just covered. I was a little surprised when he mentioned it first.

"I still can't believe all this is happening," he said as I walked him to the door. "But I do want to know anything you might find out about Denny's whereabouts, or if you learn anything at all about Jim's or Mike's deaths."

He paused, as we shook hands and looked at me intently. "I have no reason to hope I might rely on you not to make things worse—if that were possible—but I have very little choice, and you have no idea what all is at stake here."

Actually, I did have a very good idea. I assured him again that it was not my intention to cause him any more trouble than was already looming over his head, and that I wasn't the slightest bit interested in what rocks Tony T. Tunderew had been planning to turn over (except for those under which there were dead people). I did make it clear that I *was* interested in exactly what was going on and intended to find out with his help or without it.

"Whatever I can do," he said as we released our handshake and I opened the door.

As the door closed behind him, I was already making plans to somehow speak to Barbara Dinsmore and probably to her brother, Residents' Administrator Mel Hooper, as well.

I called Evergreens to tell Jonathan I was on my way, turned out the lights, and left the office.

* * *

Jonathan was pretty quiet on the way to Rosevine, the cemetery where the city's crematorium was located. When it was founded back in the late 1880s, Rosevine had been on the far outskirts of the city, which had slowly flowed around it and moved ever outward, leaving it an oasis of calm, green, and quiet in the midst of the city's sprawl. It had some magnificent old trees which had survived while its neighbors beyond the cemetery's wrought iron gates were cut down to make room for houses and parking lots and mini-marts and pizza parlors. The crematorium sat in the middle of the cemetery—a large, solid, ornate fortress-like building of rough stone. Its Victorian exterior belied the fact that its interior had recently been totally renovated to make it state of the art for the prompt and efficient reduction of human bodies to a small pile of ashes.

Adjacent to the crematorium was a much smaller building of the same materials but in a less ornate style, which served as the cemetery's and the crematorium's office. We pulled up into the small parking area beside it and I turned off the engine.

"Do you want me to go in with you?" I asked, and Jonathan gave me a small smile and a shake of his head.

"No," he said. "I think Randy'd like for me to do it. You don't mind, do you?"

He had made no move to open the door, and I reached over and laid my hand on his leg.

"I don't mind." I said, "and I think you're right. Randy'd want you to do it."

He took a deep breath, grabbed my hand and squeezed it quickly, then opened the door. "Be right back," he said.

About ten minutes later, he emerged from the office carrying a small, plain wood box, only a little larger than a cigar box. He carried it in both hands, as though afraid he might drop it. He came over to the car, set the box carefully on the hood, opened the door, picked up the box, and got in, carefully putting the box on his lap before reaching over to close the door.

"We can go home first before we go over to Tim and Phil's, can't we?" he asked.

"Sure," I said, as I backed out of the parking place and headed down the winding drive to the main gate.

"Good," he said. "I thought we'd put him in the guest bedroom, since he's stayed there before."

All the way home, he kept his eyes fixed on the box in his lap. Finally he said softly, more to himself than to me: "I can't believe this is Randy," he said.

"It's not, babe," I said gently.

"Where do you suppose Randy is?" he asked. He had turned his head to look at me as if expecting me to have an answer.

"I think Randy is exactly where he was before he was conceived," I said.

"No heaven?" Jonathan asked.

I shook my head. "No heaven. No hell. Just nothing at all—infinity."

He kept looking at me, studying my face. "I think I believe in heaven," he said.

I reached over to take his hand. "Then do," I said.

"And Randy's there," he said.

"Then Randy's there," I replied.

We rode the rest of the way in silence.

* * *

Dinner at Tim and Phil's was exactly what Jonathan—and I—needed. We all studiously avoided talking about anything heavy or philosophical. Jonathan and Phil spent a great deal of time talking about fish. Jonathan related the trauma of realizing that bigger fish eat smaller fish, but he diplomatically did not mention that it was Phil's namesake who was a main perpetrator.

Phil and Tim had just gotten a couple of new fish for their large aquarium…gloriously iridescent creatures I don't recall ever having seen before. Jonathan, of course, was enthralled, his enthusiasm for immediately running out and buying a couple for his own tank dampened only by being reluctantly told—at Jonathan's insistent prodding—how much they had cost.

We talked and laughed until nearly midnight, at which point we said our good-nights headed for home. While Jonathan's spirits had lifted considerably it did not escape me that, as we walked down the hall to our bedroom, Jonathan stopped at the guest bedroom to quietly close the door and say softly "'Night, Randy."

* * *

A dream. Dusk. Some little country town. I'm in a car, in the back seat. There are two men in the front seat. Jeffrey Dinsmore is driving. There's a very attractive, obviously gay young blond in the passenger's seat. I can't make out many of the words, but they're both obviously upset. The kid saying he doesn't want to go. Dinsmore saying he has to. Then Dinsmore alone in the car, parked by some sort of building. There's a bus in front with the door open. The young man appears from somewhere—the building?—and gets into the bus. Suddenly, he gets back off and comes quickly over to the car. The young man is upset. Dinsmore opens the door...

I know, I thought as I stood in front of the mirror and lathered shaving cream over my face, *...a dream's just a dream.* I have them all the time; I just don't remember most of them. And as far as the power of dreams to provide revelations of mysteries, I put them pretty much up there with examining the entrails of an owl or reading tea leaves. But this one stuck with me, though I didn't know why.

I'd not really had much time since Dinsmore left the office to think about him and try to figure out if I thought he was being sincere or trying to con me. I didn't believe for one second that Randy had been the first guy Jeffrey Dinsmore had had sex with. And it struck me as a little more than coincidence that out of all the residents at New Eden, the office help all seemed to be male hustlers—until now, I realized, as I remembered that it had been a woman who had answered the phone when I'd called. I might be making a stretch here, but it occurred to me that Mrs. Dinsmore might have instigated the gender change in office staff after finding her husband *in flagrante delicto* (I love that phrase) with Randy.

"Are you going to actually shave or just stand there all day?" Jonathan's voice said behind me, and I raised my eyes into the mirror and saw him standing there behind me, toweling his hair dry.

"Sorry," I said. "Just thinking."

He slung the towel over his shoulder and ran his hand over my butt and moved it across my hip and around toward my front.

"So was I," he said with a devilish grin.

What the hell…it was Saturday!

* * *

But not for long. Before I knew it I was pouring water into the office coffee maker on Monday morning ready to start a new week without knowing where the last one had gone.

I had been able, however, largely to keep my mind off the Tunderew case. I realized, as I sat at my desk going through the newspaper, that it was beginning to tiptoe back into my consciousness.

What *did* I make of Jeffrey Dinsmore? The fact that I was thinking of him was my way of telling myself that he'd moved to the top of the list, and that the others…Larry Fletcher, the Bernadines, and even Catherine Tunderew…had pretty much dropped off the radar screen. Everything was pretty much pointing at the good Reverend. He'd said it himself: Tunderew's book would destroy just about everything he'd worked for.

But that was if he'd known Tunderew was writing a book about him and New Eden. That's *if.* Tunderew was pretty devious. Unless Randy had told him, how really would Dinsmore have known? He seemed genuinely shocked when I told him I thought he was the subject of the next book.

Yeah, like you've never been conned before, my mind voice observed.

Well, yeah, I'd been conned. More times than I'd like to admit, but I'm a trusting guy.

Uh huh, my mind-voice said.

But why would Dinsmore bump off guys he'd been having sex with?

Maybe because he'd been having sex with guys? And maybe because he didn't want to risk them telling his wife?

Which brings up the subject of the Reverend *Mrs.* Dinsmore. Could she *not* have known her husband had an eye for the boys? Well, it's possible she didn't—people tend not to see things they don't want to see. And Dinsmore certainly did not strike me as being stupid. She did travel a lot. I didn't know who made the work assignments at the various New Edens, but it would be relatively easy for Jeffrey to select who worked in the residence office. If Mrs. Dinsmore *didn't* have a clue, she might even have preferred a guy working in the home with her husband when she was away, rather than risk his being tempted by some "other woman."

Hmm.

* * *

I like it when things start coming together. I realized that by quietly moving the other potential suspects out of the way, it was pretty much a process of elimination, and only Jeffrey Dinsmore—and perhaps Barbara Dinsmore; I hadn't had a chance to look at that possibility yet, but I would—remained. But regardless of which Dinsmore it might be, I was increasingly positive that he or she (maybe   *they?* Unlikely, but...) was responsible for Tony Tunderew's murder, and Randy's death.

I was feeling pretty damned smug.

And then the phone rang.

Chapter II

"Hardesty Investigations," I said, picking up after the second ring.

"Dick," the familiar voice said. "It's Glen O'Banyon. Are you still working on the Tunderew case?"

"Yeah," I said, a little curious as to why he'd be asking.

"How's it going?" he asked.

"Pretty well, I think," I said. "I feel I'm getting close."

"Well, I've been wondering about how you were doing, and I just came across a piece of information you might find interesting, if you're not already aware of it. Would you like to meet for lunch? We can talk about it."

"Sure," I said. "Etheridge's?"

"12:15," he replied. "Same time, same station."

"I'll see you there," I said, and we hung up.

Why wasn't I feeling quite so smug?

* * *

I was early, as usual. Alex, the really hot waiter, was as usual on duty and, even though I hadn't been there in quite a while, showed me to O'Banyon's table without being asked. He poured my coffee, laid out two menus, and went about his business.

At 12:20—early for him—O'Banyon entered and, exchanging a nod with Alex, came directly to the table. We shook hands as he sat down, and Alex appeared from nowhere to pour his coffee and refill my half-empty cup.

"Need a minute?" he asked. "Today's special is Eggplant Parmesan, so you'll know."

O'Banyon and I looked at one another, then said in unison: "Sounds good."

Alex nodded, jotted the order down on his pad, then headed for the kitchen.

"So," O'Banyon said after taking a sip of his coffee, "tell all." And I did. He seemed duly impressed, and obviously surprised by the New Eden related deaths.

Alex returned with our lunch just as I finished, and we ate in silence for a few moments.

"Very interesting," O'Banyon said finally.

I finished swallowing a mouthful of eggplant, then said: "Indeed. So why do I get the feeling you've got a monkey wrench to drop into my well-oiled machine?"

He took another sip of coffee and grinned. "Well, maybe it is, maybe it isn't," he said. "But were you aware that Bernadine Press had a $1.5 million life insurance policy on our friend Mr. Tunderew?"

Wrench dropped.

"No," I said, not immediately quite sure how to take that bit of information. "I wasn't. I had no idea a publisher could take out a policy on one of its authors."

O'Banyon nodded. "It's not common, but not unheard of under the 'protection of investment' classification. Think about the Hollywood studios insuring Ann Miller's legs. Usually it's a publicity gimmick. But Bernadine didn't make a peep on this one. I really can't think of another publisher who's done it, but from what you've told me and what I gathered from my brief association with the late departed, it was a damned shrewd move on Bernadine Press' part. It's a pretty expensive gamble, especially for a company in as precarious a financial position as Bernadine is…or was. Unless, of course, they somehow found a way to hedge their bet."

"Obviously, it paid off for Bernadine," I said. "They get the second book *and* cash in on the insurance! If I were the suspicious type, I might say it wasn't a bad motive for murder. I'd venture to guess that had Tunderew lived long enough to actually sign with another publisher, the policy would be void."

O'Banyon nodded again. "Since their interest/investment would be thereby voided, yes. So Tunderew's dying when he did was really a stroke of good luck for them."

While O mulled that over, we relaxed and small-talked until

Alex returned to refill our coffee, take our plates, and ask if we wanted dessert. We passed.

As we parted company outside the restaurant and I watched O'Banyon cross the street to the City Building, I made a mental note to have another little talk with Peter Bernadine.

* * *

I called Bernadine Press as soon as I returned to the office, said who I was, and asked to speak to Peter Bernadine.

"Mr. Bernadine is out of the office," the receptionist said, "but Mr. Bernadine senior is in. Would you like to speak with him?"

Actually, I'd have preferred to speak to Peter, but…"Yes, please," I said.

There was a moment of silence, then the sound of a receiver being lifted.

"This is Donald Bernadine."

"Mr. Bernadine, this is Dick Hardesty. Sorry to bother you, but I have a question you might be able to answer for me."

His voice reflected his caution. "Regarding?" he asked.

I wasn't quite sure how to mention it so, as usual in such cases, just plunged in. "I understand Bernadine Press took out a rather sizeable insurance policy on Mr. Tunderew shortly before his death."

There was a long pause. Finally: "And just how might this be any of your business, Mr. Hardesty?"

He had a good point.

"As you know, I'm looking into Mr. Tunderew's death," I said, "and I'm trying to get as much information as possible before I go to the police with my suspicion that his death was not accidental. If the police open an investigation, they'll undoubtedly find out about the policy, and I'd like to be able to present them with a logical reason for your having taken it out. Perhaps it might keep them from having to approach you directly."

Another very long silence, to the point where I was about to say: "Hello?"

"The policy," he said just before I opened my mouth, " was

taken out as a form of collateral against an expansion loan. Peter thought it would be a good idea."

"The bank suggested it?" I asked.

"No, again it was Peter's idea. He thought it would strengthen our presentation to the bank."

"I see," I said. It did make sense, I suppose. "Well, thank you for the explanation. I'll definitely add it to my notes."

"If there's nothing else, then, perhaps you will excuse me. I have a busy day."

"Of course," I said. "I understand your son is out of the office. I do have a couple other minor questions for him, since he dealt more directly with Mr. Tunderew than you did. Will he be back later today?"

"I'll transfer you back to the receptionist. She can help you on that."

"Thank you again for your help," I said and heard a click on the other end of the line. A moment later the receptionist's voice saying:

"Can I help you?"

"Yes," I said, "I was wondering if Peter Bernadine would be in later today, and if so, if I could talk with him for a few minutes."

A brief pause and the sound of pages turning. "He has a 3:00 appointment today in his office, so he should be back shortly. Would you like him to call you?"

"If he would," I said. I toyed with the idea of suggesting I just drop by the office, but didn't want to run all the way over there and then find him not available. If he didn't return my call today, I could always use an office drop in as Plan B for tomorrow.

I gave her my number, and hung up.

* * *

I'd been sitting at my desk doodling: names with arrows pointing at other names and lots of question marks and exclamation points and underlines and squiggles, and all, in the end, totally pointless and totally confusing. I did notice, though, that the case was definitely going off in two directions. There was way too much stuff relating to New Eden and the Dinsmores that didn't have anything at all to do with Randy's death. Unless the Dinsmores were responsible for Tunderew's accident, which would tie it all back together. Sort of.

Damn!

Luckily, the phone rang before my frustration level could mount much higher.

One ring. Two rings. "Hardesty Investigations."

"Peter Bernadine here," the all-business voice announced.

"Mr. Bernadine," I said. "Thanks for returning my call. I had a few more questions I wonder if you could answer for me."

"Such as?"

"I was curious about the reasons for your taking out an insurance policy on Mr. Tunderew. I understand it is not unheard of, but I'd assume the premiums would be rather steep, and at a time when Bernadine Press was pressed for cash…"

"Strictly to protect our interests," he said. "I had very sound reasons for doing so, and I'm afraid they are not for public disclosure."

I took a wild stab. "Might one of them have had anything to do with Mr. Tunderew's drug usage?"

That one got him, I could tell. There was a long pause followed by an almost-equally-long sigh. "That was one of the considerations, yes."

I tried another long shot. "You had personal knowledge of his…problem?"

"I did," he said.

"May I ask how?" I asked.

"I knew almost from the publication date of *Dirty Little Minds*," he said. "The book's success really went to his head—in more ways than one. He's made a lot of money on *Dirty Little Minds*, but he's gone through it almost as fast as he made it, and I'm pretty sure a lot of it went up his nose. He kept asking for advances on his royalties, which is strictly a no-no in the business, but we wanted that second book, even though we were fully aware that he might be tempted to try to dump us and go with a bigger house for a huge advance. So we insisted there be an insurance policy which we would take out for purposes of control, so if something were to happen to him before the book was released, we could at least cover the advances. He wasn't happy, but he went along. And he kept asking for advances until we learned of his suit to break the contract. So we cut him off. I understand he began running a tab with his dealer, which is *definitely* not a good idea. The insurance policy was our hedge against the worse case scenario which, unfortunately, came to pass."

I'd sensed a strong undercurrent of...something...beneath everything he'd said.

"And how do you think his drug problem affected *No Door to Heaven*?" I asked, deliberately using the book's title to make him think I knew more than I did. "Mrs. Tunderew turned it over to you, I know." Actually, I didn't know, but it was a pretty safe guess.

There was a very, very long pause. "Yes, she did," he said finally.

"And?" I asked. "Is it what you'd expected?"

Another very long pause, then: "Let's just say the insurance policy was a very good idea. The book is dreck."

"Dreck?" I echoed, surprised to find myself truly surprised.

"Dreck," he repeated. "Salvable dreck, with luck. Most of the details are there, and I'm sure we'll be able to make something of it in the hands of a good ghost writer. It will be a huge success. As it stands, you can almost see the progress of his drug use from one chapter to the next."

I decided that since I was on a roll, I should push right on. "I assume the Dinsmores and New Eden are sufficiently well disguised to avoid slander charges."

There was a significantly long pause, then a very controlled and rather icy: "As our legal department pointed out with *Dirty Little Minds*, just because people may see similarities between fictional characters and certain prominent real-life figures does not mean they are the same. And like *Dirty Little Minds*, *No Door to Heaven* is purely a work of fiction."

"Of course," I said.

* * *

Well, that pretty much settled the issue (if there ever was one) of who *No Door to Heaven* might be about. But was it just me, or were things starting to spin off in too many directions, here? I mean, what the hell was I trying to do? Trying to find out why Randy died, basically. But that had led me, however unwittingly or unwillingly, to the whole New Eden mess which might or might not be directly related to what I was trying to discover.

I realized that somewhere along the line, I'd totally lost track of the starting point for this whole mess: the blackmail. I still didn't know for sure who the blackmailer was, and it was still a not remote possibility that he, she, or they and Tunderew's murderer were one and the same. Thinking back, the one potential blackmail suspect I'd been made aware of but never contacted was…that temp from Craylaw & Collier…Judy? …*Judith* Francini. She was a loose end I figured I'd better tie up just for my own satisfaction if nothing else.

I pulled out the phone book and turned to the yellow pages for "Employment Agencies: Temporary." Fletcher had said she'd worked for Manpower, so I found their number and dialed.

I explained that I had some office work that needed to be done, and that one of their temps, a Judith Francini, had been highly recommended, and wondered if she might be available for a one or two day assignment. (Actually, on looking around the office, I'd realized I could, in fact, use a little help in getting things in some semblance of order.)

I was put on hold for a moment, then the secretary/receptionist/whatever-she-was came back on the line.

"Well, as a matter of fact Miss Francini is just completing an assignment today," she said. "I'll contact her to see if she might be available and get back to you. I assume you would like her to start tomorrow?"

"That would be fine, if she can," I said.

She asked me for the standard information—my company name, address, phone number, type of work I needed done, hours to be worked, if I'd used their services before, who had recommended them to me (I told them a friend at Craylaw and Collier),etc.—then explained their fee.

I thanked her, said I would wait for her call, and hung up.

Within 20 minutes, Manpower called back to confirm that Miss Francini would be available and would be at my office at 8:30 sharp.

And with that, I decided to call it a day.

* * *

I think I've mentioned before the little mantra I have to force myself to recite from time to time: "I work to live, I do not live to work."

I kept repeating it all the way home. I determined to totally shut out any thoughts whatsoever of Tony T. Tunderew or New Eden or the three dead and one missing hustlers/New Eden residents, or of Randy and how he died. The latter was a bit more difficult, since what remained of Randy was on the floor in one corner of our guest bedroom, but I would do my very best.

So Monday night was a warmly comfortable "together" night, where I just concentrated on how lucky I was to have Jonathan in my life. As a matter of fact, right after we'd finished dinner and put the dishes in the sink, I stopped Jonathan from turning on the water and instead took him by the hand and led him—a bit puzzled but willing—into the bedroom.

I've observed over the years that there are—at least for me—two kinds of sex: lust sex and love sex. Most of my life had concentrated on the former; even with Jonathan, while it was always a combination of the two, usually the lust was the major component (that's what made our little "games" such fun). But this time the emphasis was definitely on the love, and I did my very best to let Jonathan know without the use of words how I felt about him (if he didn't know already).

We were lying there in the dark after the lust had finally overtaken the foreplay, as it inevitably does, considering who would get up to turn out the lights in the rest of the apartment, when the phone rang. I was very grateful it had not rung half an hour earlier.

Jonathan scooted out of bed and went to answer it. I couldn't make out what he was saying until he called out: "It's Jared. He's coming to town this weekend and wants to know if we want to get together with him and Jake for dinner Friday."

"Sure," I said. "You didn't have anything else lined up, did you?"

"Huh-uh," he said, then returned to his conversation with Jared.

A few minutes later he returned to bed. "Eight o'clock at Napoleon," he said. "It'll be nice to see Jake again."

Yeah, I thought as Jonathan plumped his pillow and settled in beside me. *Maybe I can find out a little more about what's going on at New Eden.*

Well, so much for mantras.

* * *

I arrived at the office a little before eight, so I could figure out exactly what she might be able to do to help create order where there was none. I knew where things were, for the most part, but I realized I could benefit from a little more organization. My main purpose in having her come in, of course, was to find out what I could about her relationship, if any, with Tunderew, but as long as she was here....

At exactly 8:30, there was a gentle tap at the door, which then opened before I could say anything, and in walked my temp for the day. Judith Francini was a short, thin brunette with medium length hair which she kept tied back. Simply but neatly dressed, her outfit was clearly designed to allow her to fit into practically any office in the city. She was rather pretty and was a noticeably...ah...what used to be known in Teddy Roosevelt's time as "buxom." (I've always found it interesting how straight men's fascination seems to focus frequently above the waist, while gay men's points below.)

After our introductions, I showed her where she could put her large shoulder bag—on the floor beside the couch. I'd moved the typewriter stand and a folding chair over by the file cabinets to give her some room to work. When I'd first opened the office, I'd bought myself a Rolodex but had never gotten around to actually using it. So I had gone through the top drawer of my desk and filled a large manila envelope with the business cards and various scraps of paper on which I had scrawled client and contact telephone numbers over the years. I decided to let typing up Rolodex cards be her first project.

I really wasn't used to having other people around the office other than the occasional client, so it was just a bit awkward finding something to do that wouldn't give her the impression that I didn't do anything. I let her get about half an hour into the project before breaking the silence: "I understand you've done work for Craylaw & Collier."

She stopped in mid keystroke and turned her head quickly to look at me. "Yes," she said, and I could clearly hear the suspicion in her voice, though she tried to hide it. "I've had a couple of assignments there."

At that point, the phone rang.

"Would you like me to get it?" she asked, starting to get up.

"No, that's fine," I said. "I can get it." I had no idea who it might be, but knew anyone who called regularly would be a bit startled to have a woman answering my phone.

"Hardesty Investigations," I said.

It was a woman from Manpower calling to ask if Miss Francini had arrived and if she was working out to my satisfaction. I assured her everything is fine, and we hung up.

"You worked for Tony Tunderew, I understand," I said, picking up where the call had interrupted our exchange—it wasn't exactly a conversation.

Her eyes narrowed and her face reflected a mixture of suspicion and a touch of anger. "That's correct," she said, and deliberately resumed her typing, though I could tell I had struck a nerve.

"I was wondering..." I started to say when she pushed back her chair and stood up.

"I'm afraid I should leave," she said sharply. "I should have realized when they told me a private investigator had specifically requested me…" she turned and crossed the room to the sofa to pick up her shoulder bag.

I held up my hand to stop her. "Please, Miss Francini," I said. "This isn't any sort of trap. It's not my intention to cause you any difficulty or problem at all. I just really need some information."

She stopped and turned toward me again. I could see she was still angry.

"He hired you, didn't he?" she asked. (Well, it was more of a statement and a demand than a question.)

"Yes, he did," I admitted. "But he did not hire me to investigate you specifically, and in any event now that he's dead, the entire matter is moot. Please, sit down. And if it will help, I can tell you that I quit on him, and that I considered him a totally obnoxious excuse for a human being."

She was watching my face through slightly narrowed eyes, as if trying to tell if I were telling the truth or not. Apparently satisfied, she rather reluctantly returned to the typing desk and her chair, which she swivelled to face me.

"Please," I said again, gesturing to the more comfortable chair closer to the desk, and she took the three or four steps to it and slowly sat down.

"Tell me about your rela…about your association with Mr. Tunderew."

She was still watching me closely, but her eyes were no longer narrowed.

"I had a two month assignment with Craylaw & Collier," she began, readjusting her position and sitting up quite straight, shoulders back as though she were practicing a finishing school exercise on proper posture. "I was working with Mr. Tunderew on a special fund raising project for the Eternal Light Foundation. When I happened to mention that I'd recently moved here from Dallas, Mr. Tunderew asked if I might have read or heard anything negative about the New Eden there. I told him no, of course—it's very highly regarded by everyone who knows of it. When I said that it had been a real shame when that young man who'd lived at New Eden was murdered, he became very interested. He said he was an amateur crime buff, and wanted to know everything I could tell him about it." She looked off into the corner as she continued.

"Well, I have something of a photographic memory, as it happens. Mostly for dates and numbers, but also for things I read. I was able to recite the entire newspaper article I'd read on it–and that was some time ago. He was very impressed. I told him my mother's cousin, Pres—that's short for Prescott—was a deputy sheriff in Kaufman county—that's where New Eden is—and he'd been in on the entire investigation. They don't have all that many murders in Kaufman County, and I told Mr. Tunderew that Pres kept a huge scrapbook of all his cases. Mr. Tunderew asked if I'd seen what it had about the New Eden murder, but I hadn't."

Now it was I who was doing the close watching. "And did you and Mr. Tunderew develop any kind of personal friendship about that same time?" I asked, and saw her look quickly at the floor and blush. Then embarrassment was replaced, again, by anger.

"I thought we did, yes," she said. "But he was only using me, of course."

"How so?" I asked, though I was pretty sure I could guess.

"When I first began working with him," she said, drawing in a long breath and again squaring her shoulders, "I thought he was rather aloof. But I think talking about the New Eden murder sort of broke the ice between us. He really became quite friendly; always complimenting me, smiling…flirting, actually. I knew he was married, but he is…was…a very handsome man. As we got to know each other better, he told me in confidence that his marriage was coming to an end."

"Which led you to believe…" I started to say, but she merely blushed again and cast her eyes to the floor, nodding.

"And what made you change your mind about him?" I asked after a moment.

Her eyes rose to meet mine.

"He lied to me," she said simply.

Gee, imagine that! I thought.

"What happened?" I asked.

She ran her hand lightly across the side of her head to push a lock of hair back into place behind her ear, then continued. "He kept asking me about the New Eden thing, and how close I was to my mother's cousin, and when I told him we were fairly close, he wondered if I'd ever seen his scrapbook. I told him that it was Pres' pride and joy, and that he'd show it to almost anybody who stopped by."

She gave a huge sigh and shook her head. "I was so *stupid!* Just a few days later, Mr. Tunderew..." she paused, then looked at me with an expression that was equal parts bemusement and disdain. "Do you know I never once called him 'Tony'? Even after..."

"Did you socialize outside of work?" I asked, not wanting to force her to go somewhere she didn't care to go at the moment.

She shook her head firmly. "I'm getting to that," she said, "but no. Not until...well, he said his wife was insanely jealous and kept constant tabs on him, and that, while he wanted very badly to take me to dinner to show his appreciation for my help, he just couldn't do it. He seemed very sincere. Anyway, just a few days later—August 8th to be exact—he told me that the company was sending him to the Dallas New Eden to have a talk with Mr. and Mrs. Dinsmore about the project, and that he would like for me to come along to help him. I thought that was very odd, since the Dinsmores are living at the local New Eden now. He said the Dinsmores would be at the Dallas New Eden for a week or two—they maintain a home at all of the New Edens, I understand—and that it was some sort of urgent meeting and no one was supposed to know about it, so I wasn't to tell anyone."

She obviously read the expression on my face, and sighed. "Yes," she said, "*stupid* is the word you're looking for. There was no reason at all why he'd need me to go along on a business trip with him but, well, I'm only human and he *was* a very handsome man. He said it would give me a chance to spend some time with Pres and his family while he was meeting with the Dinsmores Saturday afternoon, the 12th of August, and then Saturday night I could help him with his notes, and we'd come back Sunday. I don't know what I was expecting or hoping for, but...well, I agreed."

She was quiet a moment, lost in thought, then continued: "So we took an early flight to Dallas on Saturday morning and got there around noon. We rented a car and drove right to Kaufman, which is only about 20 or so miles away. I'd called Pres to let him know I was coming, and when we got to Kaufman, Mr. Tunderew…isn't it silly of me not to be able to call him Tony?…said he had some time to kill before his meeting at New Eden, and I naturally invited him to come in and meet Pres and his family."

She sighed and shook her head slowly. "Which is exactly what he'd intended all along, I realize now. We weren't in the house more than five minutes than he was asking Pres about the New Eden murder—that's what folks around Kaufman still call it—and Pres had his scrapbook out. They sat there at the dining room table for a good hour going over it, with Mr. Tunderew asking all sorts of questions, until I reminded him about his appointment with the Dinsmores. He looked almost surprised, and said he'd better get going."

So it's possible Tunderew had met the Dinsmores! Why hadn't Jeffrey Dinsmore mentioned that? I wondered. Then it occurred to me that it was equally likely that the whole "meeting with the Dinsmores" story was a setup—that Tunderew had just used it as an excuse to find out more about the murder—and probably add Judith Francini to his list of conquests.

Well, one of my mind voices said just a little impatiently, *maybe you should just stop thinking and let her finish her story.*

Obviously, she'd noticed that I had wandered off, and had stopped talking.

"Excuse me," I said, lamely. "I was just making some mental notes. So Tunderew went off to the meeting. How long was he gone?"

She pursed her lips in thought, then said: "Not all that long, now that I think of it. He was back within an hour and a half. Jody, Pres' wife, asked if we'd like to stay for dinner, but Mr. Tunderew said we really should be getting back to Dallas. He said he'd called the hotel to confirm our reservations and was told there had been some mix up due to a convention at the hotel, and our rooms weren't available so we'd have to find another. Our flight back was for at 9:17 Sunday morning and he wanted to stay somewhere near the airport."

She gave a deep sigh, shaking her head. "How could I have been so incredibly *stupid?*" she asked. "How could I not have seen him for the…well, please excuse my language, but…for the *bastard* he was? And then for me to find out he was…well…"

Before I let her head off in the direction my gut told me she was going, I wanted to finish up the Dallas trip first.

"So what happened when you got back to Dallas?" I asked, interrupting her from changing to what I suspected was a totally different subject.

She readjusted her posture yet again and paused to gather herself together.

"He'd told me he'd booked rooms at the Sheraton," she continued, "and then came up with that pathetic 'overbooked' excuse. We ended up at some third-rate motel directly under the incoming flight path. It didn't even have a restaurant! But there was a roadhouse next door, and as soon as we checked in I asked Mr. Tunderew when he wanted to start on whatever it was he had brought me along to help him with. He suggested we first have an early dinner at the roadhouse, and I agreed. *Stupid, stupid, stupid!*"

To save her having to go into too much detail of what I was pretty sure happened next, I said: "So the 'early dinner' turned out to be a little more than dinner," I said.

She shook her head. "He suggested we have a cocktail first. He was so attentive. I know now he manipulated my ego like it was a balloon and he certainly had more than enough hot air to fill it. One cocktail led to another, one compliment led to another, and one thing led to another and…well, you know."

I knew.

Another long sigh, then: "We never did get any work done. I'm sure he never intended that we would. But he got what he wanted. We got back from Dallas on Sunday, and Monday at noon they called me in to Personnel and told them that my assignment was over. I was supposed to be there another two weeks. I asked them if anything were wrong, and they said no, that Mr. Tunderew had completed his project early and no longer needed me, and that I didn't even have to finish out the day. I went back to his office to pick up my things and to ask him what was going on, but he had conveniently left for lunch. I never saw him again."

Jeezus, what a total lowlife!

I knew there was something more to all this, and I hadn't lost track of where she had started to go earlier when she mentioned "finding out" something. Now seemed like a good time to switch to that track.

"Do you remember a young man named Larry Fletcher from Craylaw and Collier?" I asked.

Her reaction was exactly as if someone had snuck up behind her and yelled "Boo!" I could swear her whole body twitched for a second there. Her expression hardened, and her eyes narrowed.

"Yes. He was how I found out…" She lapsed into silence.

"Did Larry Fletcher tell you Tunderew was gay?" I asked.

She looked alternately uncomfortable and suspicious. I deliberately remained quiet until finally she said: "Not in so many words. I told you I am good with numbers, and it doesn't take much to put two and two together. Larry was always around. Everyone in the office knew he was…gay, and it was plain as day that he had a huge crush on Mr. Tunderew. Mr. Tunderew would always make nasty comments about him when he wasn't around, but every time he came in to Mr. Tunderew's office where no one else was around but me, Mr. Tunderew was all smiles. Twice I saw them together in the parking lot first thing in the morning as I was coming in to work, and I sensed something was going on between them, but I didn't *know* at first, if that makes any sense."

Oddly, it did.

"And when did you know for sure…if you ever did," I asked.

"Well, I never saw them…*doing* anything, if that's what you mean. And I didn't put it all together until…well, as I was leaving the office with my things that day I was let go, I ran into Larry in the hall. We rode down to the lobby together in the elevator. I didn't tell him I'd just been let go. Larry said he was just on his way to do some errands for 'Tony', as he called him, though it was always 'Mr. Tunderew' in the office. I commented that he seemed particularly happy, and he took a check out of his shirt pocket and showed it to me. It was one of Mr. Tunderew's checks—Number 2501—in the amount of $375. He told me that 'Tony' had given it to him—a deposit on his new apartment."

So she had seen and remembered the check number and the amount, had put two and two together, and come up with six.

"Is that when you decided to blackmail Tunderew?" I asked, casually.

Chapter 13

Her face went ashen, then flushed. "I...I don't know what you're talking about," she stammered, but she wasn't a very good liar.

"That's okay," I said. "As I said earlier, with Tunderew dead it doesn't really matter much now. I was just curious."

"He *used* me!" she said. "And then he had me fired the very next day! And then that very same day he gives his *boyfriend* a check for $375! He might as well have slapped me in the face! I tried to put it all behind me, to forget he even existed. And then all of a sudden he's a famous author, and it all came back to me! There has to be some justice in the world! People can't just go around using people and then throwing them away!"

"Well," I said, "I think you can consider the debt paid now."

We sat silently for a moment or two while she once again gathered herself together. When she at last looked up at me, I said: "Oh, and I'm curious about one more thing. You said you saw Tunderew and Larry Fletcher in the parking lot. What kind of car do you drive?"

Her expression was blank. "I don't," she said. "I've never driven. The bus stop is right by the parking lot, and I'd cut across to get to work."

Ah, well, my mind sighed, *scratch another murder suspect.*

I'm sure we both would have felt very awkward if, after our conversation, I'd ask her to get back to work, though she volunteered to do so. I told her that she should just take the rest of the day—and the next day, since I'd more or less committed to two—off, and that I'd give her a glowing recommendation. She gave me her time sheet and I wrote in two days' worth of hours, signed it, took my copy, and thanked her for coming. And that was it.

* * *

Okay. Case over. I was hired to deal with Tunderew's blackmailer— though he was of course totally wrong about who the blackmailer was. I dealt with Tunderew's blackmailer. That's it. End of story.

Sigh.

If Tunderew hadn't been such a homophobe, he might have at least told me about Judith Francini and why she might possibly be considered a suspect. Granted, she hadn't signed a confession and had it notarized, but I was satisfied. Other than my retainer, I hadn't been paid one cent, of course.

Partly satisfied.

That *still* left me with having to find out who had killed the bastard so I could know who had been responsible for Randy's death. I knew now it almost certainly wasn't Judith Francini—she didn't have a car and didn't drive. There was still Catherine Tunderew and the Bernadines, of course. But why did my mind keep going back to the Dinsmores? Probably because neither Catherine Tunderew nor the Bernadines had at least two unsolved murders and one unexplained disappearance already skulking around in the shadows. And I'd followed the ex-Mrs. Tunderew and the Bernadines about as far as I could at the moment. The Dinsmores were another story. There was still an awful lot I didn't know.

The first thing I wanted to double check was whether Tunderew had indeed ever met with the Dinsmores during his trip to Dallas with Judith Francini, or if it was, as I suspected, just a ruse to find out more about Mike Barber's murder and put another notch in his bedpost at the same time.

I picked up the phone and dialed New Eden. Of course they wouldn't put me directly through to Jeffrey Dinsmore, but I left a message saying I had a question about "Mr. Barber." I suspected that would get his attention.

Sure enough, about ten minutes later, just as I was getting ready to run downstairs to the diner—and I'd been doing just that; taking the stairs six flights up and down rather than the elevator, ever since Jonathan made the near-fatal mistake of teasing me about my developing 'love handles'—the phone rang.

It was a very businesslike Jeffrey Dinsmore.

"Mr. Hardesty, I'm returning your call as a courtesy, since I am grateful to you for having brought this book matter to my attention. I have contacted our lawyers to look into it. If there is any truth to it, they have been instructed to take the strongest possible legal action to prevent its publication. However, I think this will have to be the end of our contacts. I've told you everything I can possibly tell you about…the incidents to which you referred…and I can't see what more you might need from me."

"I understand, Reverend, and it was never my intention to cause you any problems. But if you could just tell me whether you might remember having in fact met with Mr. Tunderew at the Dallas New Eden, while he was working for Craylaw & Collier."

There wasn't the slightest pause. "I told you I have never met Mr. Tunderew and had never even heard of the man until his book made the best seller list."

Damn! "This would have been on…" *Damn again! what date did Judith Francini say?* "…the 12th of August of last year. A Saturday."

"No," he said emphatically. "That would have been impossible. August 12th is my mother's birthday, and the family gathers in Atlanta every year to celebrate. Will that be all?"

"Uh, yes, I believe so," I said, knowing full well that ten seconds after we hung up I'd probably have 126 additional questions. "Thank you again for talking with me. And please be assured that everything we discussed earlier will go no further than the two of us."

"I'd appreciate that," he said.

And with that, we exchanged good-byes and hung up.

* * *

So it was pretty much what I'd suspected: the Dallas trip had just been Tunderew's excuse to see what he could find out about Mike Barber's murder from Judith Francini's second cousin, and to take the opportunity to boff Judith at the same time.

But regardless of what was going on at New Eden, I really had the impression that Jeffrey Dinsmore was telling the truth about not knowing who Tunderew was, other than the author of *Dirty Little Minds* . And if he really didn't know about   *No Door to Heaven*, what motive would he have had to kill Tunderew?

A deep rumble from my stomach put broke my train of thought, and I got up and headed for the stairs.

* * *

A phone message waiting when I returned to the office put the whole Tunderew matter on a back burner. It was a call from a prospective client who needed my services and, I had every reason to hope, would even   *pay* for them. I returned the call immediately, and set up an appointment for later the same afternoon.

Since we're mainly concerned with the Tunderew case here, I won't go into too much detail. Suffice it to say that the owner of a large furniture store in The Central believed he was being ripped off by one of his two-man delivery crews: a helper and a crew boss. The store had a policy of offering free delivery, which consisted of bringing the item into the customer's house, putting it where the customer wanted, and leaving. But if, as often happened, the customer decided that he/she thought, after having the furniture put where the crew was told, that it really would look better over there...or maybe over *there*, which could result in a lot of rearranging and a lot of extra time...the store's sales contract specified that an additional charge would apply. That was logical, since the delivery time schedules were tight; the more time wasted with each delivery, the fewer deliveries that could be made. If ten deliveries were scheduled, and only eight made, that would result in two unhappy customers.

The suspect crew was always behind schedule, and the owner believed it was because they were not reporting the "extra moves" and pocketing the money. Sounded pretty innocent, but as the owner pointed out, not only did the store lose money on the "extra moves" fee—as much, he estimated, as $400 a week—but lost money on the slower delivery schedule and unhappy customers.

He wanted to put the helper on a special in-warehouse project and hire me to work with the crew boss to see what was going on. He figured it shouldn't take more than three or four days: if the suspect offered to let me in on the deal, we'd have him dead to rights. And if he didn't and the delivery schedule picked up as a result, it would also be a good indication that the boss's suspicions had been right and the crew boss was just being cautious with a new man around.

I wasn't in a position to pass up the opportunity to actually be paid for a case, and I thought the exercise would do me good. Tunderew and Randy were already dead; there wasn't anything I might do on that matter that couldn't be put off a few days.

I took the job.

* * *

I showed up at the store Wednesday morning at 7:30, met my "crew boss"—a guy named Fred, who had a body to die for and a face that could stop a clock. I really don't like to make that kind of judgment of other people's looks. We all have to live with what nature gave us, but let's just say he was most definitely not *my* type—whatever that might be.

By Wednesday night, my ass was dragging. Hauling sleeper sofas up three flights of stairs ain't a stroll in the park. The day had gone without a hitch. One elderly lesbian (I gathered her sexual orientation by the fact that she lived in a residential section of The Central, and by the number of photographs around the apartment—all of women) did ask if we could move a couple of pieces of heavy furniture to make her new love seats fit in, and wrote a check to the store for the extra time involved.

At the end of the day, as we were heading back to the store after our last delivery, I told Fred I thought moving furniture all day was a hell of a lot more work than we were getting paid for. He just grunted and nodded (Fred was the strong, silent type. Not unfriendly, just quiet.)

* * *

I made a point of stopping by the office after I got off work at the store to check for messages. I definitely took the elevator up and back. There were a few calls, but nothing that needed immediate responses, so I headed home.

Jonathan had obviously guessed that I'd had a pretty rough day, physically, and when I walked into the apartment I saw his large book bag on the floor next to the sofa. He suggested that before we have dinner we might play a game of The Overworked Private Eye and the *Very* Professional Masseur. We hadn't played that one before, but it sounded like exactly what I needed. As always, Jonathan was able to immerse himself totally and instantly into his "character," who told me his name was Lance and asked which of three types of massage I would prefer: basic muscle relaxer, full body massage, or 'the works.' I told him I thought I'd go for 'the works.' A couple of weeks earlier, he had picked up small gift box of Exotic Body Oils at the place we got our hair cut. I'd asked him at the time what he thought we were going to do with it, and he just shrugged. "They smell nice," he said.

"Lance" asked if I would prefer the sofa, the floor, or the bed for the massage, and I opted for the bed. I showed him where the bedroom was (I was getting pretty good at this games thing, too) and he picked up his book bag and followed me. Once inside the bedroom, he instructed me to strip down to my shorts while he opened his book bag and took out a clean white sheet, which he very carefully spread across the top of the comforter. While I was finishing undressing, pretty much into the mood of the game by now, he dug back into the book bag and took out three small bottles that I recognized as having come from the Exotic Body Oils kit. When I was stripped to my shorts, he instructed me to stretch out face down on the bed, which felt *very* good, and just relax a minute. I had my head turned away from him so I couldn't tell what he was doing. When I turned to look I saw that he'd also gotten totally undressed except for a very skimpy bathing suit he'd insisted on buying despite my telling him I'd never let him wear on any beach. I reached out to touch him, but he gently slapped my hand away.

"Behave," he said. He then announced that I had my choice of Coconut, Musk, or Sandalwood oil.

"Surprise me," I said.

He smiled his Lance persona smile and said: "Oh, I intend to."

He opened one of the bottles, poured a dab into one palm and rubbed his hands together briskly. I could smell the Sandalwood.

"Just close your eyes and relax," he said, and I did (well, most of me did), though one of my mind voices, which I recognized immediately as my crotch, observed that Jonathan made a very attractive "Lance." A moment later I felt him climb onto the bed and straddle me, then the drip of oil at the base of my neck. Next, he put his hands on either side of the base of my neck at the shoulders and began gently rubbing the oil in, kneading the muscles, moving his hands slowly outward and back. It felt fantastic. After a few minutes of that, and despite my growing enthusiasm for the game, I almost fell asleep. After working down to just below my armpits, he moved his hands to put the heels of his palms on either side of my spine, just below the shoulders, fingers splayed wide. He pushed down quickly three times in rapid succession, hard enough to make me grunt with each push, then with his full hand moved slowly outward from the spine to beneath my armpits, alternately pushing down to stretch the skin away from the spine, and kneading strongly. When his fingers had almost circled around my side to my chest, he released, then started the same motions again, a little lower on the spine. He repeated these movements, alternating with a strong, cupped palms upward pushing, all the way to the small of my back. From time to time I could feel a few drops of oil being poured directly on my skin.

"Lance, you're hired!" I muttered, eyes closed.

I felt him scoot down on the bed until he was at my feet, and he began massaging my ankles, thighs, and calves. When he reached my butt, he said: "Lift your ass." I did and felt him sliding my shorts off.

"We don't want to get oil on your shorts," he said in a

professional tone. Then the strong kneading continued.

"Roll over," he said, and I did.

"Well, well," he said: "What have we here?"

Without waiting for an answer, he moved quickly back down to my feet, concentrating on massaging the inside of my ankles, then slowly up the front of my legs to my waist.

Ignoring the obstacle, he worked around it without touching it, up my stomach and chest to my shoulders and the base of my neck. He rocked slowly forward to kiss me, and while he was raised up, pulled his bathing suit down. Pouring more oil onto his hand, he reached behind him, then settled himself backwards, slowly...

Have I mentioned that games can be *really* fun?

* * *

Thursday was pretty much a repeat of Wednesday, though most of the deliveries were either to the ground floor of houses or in buildings with freight elevators. Two customers asked for "extra" help: one to move a bed from one bedroom to another, another to take an old recliner out to the curb. Again both times the customer paid—one with a check, one with cash. Fred put both into his shirt pocket. I was wondering, as we went through the day, how the store owner figured he was losing so much money on pocketed "extras". We'd only done three extras in two days, and only one of those was in cash.

Once again, toward the end of the day, I observed to Fred that we didn't get paid nearly enough for the amount of work we had to do. Fred reached in his shirt pocket and took out a $10 bill: I assumed it came from the cash the customer had given him. "Here," he said. "Consider it a bonus."

"Great!" I said. "Thanks."

I realized that was probably all the evidence I or the store owner needed, but figured I'd go another day to see if anything further developed.

* * *

* * *

Thursday was Jonathan's class night, so I decided to just relax—no time before class for another episode with Lance, unfortunately. When Jonathan went off to school, I did the dishes, half-heartedly watched a little TV, and caught up on the newspapers I'd not had a chance to look at for the past couple of days. The Wednesday edition always carried a few pages of local religious news, which I usually managed to skip over without even slowing down. However, something caught my eye just as I was turning the page to more important stuff like the comics: the name "Dinsmore". I turned back to it, and saw the heading: 'Dinsmore to Receive C.M.L.A. Honors'. I hadn't a clue what the C.M.L.A. might be, but decided to find out.

Reverend Jeffrey Dinsmore will be honored by the Christian Men's Leadership Association on the 27th of this month at a ceremony following the annual week-long C.M.L.A. retreat in Holy Hill, Arkansas. Reverend Dinsmore, a leader of the Eternal Light Foundation and the founder of New Eden Farms, will receive the Good Works for Glory Humanitarian Award for his tireless devotion to…

Interesting. That meant that Jeffrey would probably be out of town the next week, and since it was a Christian Men's retreat, it was unlikely that the Reverend Mrs. Dinsmore would be going with him. All I had to do now was figure out a way to get to see her in person. And after that, maybe her brother? Though definitely not at the same time. It was unlikely that either of them would know any more than Jeffrey knew, but it would help verify that his protestations of knowing nothing about the book were legitimate. And if they were…well, I'd think about that when the time came.

But, my mind said, ignoring my decision to let it rest, *if Dinsmore didn't know or suspect that he and New Eden were the subject of Tunderew's new book, he wouldn't have had any reason to kill him.* In that case, I'd not only be back to square one but facing two totally separate cases: the New Eden murders, and Tunderew's—and again by extension, Randy's— murder. Also in that case, the New Eden murders were totally and completely none of my business. That's what the police are for. I sure as hell can't afford—literally—to get involved in every murder, suspicious death, and disappearance in the world. I'm good, but I'm not *that* good! If Dinsmore wasn't involved in Tunderew's murder, I'd just have to let the whole New Eden thing drop and get on with my life.

Uh huh.

* * *

Our first delivery on Friday morning was a dining room set that King Arthur might have fancied—a huge solid oak table with four leaves and eight gigantic chairs, an eight-foot high hutch and a nine-foot long credenza. The house was in the Briarwood area, not far from the Birchwood Country Club. Fred asked the boss to give us another helper, but was told no one else was available and we'd have to manage ourselves.

The house was brand new, one of four side-by-side mansions in various stages of construction. Each one of them would have been beautiful if set in the middle of two or three acres of lawn, but all four of them were crammed nearly cheek-to-jowl on what appeared to be the equivalent of two city lots. Landscapers were busily working on the minuscule front lawn and, huge as the houses were, there couldn't have been more than eight feet between them.

The customer turned out to be one of those piss-elegant snobs I always want to punch out just on general principles. Tall, thin, with a habit of sucking in his cheeks and pursing his lips when anything displeased him—which apparently nearly everything did. He did deign to open both the double entrance doors and watched us like hawks, advising us pointedly to wipe our feet carefully before entering.

He did, I noticed, take a particular interest in Fred, who was wearing a form-fitting tee shirt.

The dining room was larger than most people's living rooms, but by the time we'd brought all the pieces of the dining room set in, the challenge of where to put everything was obvious. We had set everything in its logical place as we brought it in, but of course that did not suit the customer. He began to direct us to move this piece here; to turn the table crossways; to try the hutch over there. Fred pointed out to the customer that the delivery of the furniture was free, but that we were on a very tight schedule and didn't really have the time to…

"Well, I'll *pay* you, of course," the customer huffed. He exchanged a long look with Fred and then actually smiled, his eyes moving slowly and deliberately over Fred's impressive torso. "Cash," he added.

We spent the next forty-five minutes courting a hernia moving things here, then there, then over there, then…

When we were finally through, the customer handed each of us a $50 bill, being sure he pressed Fred's slowly into his hand. As we left and were headed down the walk, the customer called Fred over for a few words I could not overhear. But I didn't think I really had to.

Back in the truck, I handed Fred my $50 and said: "Here, you can give this to the boss."

He looked at me and laughed. "Are you nuts?" he said. "We worked our butts off for that money. It's ours."

"But we're forty-five minutes behind schedule," I said. "The boss…"

"We had a flat tire," Fred said.

Good bye, Fred.

* * *

Though I ached in muscles I didn't know I had, and there was again no time when I got home to call on Lance's expert services, we managed to make it to Napoleon by 7:40. Surprisingly, Jared was already there, sitting at the small bar in what had been the living room of a private home before it converted to a restaurant. We exchanged greetings and hugs, then ordered our drinks and moved over to a small circle of chairs in front of the fireplace.

"I thought you and Jake would be coming in together," I said when we sat down.

Jared took a sip from his drink and shook his head. "He called just before I left Carrington to say he'd be running late," he said. "I told him I'd just meet him here."

"So, uh, how's it going with you two?" I asked, once again striding boldly into It's-None-of-Your-Damned-Business-Hardesty territory.

"Really great," he said. "I've never had a…'steady?'…before. I don't usually see a guy more than a couple of times." He suddenly glanced up at me. "I mean…" his eyes went to Jonathan, who just gave him a knowing smile "…well, you know."

While we'd never directly talked about it, I knew that Jonathan was well aware that Jared and I had been…uh, sexually active…for quite a while before I met Jonathan, so we all knew what he meant. Jared and I were always friends first and sex partners on the side. No emotional involvement beyond that. That's why I was curious about his relationship with Jake, which seemed to go quite a way beyond where I'd ever known him to go.

"I'm glad you're with Jake," Jonathan volunteered. "Everybody should have a lover."

Jared smiled at him. "Well, I'm not sure about that," he said. "Neither Jake nor I is exactly what you'd call the monogamous type. Besides, he's got his business down here, and I'm up in Carrington, and, well, like I say, we both like playing the field a little too much. When we're together, we're together. And we make a great team when it comes to picking up three- and four-ways."

He noticed Jonathan's look of incomprehension and reached out and put one large hand on Jonathan's shoulder. "But who knows? Maybe some day," he said, grinning.

"But you do really like him, right?" Jonathan asked.

Jared looked at Jonathan and smiled again. "Yeah," he said. "I really like him."

Apparently satisfied, Jonathan looked at me, then sat back in his chair. "Good," he said.

* * *

Jake didn't arrive until about ten after eight.

"Sorry, guys," he said as we exchanged greetings. I noticed that as usual, while we all stood up and Jonathan and I exchanged hugs with Jake, Jared and he went into some sort of clinch that looked a little more like a strangle hold than a hug. The hug was there in the eyes, though.

"Do you want to order a drink first?" Jared suggested.

"Is our table ready?" Jake asked.

"Yeah, but we can wait a bit," Jared said.

Jake shook his head. "Nah, I'll order at the table."

We moved into the dining room, Jake and Jared leading the way, and I noticed again what a great pair they made, physically. Same Tom of Finland build, same height; Jared as dark as Jake was light. I felt Jonathan's elbow poke me in the ribs. Startled, I glanced at him to see him grinning at me. "Don't drool," he said.

Dinner was, as always, great. Napoleon was definitely at the top of our favorite restaurants.

And of course, me being me, I had to try to pump Jake (*Oh, now there's a thought,* my crotch said eagerly) for more information on New Eden; especially after he mentioned the reason he was late was because of a project his construction company was doing for them.

"Still not much direct contact with the Dinsmores?" I asked as the waiter came to take away our salad plates. (Hey, I held out that long!)

Jake wiped the corner of his mouth with his napkin and put it back in his lap before shaking his head. "Not much. I see them from time to time, of course, but I still deal mainly with Mel Hooper. He pretty much runs the place on a day to day basis. I hear they're considering starting another New Eden in the San Francisco Bay area. That'll mean Mel will be going out there to manage it. But they haven't started to train a replacement for him, yet, so I guess it's still a way off."

"He a nice guy?" I asked.

Jake nodded and took a sip of his water. "Nice enough, I guess. Not exactly overly friendly. Pretty businesslike, no-nonsense kind of guy. Not much joking around. All the residents really respect him, as they'd damned well better."

"You said he's pretty protective of his sister," I said.

Jake raised his eyebrows and gave one very emphatic nod of his head. "*Oh* yeah!" he said. "Of course he keeps a close eye on all the residents. There are more guys there than women, but he doesn't allow anybody to get out of hand. No intramural screwing around on *his* watch. Separate dorms and *no* unauthorized intermingling."

"How do you think Mel would react if he found out Jeffrey was screwing around on his sister."

He nodded at the waiter, who just put his steak in front of him, then looked at me, surprised. "Is he?" he asked. "You mean you think the rumors aren't just rumors? Interesting."

"Randy was having sex with him," Jonathan volunteered, then looked at me quickly as if he'd said something he shouldn't.

"And I'm pretty sure Randy wasn't the only one," I said by way of reassuring Jonathan he hadn't been out of line.

"Well, well, well," Jake said. "As I think I said last time we talked about this, I think old Jeffy boy had better make damned sure Mel doesn't find out."

"Would you by any chance know if the Dinsmores are going to be around next week? I really need to talk to Mrs. Dinsmore without Jeffrey being around, and I'd like to meet Mel Hooper as well."

The waiter had put the last of the entrees on the table by this time, and Jake was picking up his steak knife as he said: "Jeff's going to some retreat all next week, I understand. Leaving tomorrow night, as I recall. As far as I know, Mrs. Dinsmore won't be going anywhere. And Mel never leaves the place."

I decided I'd better drop the whole New Eden subject before they all decided I should get a real life.

* * *

After dinner Jonathan suggested that we stop by either Glitter or Steamroller Junction. I knew he wanted to go dancing and I, again, felt really guilty for being such a total klutz about refusing to get out there and at least *try* to dance. But after having seen Jonathan dance—my gut ached just watching him, he was so good—I could never bring myself to do it. I'd mentioned it to Jared one night on the phone while Jonathan was in class, and he said he understood, though I'd seen him out there on the floor a couple of times and he definitely did all right for himself.

Jared diplomatically came to my rescue by suggesting that since both Glitter and Steamroller Junction tended to be both jammed and, with the wrong DJ, induced bleeding from the ear drums, we might compromise and go to Venture, which had just expanded into the building next door and put in a dance floor.

"Hey," he said, putting one large hand on Jonathan's shoulder while lowering his voice about half an octave and flexing his considerable arsenal of muscles, "if your old man won't do right by you, I will."

"And when Jared gets tired out, I can take over," Jake said.

Sexual fantasies, anyone?

* * *

It was a great night, and I managed to pretty much overlook my aching muscles. And when we got home, Lance put in an appearance and relieved a number of aches.

Sunday we met Jared, Jake, Phil, and Tim for brunch and before I knew it, it was Monday morning. I hate it when it does that.

After my coffee/paper/crossword puzzle ritual, I made out a formal report for the furniture store owner and enclosed my bill. I normally would have waited on sending the bill until the first of the month, but my bank account was beginning to look a little more anemic than usual, and even a small infusion of cash would be welcome.

I realized—after I'd emptied the waste paper basket, dumped the contents of my top desk drawer onto the top of the desk to rummage through it, tested the 32 pens I'd found there and pitched the 28 that refused to write after even the most furious scribbling, and was in the process of sharpening the two inch stub of a pencil—that I just might be procrastinating on calling New Eden and trying to arrange an appointment with Barbara Dinsmore. She'd seen me with Randy the day we went to pick up his sneakers; she might well assume that I knew about her husband's little dalliances with the male office help and wanted to exploit it. Well, I did want to know more about how she was dealing with that fact, of course, but again I was juggling two completely separate issues. The New Eden murders were one thing, Tunderew's murder…well, maybe they weren't quite that separate, but I was mainly concerned at the moment with how much the Reverend Mrs. Dinsmore might know about *No Door to Heaven* and its subject matter.

Only one way to find out. I opened the now empty top drawer of my desk and scooped everything back into it, then slid it closed and reached for the phone.

"New Eden," the female voice answered. Whether it was the same female voice as the last time I'd called I couldn't remember.

"May I speak with Mrs. Dinsmore, please?" I asked, knowing full well that the answer would be no, I may not.

"May I ask who's calling?"

"My name is Hardesty. Dick Hardesty." I said, trying to sound as pleasantly casual as possible.

There was the briefest of pauses, then: "And may I ask what this is regarding?"

Both feet, Hardesty, I thought. "Randy Jacobs," I said. "A former New Eden resident."

"One moment, please," she said. That caught me by surprise: I was sure she'd tell me Mrs. Dinsmore was not available but that she'd leave word that I'd called.

I was even more surprised when there was a click of phones being transferred and then another female voice: "This is Barbara Dinsmore. What can I do for you, Mr. Hardesty?"

Damn! I definitely wasn't expecting to actually *talk* to her right away. Well, onward and upward.

"Thank you for taking my call, Mrs. Dinsmore. We met once, some time ago…"

"When you came to pick up Randy Jacobs' sneakers. I

remember," she said.

"Then I assume you know that Randy is dead."

There was a very pregnant pause, and then: "No. No, I wasn't aware of that. I'm sorry to hear it. How did he die?"

Her voice remained calm, but I could sense...what?... surprise?...underneath.

"He was in the car with Tony Tunderew when he died," I said. "I'm sure you heard of the accident."

"Yes, yes of course. He was that...author. I knew someone else had been killed in the accident, but I had no idea it was Randy Jacobs. I really don't know what to say."

"Were you aware that New Eden was to be the subject of Mr. Tunderew's next book?"

"My husband told me he had heard a rumor that we were possibly the target of a muckraking book, and we agreed to have our lawyers look into it, but he did not mention Mr. Tunderew. Are you saying the rumor is true?"

"I'm afraid so," I said, "and I was wondering if it would be possible for us to meet in person to discuss it."

There was no pause this time. "I don't think that would be possible without having my husband and our attorneys present."

"I understand," I said. From what she'd said I didn't know if she had figured out that I was the one who'd told her husband, but if she wasn't, I'd just as soon she didn't know I'd already talked to him. "But it's been my experience that talking to one individual at a time is more productive, because frequently each person has a slightly different perspective and is aware of some small details the others are not. These tend to get lost in a group setting. And it is easier to address certain subjects on a one-to-one basis."

There was no mistaking the suspicion in her voice when she said: "Exactly what is it you are investigating, Mr. Hardesty, and for whom are you working?"

"I'm not working for anyone, Mrs. Dinsmore," I said honestly. "Randy Jacobs was a good friend of...a friend of mine..." I wanted to hold off the entire gay aspect of the case as long as possible, lest she go jumping to the wrong conclusion and think

I was considering blackmail for her husband's dalliance with Randy. "…and I am looking into the cause of his death."

"Didn't you just say he died in a car crash?" she asked. "Are you implying something more is involved?"

"It's all really very complicated, Mrs. Dinsmore," I said, "which is why I would really appreciate it if we could talk privately in person. I assure you I have no ulterior motives against you, your husband, New Eden, or the Eternal Light Foundation. I merely have some questions which really need answers."

Another pause, then: "I really don't know what I can tell you, Mr. Hardesty, but…are you sure we are the targets of this new book?"

"I'm quite sure," I verified.

She took another moment to think that one over, then said: "I know of Mr. Tunderew only by reputation, and from what little I know I find him reprehensible. On what basis he might possibly have singled out us and our organization I cannot imagine." Another pause, then: "I have a solid slate of engagements this afternoon, but if you'd care to come out around 11 this morning, we might talk for a few minutes."

"I'd really appreciate that, Mrs. Dinsmore. Thank you. I'll see you at eleven."

"Very well," she said. "Goodbye."

And we hung up.

I was just getting ready to leave the office when the phone rang.

One ring. Two rings. "Hardesty Investigations."

"Dick: Marty. I've got some news you're probably not going to want to hear."

I was pretty sure he was right, but said: "Such as?"

"Remember that missing kid I told you about? Denny Rechter, the one who had been at the local New Eden?"

I knew what was coming next. "Yeah?" I said.

"We found him. In a culvert off a dirt road just north of Pritchert Park."

Damn!

Chapter 14

It was exactly what I had thought he was going to say, but it still hit me harder than I might have expected.

"How long had he been there?" I asked

"Hard to say, but they figure anywhere from eight to ten months."

"They can't pinpoint it any closer than that?" I asked, puzzled.

"There's an artesian spring just upstream of the culvert," Marty said, "and the water's pretty cold. It could have slowed decomposition considerably. They found his billfold with some I.D. inside, but they'll be comparing dental records just to make sure. Not much doubt, though. The odd thing is the body was within clear sight of a popular walking trail. I think whoever put him there wanted him to be found. Ironically, though, the trail was closed when a guy who bought a piece of property the trail passed through put up a barrier to keep people from using it."

I heard myself sigh. "Thanks, Marty," I said. "Keep me posted if you find out anything else, would you?"

"Sure," he said.

* * *

I drove past New Eden's main gate at 10:45—driving past because of course I was fifteen minutes early and it was less than a two minute drive from the gate to the main house—and proceeded down the road, checking the place out. A white wooden fence apparently surrounded the entire property, and I noticed large tracts of neatly tended gardens of some sort or other, obviously vegetables, alternating with sections of endless rows of various flowers, some of which were in brilliant bloom. In the distance behind the flower beds were several large buildings that I assumed to be greenhouses. I knew New Eden supplied florists throughout the state, and that flowers were a large part of New Eden's economic base. I came to a crossroad and noted that the white fence continued on the other side; it paralleled each side of the side road as far as I could see. Behind the fence on the other side of the road appeared to be pasture, and I could see cattle (I took a wild guess they were cows) standing under a clump of trees near a pond.

I had no idea how much further the white fencing went, but I was dutifully impressed with what I'd seen. I was driving pretty slowly, taking everything in, and not paying much attention to the road behind me. So I was a little startled when a large red pickup passed me, three men in the passenger compartment, one in the truck bed; the front 3/4 of the truck bed was stacked high with wooden crates marked "New Eden Farms." As it pulled ahead of me, I noticed that while the tailgate was up, there was some sort of box-like platform extending out maybe two feet from the rear of the truck. It took me a minute to figure out what it might be for, then I realized that it was probably a work platform for the farm workers to stand on while filling the truck. A lot more sturdy than trying to stand on the tailgate, I'd imagine.

I followed the pickup to the next crossroad, where it turned right onto a dirt road. I slowed as I approached the crossroad and made a u-turn, heading back toward the main gate.

It was twelve after as I pulled up the long driveway and parked beside the house. I walked to the front door and rang the bell. A moment or two later, the door opened.

"Mr. Hardesty," Barbara Dinsmore said, extending her hand. "It's nice to see you again."

"I do appreciate your seeing me," I said as we exchanged a very quick handshake.

She stood back, holding the door open. "Please, come in," she said, and I did. "I thought we might talk in the study."

She led the way through the comfortable-looking living room, which was furnished tastefully but certainly not ostentatiously, to an equally comfortable-looking room at the far side of the house from the parking area. There was a really nice desk of a wood I couldn't determine, flanked by two small floral-patterned armchairs facing one another in front of the desk. A large bookcase stood against one wall beside a smaller writing desk. There was a cross on the wall above the desk. Mrs. Dinsmore herself was wearing a nice looking full-skirted dress with a very subtle floral design. Though it was still morning, she wore a small strand of black pearls and small black pearl earrings. Her understated makeup and hair were—from my decidedly non-expert point of view—flawless.

She motioned me to one of the armchairs and moved to close an open door in the wall toward the rear of the house. Without trying to be obvious about looking, I noticed a young woman standing beside an open file cabinet in the next room, and assumed that must be the residence office. I waited until Mrs. Dinsmore came back to the chairs, and sat down when she did.

"Now tell me what this is all about," she said.

I leaned forward slightly in my chair. "You used the word 'reprehensible' in referring to Tony Tunderew," I began, "and I'm afraid that is something of an understatement. I have reason to believe his death was no accident." Reading her thoughts clearly in her face, I hastened to add (shading the truth more than a tad): "I have no reason to believe anyone at New Eden was in any way involved—he seemed to have a magic knack for collecting people who had every reason to wish him harm—but the fact that New Eden is the subject of his new book raises a number of questions that might help me narrow down who might have been responsible for his death."

I didn't know if she bought that, but I wasn't about to stop and ask.

"Had you ever met Mr. Tunderew?" I continued.

She knit her brows and shook her head. "Never," she said. "I'm sure I'd remember if I had."

"He never tried to contact you directly?"

Again the head shake. "Never."

"And you had absolutely no idea that he was writing an expose of New Eden?"

She visibly stiffened in her chair. "Absolutely none," she said sharply, and there was frost on the edge of every word "...and I'm afraid I strongly resent your implication that there might be anything to 'expose' here!"

"Well," I said, knowing I probably shouldn't but unable to resist the temptation and wanting to see her reaction, "there is the matter of the murders."

She looked alternately stunned, puzzled, and angry. "What are…" she began, then stopped and took in a deep breath. "If you are referring to the tragic death of Michael Barber, you must know that it had nothing whatever to do directly with New Eden. My husband and I have prayed for Michael every single day since his death, and if there were anything at all we could have done to prevent it…"

She looked truly sad, and I could tell her eyes were misted.

But I couldn't stop now.

"Mike Barber, yes," I said. "But also Jim…James…Temple, and Denny Rechter."

She looked at me, uncomprehendingly. "Are you saying they are dead?" she asked. "*Murdered?*"

I nodded. "I'm afraid so," I said.

She sat in silence for a moment, as if trying to make sense out of what she'd just been told.

"But James Temple was from our Atlanta location…I remember him because he worked in the residence office there. If anything tragically happened to him, it surely had nothing to do with New Eden. He just left, as all our residents do eventually. There was nothing unusual about it. Surely if anything had happened to him, we'd have heard about it."

That was pretty much what her husband had said, and it was a logical assumption.

"His body wasn't discovered until fairly recently," I said.

She looked at me, as if still not quite comprehending. I say "as if" because I really couldn't tell if she was being sincere or faking it. I leaned toward sincerity, but had been fooled too many times in the past to buy it outright.

"And Denny Rechter?" she asked after a moment. "That's impossible. He left suddenly, it's true, but from what I understand from a policeman who called shortly after he left, Denny had run

away from home and his parents had heard he was at New Eden.
He apparently found out they were coming for him, and ran away
again. I wish this sort of thing didn't happen, but when you
consider the background of many of the young men and women
who come to us..."

Again a moment of silence, then: "Are you sure he's dead,
too? When? How?"

"I'm not sure of the details," I said. "I just found out about it
this morning."

She looked at me closely with just a hint of suspicion on her
face. "And exactly how did you come by all this information?" she
asked.

I shrugged. "Putting bits and pieces of information together
is what I do for a living," I said. "One bit of information leads to
another, which leads to another. And everything I have been able
to piece together seems to have two common denominators: Tony
T. Tunderew and New Eden."

She shook her head. "I'm sorry, Mr. Hardesty, but it simply
does not make sense. For you to tell me that three former
residents of New Eden have been murdered horrifies and saddens
me beyond words. But again you must remember what New Eden
is and who comes to us. These young people are society's rejects.
Some have run away from home, others have been thrown out of
their own families. Too many have been abused in ways that
sicken the soul to even contemplate. Many are drug abusers. New
Eden offers them safety, shelter, and stability—a chance to learn
and grow until they're ready to go back into the world. We don't
always succeed, I'm sorry to say, but we sincerely try."

I had to admit I was impressed. The look of sadness on her
face as she talked really got through to me.

We lapsed again into silence until she said: "Have you any
proof of a direct link between any of these three terrible deaths
and New Eden? There seems little connection. James Temple was
at our Atlanta location; Mike Barber from our Dallas facility;
Denny Rechter from here. But only one—Mike Barber—has a
direct link, that I can see. And that is only because he was
tragically murdered within hours of leaving New Eden. And each

of them was...well...lost even before they came to us. While we don't like to think of it, I'm afraid it is a fact that too many of our residents return to the world from which they'd come. That Mr. Tunderew might try to profit from this fact and from these sad deaths is beyond comprehension and beneath contempt. What other evidence do you have?"

I could see thin ice ahead and had to think a minute before proceeding. I really didn't want to directly address the sex issue on the chance that she really didn't know about her husband's dalliances other than the one she caught him at, with Randy. Destroying lives and marriages isn't something I do willingly. I decided I couldn't avoid the thin ice, but would try to step as carefully as possible.

"All three...four, if you include Randy...of the dead men worked in the residence office, isn't that correct?"

A brief look of...what?...shock?...realization?...crossed her face.

"Yes," she said, almost to herself. "Yes, they did."

"And they all had access to certain of New Eden's books and records, true?"

"Well, yes, but on a very limited basis. And we certainly have absolutely nothing to hide in any event. What are you saying?"

Good point: what *was* I saying? Ah, yes: "I have reason to suspect that perhaps Randy, at least, might have been trying to gather some sort of information on New Eden's operations to pass on to Mr. Tunderew for the purposes of his book."

I waited while her look of shock faded, and I took the opportunity to prepare to step out onto the thinnest of the ice. "How, may I ask, did Randy come to work in the residence office to begin with?" I watched her face carefully for her reaction.

"He volunteered, as I recall," she said. "When each new resident comes to us, either my husband or I meet with them to determine how best New Eden can be of benefit to them. We turn away very few applicants, but there have been a few cases in which we have had to refer them to other agencies which might offer more than we can provide. One of the things we try to determine is where they would best fit into our work structure.

Randy apparently..." here I noticed a distinct flash of discomfort "...impressed my husband when he mentioned his office skills."

Office skills? Randy? If he had had any before he came to New Eden, it was news to me. But then, I really didn't know very much about him or his past.

"Our residence office worker at the time," Mrs. Dinsmore was saying when I yanked myself back to the moment, "had been with us for several months...since Denny left, as a matter of fact...and had just accepted a job at an office in the city through our job referral program."

Though I'd asked the same question of Jeffrey Dinsmore, I wanted to raise the issue of Tunderew's Dallas visit to see if there might be any difference at all in the answer I got.

"From what I understand," I started, "Mr. Tunderew made a trip to Dallas in August of last year as part of his job with Craylaw & Collier to meet with you and your husband on some project."

She looked puzzled. "I'm sure you're mistaken," she said. "As I've told you, neither I nor my husband had ever met Mr. Tunderew. I had no idea he might have worked for Craylaw & Collier."

"But you were at the Dallas New Eden in August, I believe?"

She thought a moment. "Yes, we try to spend two weeks at every location several times a year. We were in Dallas until the 10th, as I recall, then went on to Atlanta. My mother-in-law's birthday is the 14th and the entire family gets together in Atlanta on that date to celebrate with her. We left Atlanta around the 24th or so and returned here. I can assure you we had no contact whatsoever with Mr. Tunderew, either then, before, or after."

I heard a clock somewhere striking, and decided it was about time to leave. There were a couple of other questions I would have liked to have asked, but didn't want to press my luck. We had completely skirted the sex issue, and I figured it was best to leave it at that.

"I've taken up enough of your time, Mrs. Dinsmore," I said, edging forward in my chair. "I very much appreciate your cooperation." We both got up and began to walk toward the front door.

"Oh, one more thing," I said as we passed through the living room. "Do you suppose I might speak with Mel Hooper? I understand he manages the day to day operations of the farm, and I'd like to ask him some questions about whether there may have been any problems between Denny Rechter and the other residents."

We reached the door and she opened it for me. "He's working in the fields today," she said, "and they usually don't come in until five or so, but I'll ask him when I see him. If you'll give me your card, I'll have him call you."

I paused in the doorway long enough to extract a business card from my wallet and hand it to her. "Thank you," I said. "I'd appreciate it. And thank you again for your time."

"You're quite welcome," she said, and closed the door behind me.

* * *

I thought of stopping by Evergreens to see if Jonathan might like to go to lunch (even though he took his lunch to work every day) but realized he was probably out on a job somewhere. I stopped anyway, just in case, and as I'd thought, he was with his boss delivering trees somewhere in Briarwood. I wondered idly if it might be to one of the four new mini-mansions where I'd helped deliver the dining room set.

There was a Cap'n Rooney's Fish Shack (one of about 100 of the franchises scattered around town, but they were pretty good, considering) between Evergreens and the office, and I stopped for some fish & chips. Both Jonathan and I liked Cap'n Rooney's—I because their chips were crisp and thick and they came with lots of vinegar, and Jonathan because most of the franchises had large fish tanks he could stare at while we ate.

As I opened the office door, the phone rang. I hurried to pick it up before the machine did.

"Hardesty Investigations."

"Dick Hardesty?" the very male voice asked.

"Yes," I said.

"This is Mel Hooper. I want to talk to you."

Interesting how the same words can be said in several different ways, and each way conveys a very different messages. I readily recognized this one as a command.

"I'm glad you called," I said, "though I didn't think it would be this soon. I..."

"There's a coffee shop next door to the SuperFoods warehouse on Fearn Drive," he interrupted. "Meet me there at two thirty."

And if I don't? I wondered. But all I said was: "Okay." Then I hastened to add: "How will I recognize you?"

"You won't have to. I've seen you before. Two thirty," and I heard the click of his hanging up.

He's seen me before? Then I remembered...the day Jonathan, Randy, and I had gone to the house to pick up Randy's sneakers—the guy I'd seen walking through the living room.

Well, this should be fun, I thought. *I wonder what happened to 'working in the fields until after five'?*

* * *

Daisy's was to diners what Rockwell was to painters. It was so wholesomely American I was surprised it didn't have a flagpole out front. It sat there, all bright blue with bright white trim and shiny windows looking chipper as all hell, surrounded by featureless brown, grey, and dirty white nondescript commercial buildings, a very-used car lot and an "Everything Must Go!" furniture store. The SuperFoods warehouse directly next door was a sprawling horizontal monolith whose surface was broken only by six large loading docks, four of which had tractor-less semi trailers backed up to them, and two smaller docks. At the one closest to the semis I noticed what I was sure was the same red pickup truck that had passed me on the road at New Eden.

I turned into Daisy's parking lot, which only had about five cars in it, and pulled into the closest spot near the front.

I don't have to describe the interior. Just close your eyes and remember: shiny plastic-padded booths under the windows on either side of the front door, long formica counter with stainless steel trim and backless swivel chairs on poles, menu board on the wall behind the counter with the day's specials spelled out in removable letters. You've been there.

I took a seat at a booth against the outside wall closest to where I'd parked the car, and the waitress came out from behind the counter to bring me a menu. She was wearing a crisp blue one-piece uniform with a spotless white apron and—I'm not kidding, I swear!—one of those cloth tiara-like white starched caps! God, I hadn't seen one of those in years. But it sure fit the image.

I told her I was expecting someone, but would have coffee while I waited and she smiled and moved off to get it.

At exactly two-thirty I saw the red pickup move past the front of the diner and pull into the parking lot. A moment later, a very large man walked past the window and to the door. He entered, looked around briefly, spotted me, and came over. He reminded me of a Marine drill sergeant I'd had in the service: close cropped hair, rugged, not-unhandsome face, somewhere in his mid-40s. He extended his hand without a word and I leaned forward to take it. He slid into the booth opposite me, and the waitress came over with two menus and a mug of coffee to match my own, setting it in front of him. They exchanged small smiles and a nod which clearly indicated to me he was a regular here.

Neither of us had yet spoken a word until the waitress went back behind the counter in response to the ding of a small bell indicating an order was ready. Then he looked at me and said: "So exactly what's your game?"

Jake had been right: Mel Hooper obviously didn't believe in wasting much time in chit-chat.

"I'm not sure I follow," I said.

He was staring at me. Not particularly a hostile stare, just intense. "What do you want from the Dinsmores?" he asked.

I deliberately took a sip of my coffee before answering. "Information," I said. "I'm trying to find out who killed Tony Tunderew."

He also took a swig of coffee and set the mug carefully back on the table. "The author? What does he have to do with the

Dinsmores?"

Now, I didn't know exactly how much of a little game we were supposed to be playing here. I had no idea what he knew or what he didn't know. Obviously, Mrs. Dinsmore had to have spoken to him very shortly after my meeting with her. What she'd said I couldn't imagine, but it was fairly obvious his big brother instincts had been strongly triggered.

"Your sister didn't tell you?" I asked. "I hate to go over the same ground if she did."

He was still looking at me, but there was a subtle downgrading from a stare to a look. "Reverend Dinsmore mentioned some rumor about a book last week, I think it was, and that they'd alerted the lawyers. But she said something about there maybe being a link between some supposed murders and New Eden. I didn't see the connection, and still don't."

"Did you ever meet Tunderew?" I asked. Apparently the question caught him by surprise.

"No. I never even heard of him other than to know he'd done a hatchet job on Governor Keene."

"You didn't read *Dirty Little Minds*?"

He almost smiled, but not quite. "Do I look like the kind of man who would?" he asked. He had a point.

"So you weren't aware he'd been writing a new book centered on New Eden?"

"Bar...Mrs. Dinsmore said that's what you'd told her, and that really upset her. And when she gets upset, *I* get upset, if you know what I mean."

I think I knew.

"Look," I said, "I'm not out to cause any trouble for New Eden, the Dinsmores, you, or anyone else. All I'm trying to do, as I said, is to try to find out who killed Tony Tunderew."

"And why should you care?" he asked.

"Because Tunderew wasn't the only one killed in that crash. He was a rotten excuse for a human being, but Randy Jacobs didn't deserve to die with him. You knew he was with Tunderew, I assume."

He shrugged. "Yeah. The police called trying to locate his

family. I couldn't help them. Every resident fills out a form when they first come to us. A lot of them leave the 'Family Information' part blank. Jacobs had just written in 'None.'"

"Did you tell your sister or brother-in-law that Randy was dead?"

He shrugged. "I told Jeffrey."

"But not your sister?"

"No reason she had to know. She's got enough to worry about. I didn't want to upset her. Nothing she could do about it anyway. Part of my job is to act as a buffer between the Dinsmores and what goes on on the farm and with the residents. I try not to bother them with all the details."

"A former resident's death is a 'detail'?" I asked.

He shrugged again. "You know what I mean," he said. "But given everything else they have to deal with every day, yeah, it's a detail."

The waitress came over to refresh our coffee and ask if we'd decided what we'd like. Hooper asked what kind of pie they had, and she ran through the list: Apple, Cherry, Banana Creme, and Rhubarb.

"Rhubarb," Hooper said.

"Sounds good," I said.

She filled our cups and returned to the counter for the pie.

"So you had no idea Tunderew was writing a book about New Eden?" I asked.

He shook his head. "Not a clue," he said.

"But the news about the murders didn't surprise you?"

He gave a deep sigh and shrugged. "The only murder I know about is Mike Barber in Dallas. She mentioned there being two more...one from Atlanta and one from here. But look, New Eden isn't exactly a finishing school for the children of the wealthy. The kids who come to us are already pretty damaged goods. They lived on the edge before they got to us, and too many go back to it when they leave. We do what we can, but that's all we can do. We can't save everybody."

The waitress brought our pie, and we ate in silence for a few minutes until he resumed talking.

"If you knew Randy Jacobs, you know what he did for a living. He hustled his ass on the streets. A lot of our residents did that, or worse. That three former residents got themselves killed, out of the hundreds and hundreds who pass through our program every year, is hardly surprising, I'd imagine."

I finished a forkful of pie before saying: "I suppose you're right. But all three...and Randy, too, for that matter...worked in the residence office."

He shrugged. "Coincidence," he said.

Sure.

"How do you get along with your brother-in-law?" I asked.

He looked at me sharply, his fork halfway to his mouth.

"We get along fine," he said. "Why would you ask that?" He finished conveying the pie to his mouth and replaced the fork on his now empty plate.

"Just curious. I'd heard some talk that maybe you weren't the best of friends."

He picked up his coffee mug and took a sip.

"Don't know where you'd have heard anything like that," he said.

"So it's not true?"

Another slight shrug, then: "Look," he said, "my mother died when Barbara was seven. I was seventeen. Our father was an important man, and a busy one. He loved us, but he just wasn't able to be around as much as he wanted. So it fell mostly to me to look after her. I've done the best I could ever since. She'll always be my little sister, so I guess it's only natural that I wouldn't think *anyone* was good enough for her. But she loves him, and that's good enough for me."

I gave a small laugh. "I guess if I were Reverend Dinsmore, I'd better watch my step."

He looked at me, his eyes narrowing for just the fraction of a second.

"What's that supposed to mean?" he asked.

"Nothing," I said. "Nothing at all. Just an observation."

He excused himself to go to the bathroom and I took the

opportunity of his absence to allow some of the thoughts that had been piling up in my head to air themselves. Either he, his sister, and Jeffrey were all very good at conning me, or they really *didn't* know about *No Door to Heaven*. And if they didn't know about the book, what motive would any of them have had to kill Tunderew? Hooper had been right about it maybe not being surprising that three former New Eden residents had met untimely deaths, given their lifestyles.

But the residence office connection? That's stretching coincidence way past the breaking point.

Did Hooper know the good Reverend had been playing around with his residence office staff? I had little doubt from meeting him and from what I'd heard that if he thought for a minute that Jeffrey had been betraying Hooper's little sister, he'd snap him like a twig.

So if Tunderew hadn't been killed because of what he was writing about New Eden, who did kill him and why? Back to Catherine Tunderew, the Bernadines, and the way-in-the-rear contenders, Larry Fletcher and Judith Francini.

Sigh.

* * *

The waitress brought the check, and I quickly reached into my wallet to hand her a bill to cover it and the tip. Hooper returned to the table, slid back in long enough to drain the coffee from his cup, then said: "Well, I've got to get back to the farm. I'm glad we had a chance to talk. But I think you know where I stand when it comes to asking the Dinsmores any more questions. You need information, I suggest you get it somewhere else."

He obviously read the expression on my face, and hastily added: "That's not a threat…it's a strongly worded suggestion."

He motioned to the waitress for the check, but she merely pointed at me and nodded.

"Thanks," he said.

"You're welcome," I said, and yet another little ritual of

civilization was observed.

We got out of the booth at the same time, and he extended his hand. We shook, and I followed him to the door and outside. We didn't say a word as he walked three paces ahead of me, without looking back, to his pickup, which was parked right next to mine.

As I walked behind it, I took a closer look at that extended platform I'd noticed when it had passed me on the road. It was a pretty solid looking affair, unpainted steel, apparently. A perfect, rectangular box about two feet deep and two feet wide, running the width of the truck. It had slightly recessed brake lights built in, but I doubted the back-up lights could be seen if he needed them. And I noticed that it wasn't, indeed, quite a perfect rectangle. There was a slightly pushed-in section on the corner of the driver's side.

The blood rushed from my head and I actually saw little flashes of light behind my eyes as every one of my mind voices realized what I realized in that instant, and yelled in unison:

Jeezus H. Kryst, Hardesty!!

Chapter 15

I managed to get into my car and even exchanged a wave with Hooper as he backed out of his spot and proceeded up to the street, where he turned left. I waited until he was out of sight, then got back out of the car and returned to the diner. I'd noticed the ubiquitous pay phone in the short hall leading to the restrooms, and fished around in my pocket for change.

I dialed the number, asked for the extension, and prayed he'd be in.

"Lieutenant Richman," the voice said.

* * *

I made it to the City Hall Annex in what seemed like record time, though I couldn't actually be sure because my mind had been racing so furiously all the way from the diner, I really had little awareness of the time. I was lucky I didn't get into a traffic accident—I do remember running a yellow light and being grateful there wasn't anyone around to see it, or to collide with.

After parking the car in the Warman Park underground garage, I'd practically sprinted the two blocks to the Annex.

I found myself pacing back and forth in the elevator on the way to Richman's floor.

"Come," the familiar voice said in response to my knock. I opened the door to Richman's office and went in, only mildly surprised to see Marty Gresham was there as well. We did our little hand-shaking ritual, and Richman gestured me to one of the seats in front of his desk, next to Marty.

"I asked Marty to sit in since he already knows a little bit about what's going on on this Tunderew matter," Richman said as we all settled in.

"That's fine," I said. "I'm really glad you agreed to hear me out."

"No problem," Richman said. "So, we're listening."

And the verbal dam burst.

Even as I heard myself talk, I was aware of a part of my brain that was somehow removed, and far more objective than the rest of me was at the moment. *It's really weird how things happen,* it observed. *I'd been working on Tunderew's murder for what seemed like months, bouncing from one clue to the next. And then in the space of two seconds...*

I heard my voice explaining that it wasn't Tunderew's murder I should have been working on all along, it was Randy's! While any number of people might have eventually murdered Tunderew if they'd had the chance, they didn't. Instead of Randy being coincidentally in the car when Tunderew was murdered, it was exactly the other way around.   *Randy* had been the intended victim.

Why in hell hadn't I seen that?

I heard myself laying out the scenario of the night Tunderew and Randy—make that Randy and Tunderew (see how perceptions make all the difference?)—died. We'd gone to New Eden to pick up Randy's sneakers. As I stood at the front door, I'd seen whom I now know to have been Mel Hooper walking across the back of the room. All he had to do was look out the kitchen window and he'd have seen Randy.

Hooper had known all along about Jeffrey Dinsmore's taste for male hustlers. How he'd found out I had no way of knowing, but he did keep a tight rein on all the residents and what went on on the premises.

I heard Lieutenant Richman interrupt me.

"Why," he asked, "if Hooper knew Jeffrey Dinsmore was cheating on his baby sister, didn't he simply kill Dinsmore?"

That had been one of the questions I'd asked myself on the way from the diner.

"I think," I said, "it was probably simply because his sister loves the guy, and Dinsmore's death would hurt her too much. I think he wanted to send Jeffrey a loud and clear message when he murdered Jim Temple and threw his body into the

Chattahoochee. He almost surely assumed it would be found downstream somewhere. But fate intervened, and Temple's body got snagged along the bank in a remote area where nobody noticed it. When it hadn't shown up in several weeks, Hooper tried another message by sending Dinsmore Temple's bible, which Hooper had probably taken from him before or after the murder.

"It wasn't as clear a message, but Hooper probably figured Dinsmore would get it. He didn't." The Lieutenant nodded.

"How Dinsmore could possibly have missed making the connection when Mike Barber was killed is almost beyond comprehension, but incredibly, Dinsmore apparently missed it. I wouldn't be surprised if Hooper had set Mike up to get booted out of New Eden—he was always careful not to have too direct a link between the deaths and New Eden itself—and have Mike show up dead within a day *still* didn't register with Dinsmore! Dinsmore isn't stupid, but the only possible reason I can think of as to why he could have been so dumbfoundingly dense is that it may just never have occurred to him that someone actually knew what was going on. He gave himself too much credit for being discreet."

Both Richman and Gresham just sat there, watching me, saying nothing. Maybe they figured they wouldn't be able to stop me if they tried. They were probably right. So I went on.

"Denny Rechter was dumped in a place where Hooper again assumed the body would be quickly found. Again, it wasn't. In a way, Hooper was as unlucky in sending his messages as Dinsmore was dense in ignoring them."

When I paused for breath, Richman took the opportunity to step in. "How could Dinsmore have been sure the guys he was having sex with wouldn't expose him?" he asked.

"He probably bribed them with promises of a good job when they left New Eden in exchange for their silence," I said. "Randy had hinted as much before Mrs. Dinsmore caught him and Dinsmore in the act. I kind of doubt that Mrs. Dinsmore told Hooper about it. She might well be afraid of what Hooper might do to Jeffrey. But Hooper undoubtedly figured it out when she demanded Randy be thrown off the property. Whether Hooper wanted Randy to be another message or whether he was just out to punish Randy for Mrs. Dinsmore's having actually seen him servicing her husband, I don't know." I could feel Marty's big brown eyes focused on my face as I spoke.

"Anyway, Hooper undoubtedly followed us when we left New Eden. I wasn't expecting to be followed, of course, so I didn't pay any attention to who might be behind us. We dropped Randy off at the bus station, and Tunderew probably picked him up almost immediately, or Hooper might have made a direct move on him, and Tunderew would never have been involved."

"And the accident itself?" Richman asked.

"I'd guess Hooper just followed Tunderew into the foothills, then when he knew there weren't any major side roads for Tunderew to turn off on, Hooper pulled past him until he came to that convenient curve. When he was out of Tunderew's line of vision, all he had to do was to shove the pickup into reverse and back around the curve and directly at Tunderew. It was raining, and the platform at the back of Hooper's truck blocked Tunderew's ability to see the back-up lights. By the time Tunderew saw him, it was too late: he tried to swerve around him, but the platform hit the passenger's side fender, smashed the light, and sent the car swerving out of control and over the edge. The platform was unpainted steel; it wouldn't have left any paint residue on Tunderew's car. But you should be able to match up the impression it left in Tunderew's fender to the dent in the platform."

And all of a sudden, I felt like a balloon whose knot had been undone, and all the air was gone. I just sat there, feeling both relieved and not a little tired.

Marty Gresham grinned at me. "You're good, Hardesty," he said approvingly.

"Yeah," I heard myself saying. "If I'm so good I should have figured it all out a long time ago."

* * *

Mel Hooper was arrested for the murders of Randy Jacobs and Tony Tunderew. Investigations were launched into the deaths of Denny Rechter, Mike Barber (by the police in Kaufman County, Texas), and in Atlanta for the death of James Temple. The full weight of the Eternal Light Foundation was thrown into keeping the exact motive for the crimes from becoming public knowledge. Jeffrey Dinsmore left the area for San Francisco shortly after Mel Hooper's arrest, to finalize plans for the next New Eden. Barbara Dinsmore remained behind in semi seclusion to be near her brother and aid in his defense.

And the world goes on.

* * *

On Sunday morning, early, we drove out of the city, taking the Neeleyville turnoff toward the hills. Jonathan sat quietly, the small box in his lap. We headed up the hills, passing the spot where Tunderew's car had gone through the guardrail. I didn't point it out to Jonathan, but he spotted it and turned his head to look as we passed.

We drove on to the where the road crested the ridge, then took a dirt road that went even further up the hill. When the road ended in a small turn-around, we parked the car and took a narrow trail winding upwards through the woods. This was one of my very favorite secret places, but for some reason I'd never brought Jonathan there before.

The trail ended at a small clearing on the edge of a granite bluff which looked out over the forested hills and the wide valley. To the right, far below, was a small lake, glinting in the sun. To the left, in the distance, was the haze of the city.

Jonathan handed me the box while he took a small folding knife from his pocket and cut the seal on the box. Then he took the box from me and walked alone to the edge of the bluff. A sudden breeze from behind ran its fingers through his hair and ruffled his shirt.

Holding the box in one hand, he opened the top with the other. As he tilted the box, a wisp of grey dust tentatively escaped and then, as the box tipped further, the wisp became a small grey cloud which quickly dissipated, joining the wind as it rushed out over the valley.

"So long, Randy," Jonathan said.

He stood looking out over the valley for a long moment, then slowly closed the box and turned back to join me.

THE END

OTHER BOOKS IN THE
DICK HARDESTY SERIES

The Butcher's Son

1-879194-86-4   US $ 14.95
Lambda Award Finalist

The 9th Man

1-879194-78-3   US $ 14.95

The Bar Watcher

1-879194-79-1   US $ 14.95

The Hired Man

1-879194-76-7   US $ 15.95
Lambda Award Finalist

The Good Cop

1-879194-75-9   US $ 15.95

The Bottle Ghosts

1-879194-73-2   US $ 15.95

Order directly, with author-signed bookmark, from:
GLB Publishers, POBox 78212, San Francisco, CA 94103,
Include $3.00 S/H for each book

Web site:www.GLBpubs.com

All Dorien Grey books are also available as e-Books (Downloads) on the GLB Publishers' Internet Site in your choice of printable formats

The Butcher's Son
1-879194-86-4   US $ 8.00
              Cover   US $ 1.00
www.glbpubs.com/tbs.html

The 9th Man
1-879194-78-3   US $ 8.00
              Cover   US $ 1.00
www.glbpubs.com/9th.html

The Bar Watcher
1-879194-79-1   US $ 8.00
              Cover   US $ 1.00
www.glbpubs.com/tbw.html

The Hired Man
1-879194-76-7   US $ 8.00
              Cover   US $ 1.00
www.glbpubs.com/thm.html

The Good Cop
1-879194-75-9   US $ 8.00
              Cover   US $ 1.00
www.glbpubs.com/tgc.html

The Bottle Ghosts
1-879194-73-2   US $ 8.00
              Cover   US $ 1.00
www.glbpubs.com/tbg.html

Web site: www.GLBpubs.com